THE CHEST

THE CHEST

Hidden Secrets

Tania Park

Tania Park Publishing

A catalogue record for this book is available from the National Library of Australia

ISBN: 978-0-6485565-4-1 (Paperback)
ISBN: 978-0-6485565-5-8 (Ebook)

Printed & Channel Distribution: Lightning Source | Ingram (USA/UK/EUROPE/AUS)
Cover Designed—Laila Savolainen, Pickawoowoo Publishing Group
Publishing Consultants/Interior Design—Pickawoowoo Publishing Group

Tania Park Publishing
For enquiries, write to: rights and permissions via publisher.

This book is the result of two seasons of NaNoW-riMo plus the intervening months of editing and re-writing followed by more editing. The idea came from a glance at my own cedar wood chest, which holds a life-time of mementos.

I can't recall the number of people who had a hand in making suggestions but to each one, a mighty big thank you.

Special thanks go to Karen Woodward and Leonie Gorman who pulled each chapter apart, one by one and used their extra-picky hats to point out punctuation indiscretions, and the ever-present typo which occurs despite how many times one reads their own words.

Again, my friend, Maria Antonas, was invaluable in assisting me with all things Greek.

A special thank you to my husband, James, who must the most generous of men. He never comments on the hours I spend at the computer, often creeping past so he doesn't interrupt me or brings me a coffee when I have been so absorbed in getting words down that I forget time and his morning tea.

Previous Books by Tania Park

Mistaken: 2015

He never got around to telling me why he wanted me dead.

Retribution: 2015

Amy spends the next week hiding while planning to escape the clutches of Rico and his family crime gang.

Blind Justice: 2016 – Commended *2016 Christina Stead National Literary Fiction Awards*

Panic turned to terror at the sudden on-rush of two sets of feet. A rough hand clamped over her mouth to silence her.

Road Trip: 2016

Something inside her broke apart, leaving an intense sensation of emptiness. It was like he'd taken a huge chunk of her heart with him and he was only her brother.

The Swan: 2018 Finalist 2020 *The Wishing Shelf International Awards.*

I was seven years old. Do you honestly think I would tell the truth so that I could get beaten again the minute the police left.

Stalked: 2019 - Long listed *2020 Davitt Awards*

A triumphant sneer shot from the corners of his mouth at the thought of one way he could leave his mark to let her know she belonged to him.

Double Cross: 2020 - Long listed *2021 Davitt Awards.*

The weekend was awesome, right up until the time I murdered a man.

One

It was as though a kilogram of molten lead had replaced the blood in her heart. The tears she fought to keep at bay defied her wishes by washing across the surface of her eyes to make everything fuzzy. Even though her head sought to meld into her chest, she could still make out the hazy shapes of the people around her; dark like the day, which made the lead even heavier. Nearby trees gave the impression they were suffused with the same sense of gloom, their leafy branches drooped low, dripping large plops of water as though they also were shedding tears. The mournful cry of a lone black crow seemed appropriate, sending a shiver scooting across her shoulders. The only signs of brightness were the various pots of flowers, most fake, scattered around the lawn and on top of smooth slabs of polished granite and marble.

Suppressed tears were determined to leak but found a new channel, through the nose, giving her no option but to sniff since she had forgotten the basic necessity of a tissue. She winced at the resultant indelicate sound which seemed to echo in the stillness making the atmosphere even spookier. The dankness of the wet earth caught in the back of her throat as a prickle of sensation told her all eyes had turned her way but Vicky Saunders didn't dare look up. A hum of consolation whispered from across the site, confirmed they had all heard but, she guessed, it was expected she would show some form of grief. It was ridiculous to think it at this time but she wondered how many other people here also let a few tears escape. Not many, she thought.

'*Rest eternal grant unto her, Oh, Lord.*' The Anglican minister's words echoed in the gloom. They meant little to Vicky as she fought to concentrate on the reason she was here.

'*And let light perpetual shine upon her.*' For the number of people who stood around the gravesite like statues, the response was pitiful but Vicky didn't respond either for she couldn't make out the words on the printed page, didn't even know where they were up to or if she was on the right page.

'*May she rest in peace.*'

She wasn't used to a feminine voice leading a religious service and couldn't figure out why they were even having a religious ceremony for as far as Vicky knew, the person in the casket had never been to church but the request had been in the will, so a service had been arranged in frantic haste after the first meeting in the lawyer's office. It was Anglican because Vicky didn't have a clue what religious service was needed and this minister was more than willing to carry out the deceased's wishes at short notice.

'*Amen.*'

The response was louder: maybe everyone was hopeful this was the end and they could all go home to get out of this miserable weather.

'*May her soul and the souls of all faithful departed, through the mercy of God, rest in peace.*'

Faithful, what a joke.

'*Amen.*'

With her head bowed, Vicky waited for the next line but instead there was an eerie silence which became more and more uncomfortable the longer she waited. Spooked, she peeked from under damp lashes. She tried to focus on the people but since all their clothes were dark and her eyes bleary, they blended into each other in a hazy black. A swipe at her eyes cleared them enough so she could see. Damn, every single person had their eyes honed onto her. Mortified, she swung wet eyes towards the minister only to find the bible was closed and the woman also had her eyes honed onto Vicky as though she was supposed to do something. When the minister's hand wavered by her side, Vicky studied the motion for a few seconds before she remembered she was supposed to pick up a sod of dirt and cast it over the coffin. Instructions began to surface through the fog of a confused brain.

The moment she took a step closer to the dark two-metre-deep hole, others followed suit and shuffled into a snaking line behind. Too overcome to glance into the open grave, she bent at the knees, reached down, scooped up a handful of gravelly sand and cast it into the hole. She winced at the hollow thud when it landed. There was no way she could explain to anyone how she felt. Sad, yes, to a certain extent. It is always gut-wrenching when someone dies. Glad, definitely, for there would be no more suffering from continual arthritic pain. Gutted and empty, she thought, were more appropriate words to describe the hollowness of her innards. It was also a mystery as to why a sixty-eight-year-old woman with no apparent health issues would die so suddenly but at least it was a peaceful death, dying in her sleep. The body had been released after the required autopsy for sudden death but as yet, no report had been given, at least, not to Vicky.

As she moved to one side, she almost tripped when she had to avoid a deep puddle of mud. An arm circled her shoulders to steady her.

'How are you doing?' Her daughter, Gina, was more than welcome and the only one she wanted near her from this crowd of about thirty.

'I can't believe I am crying like a baby. I feel such an idiot.'

'Why? It would seem odd if you didn't shed a tear for your own mother. And who are all these people?'

Now the service was finished and other mourners could do their bit, Vicky turned, picked her way through the sodden dirt to a tree a few metres away. It was shadowed enough Vicky would be hidden while she studied the snaking file of mourners as each paused to drop held flowers or handfuls of dirt over the plain coffin.

'I have no idea,' she said to her daughter who wriggled closer, her arm still draped as though Vicky would vanish if she wasn't held close. It felt so darn good. 'Those three ladies belong to the bridge club.' She pointed to three elderly, rugged-up women who stood in a sole huddle on the far side. They had already shown their respects and now looked as though they didn't know what they were supposed to do. There was to be no wake. No tea, cake and sandwiches or any type of refreshments. Vicky hadn't expected anyone other than family to attend and family consisted of only the two of them: Vicky and Gina. They had plans to have their own private meal with a toast to Mum, at the local hotel before they headed back to the desolation of an empty house for the night to spend the next couple of days sorting through her mother's belongings. She winced at the thought for it was a task she dreaded.

'The couple on the end are neighbours and I recognise the man with the yellow umbrella. Old George from the corner shop where Mum bought her milk and papers.' Vicky cast her eyes over the other guests. 'You must recognise Meg and her husband but as for the others... I don't have a clue.' Most were now huddled in small groups, chatting in undertones. All wore a variety of protective rainwear, from clear, thin emergency ponchos pulled from dark recesses of handbags to cheap plastic macs and upmarket raincoats but all had sensible leather shoes to keep feet dry. Since the rain had held off for the service, furled umbrellas hung from elbows and hands. There were a few other faces she vaguely recognised but most were new to her, which in itself appeared odd for she thought she knew most of her mother's friends and associates.

'What about those two guys?'

Vicky followed the line of Gina's outstretched arm. She jolted when she spied the two men who stood in the wet grass about thirty metres away. There was something about them... They looked official with both garbed in similar grey raincoats which reached below the knees, like the ones you see European people wearing in the height of winter. Akubra hats slung low over the brow with sunglasses hiding everything above their noses. It was the sunglasses which gave them away for in this gloom they weren't necessary and stood out like a lone beacon perched on a sole rock in the middle of the ocean.

A shiver of unease wound its way down her spine. It was obvious the men didn't want to be recognised but why were they even here?

'They look important, which is ridiculous. Why on earth would officials be here?'

'Did Granny break the law?'

'I wouldn't put it past her, she was single-minded and outspoken on most things but I doubt it. Her arthritis kept her pretty well housebound these past few months. She wasn't capable of sneaking around the neighbourhood in the middle of the night to break into houses or rob a bank.'

Gina sniggered. 'I can picture it, Granny in her lairy P.J.s, wearing a mask, slithering over fences while hiking through backyards. Reminds me of Halloween.'

Vicky tried to swallow the gurgle of laughter, but it resulted in the escape of an awkward snort. There was one thing about her mother – she was unconventional and nothing like what Vicky thought a mother should be. Wacky, multicoloured clothes was one thing Regina Wakefield was noted for, with her hair often the same colour as the outfit of the day. She snubbed her nose at accepted conventions and was outspoken, bordering on rudeness when she believed she was right, which was most of the time. But Mum had been fiercely protective. Heaven help anyone who maligned or bullied Vicky, especially at school. You could count on Mum turning up at the principal's office the next day to ensure it got sorted to her satisfaction. When she had been a young primary school student, Vicky had been overjoyed to have her mother defend her but by the time she was ten, it had become such an embarrassment Vicky learnt to not let slip any hassles she'd had, even more so once she reached high school for it only made the torment worse. Teenagers can be incredibly cruel.

The downside to her mother's personality was the lack of motherly love. Vicky couldn't remember a single time when her mother gave her a cuddle, or hug, or kiss, even as a child. There must have been some somewhere along the line but Vicky couldn't remember any. Regina was not and never had been a touchy-feely woman. When she was old enough to understand, Vicky believed it was the reason for the non-existence of her father. Timothy Wakefield, as far as Vicky knew, never existed apart from a typed name on her birth certificate. She had never seen the man nor even a photograph. The only information she had ever been given was how he deserted her mother on the announcement of being pregnant. Vicky still didn't know whether this was fact or fiction and she no longer cared since it was obvious he never cared two-hoots about her existence.

Her own long sigh jerked Vicky back to awareness only to discover people were headed towards her. Damn, she so didn't want to do the meet and greet thing. 'Do you think we could sneak away?' she hissed out the side of her mouth.

'Too late, Mum.'

'You must be Gina's daughter,' a stooped gentleman said at the same time.

Vicky didn't like to correct him and explain she was Gina's mother and Regina's daughter. She had never heard her mother being referred to by the diminutive of her name before. It felt weird, now knowing other people used the name

Gina, when her mother had always insisted on being called Regina.

'I'm sorry for your loss,' the ancient man added with a half-smile.

'Thank you Mr...'

'Stan, call me Stan.'

'I feel awkward asking this but how well did you know my mother? I don't recall if we have ever met. My apologies if we have.'

'Oh, we dated for several years and remained good friends after she refused my proposal. Never wanted to get married again, she said at the time.'

It was difficult to hide her shock as Vicky scrambled to find something adequate to say. She knew her mother had dated and had several affairs, sometimes with more than one man at the same time. Being faithful to one person was not one of her mother's strengths but she also wasn't a wanton hussy. Regina had been discrete with her relationships and after all she was a single woman. Why shouldn't she have relationships with men? But as far as Vicky knew, Stan had never been on the radar. She glanced around, wondering how many of the other men here had shared her mother's bed. Fiddlesticks, she didn't really want to know. Way too much information.

'Maybe I should offer you condolences as well,' she said, merely as a means of saying something for she didn't know how to handle such intimate information.

The man grinned. 'She was a good woman, life of the party. I will miss her company.'

'Did you know any of that?' Gina whispered after the man hobbled away.

'No,' was all Vicky could manage before the next woman paused in front of them. It felt like she was having an out of this body experience for the next half hour while people chatted, hugged and introduced themselves. Unfamiliar hands gripped her wrist, or both upper arms while unwanted pretentious air-kisses blew past her ears. The strangers chatted, told anecdotes, laughed, cried and talked some more. Most words vanished into the muggy atmosphere, washing over Vicky who felt stunned at how little she knew of her mother's social life. It wasn't as if she never spent time with her mother, she did. She called in at least twice a week, they shopped together and attended various functions on a regular basis. By the time the last person had left, it felt as though her mother had been two entirely different people. Vicky couldn't chase away an insidious thought. Had Regina been deliberate in keeping family life separate from her social engagements?

Hurt had burrowed its way deep into Vicky's gut as they trudged through mud and puddles towards her car, where she had to wipe sticky dirt from shoe soles on the last patch of grass before getting into her car. It was familiar hurt, which managed to re-surface after being locked away years ago. Why wasn't she good enough to be hugged by her mother? And now a new pain erupted: why hadn't her mother let Vicky be a part of this other life?

Two

Even though she had slept in this room all through her childhood, Vicky felt like a complete stranger as she eyed the familiar objects. The walls were still coated in the same moss green but now hinted at the need to be refreshed. Nothing had changed furniture-wise with a white Queen Anne wardrobe still standing against the same wall. It looked as though it was embedded there for it didn't appear to have been moved a single millimetre since Vicky left home almost twenty years ago. A matching dressing table had yellowed under the glare of many years of summer sunshine which found its way through the opposite window. Carpet – same, bedside tables – same but without any adornments apart from a reading lamp which was the only new item. The layer of dust was so thin it barely registered, indicating a recent clean and there was no musty odour to suggest the room had been closed up for months on end. The scene tickled the memory banks but at the same time Vicky felt like an interloper in unfamiliar territory.

Yesterday's revelations had disconcerted her to the extent she hadn't been able to face sorting through her mother's house after the late lunch with Gina. Instead, they hit the shopping centre, window-shopped but bought nothing. Still feeling spaced-out, she talked Gina into going to the late afternoon session at the cinema after which they enjoyed ridiculous obscene ice-cream sundaes: anything to avoid sorting through the remnants of her mother's life.

A thick head accompanied her to the bathroom where steaming hot water pelted away some of the tension and gloom. Here, too, the décor hadn't changed but now wore patches of peeling paint and missing silver around the edges of the mirror nestled over the vanity. At least the room was scrupulously clean. After a vigorous rub-down with a faded towel she found hanging on the rail as though nothing had changed over the past fortnight when everything had, she dragged on old jeans, so faded they were almost white. She topped it with a dark long-sleeved fleecy cotton top before she tugged on thick socks and sneakers to keep her feet warm. While she brushed her still lustrous dark hair, she noticed the deep frown lines which had taken up residence on her face, making her look at least ten years older than her thirty-seven years. You look like a hag, she thought. Shoulders went back, chin up, chest out.

'Get over yourself, Victoria Saunders,' she chided to her image. 'Life has thrown you another curve ball so get out there and do what has to be done with a bit of grace.' She forced the corners of her lips upwards, ran a finger over the lines in a vain attempt to straighten them out before she sucked in a long breath and spun around with a new determination to make the most of the weekend with Gina. If they worked hard they could clear the cupboards of sixty-eight years of life and pile the contents into three heaps: keep, charity and discard. With her own house full of everything she needed, Vicky doubted there would be much in the keep pile although Gina might want a few things.

'Rise and shine, Sweetie,' she yelled outside the door to the spare room where they'd had to shift piles of *stuff* to find the bed for Gina to sleep in. Neither had wanted to use the bed where a dead body had lain for two days before it was discovered by the neighbour from two doors down.

'Too creepy,' Gina had mumbled when they stood in the doorway, staring at the bed stripped of all the covers, including the mattress which was nowhere to be found. Vicky had agreed but said nothing when a shiver of distaste had run across her shoulders. She had no idea who had taken care of what would have been soiled bedding or where it was. Burnt, she hoped.

The call from the police had been a shock. It had also set up a wave of guilt. Due to working a few extra hours for a friend, Vicky had cancelled dinner on the night Regina died. If only she had come, things might have been different. She might have noticed something was not right... her mother might have said she was not feeling well... might, might, might. If only... how many times in a person's life do they say those words? And she could recall a few of those times.

'Don't call me that.' The words arrived a split second before Gina's tousled head poked through the doorway.

'Why not?' Vicky grinned, knowing the endearment was not acceptable to 17-year-old teenagers, especially in front of peers. She had been chided often enough but was not about to stop. She wasn't sure if it were purely to annoy her daughter or if it was something deeper.

'It's embarrassing.' Gina stepped out, still in pyjamas covered in bright blue love hearts on a shocking pink background. Vicky didn't dare mention her daughter's penchant for wild colours might have been inherited from her grandmother for Gina was always disparaging about what Granny wore.

They both headed towards the kitchen. 'I fail to see how telling your daughter you think she is special can be a cause for embarrassment.'

'Mum.' The word was typically long with whiny undertones as only a teenager could do.

'How would you feel if I never cuddled or hugged you or told you I love and admire you or how proud I am of you?' Vicky said over her shoulder while she filled the electric jug.

'What do you mean? You have always told me.' A chair scraped across the linoleum floor, the screech causing Vicky to wince. Gina flopped into it, sending up an echoing *whoof.*

'Imagine never being told those positive things. Would you like it?' Two mugs came down from the overhead cupboard and clattered on the stainless-steel sink. Vicky dropped a teabag into each.

'No, of course not but you would never be so mean.'

With the steaming kettle held in one hand, Vicky turned to her daughter and caught her eye. 'It was how Granny was with me, which is why I make sure I always tell you... show you how I feel about you.'

A scowl wrinkled the few brown freckles across Gina's nose. 'Really, never?'

'Never.'

'That's so sad.' Gina rose and threw herself into Vicky's arms, almost tipping the kettle up. 'I love you and Daddy loved you heaps.'

The warm hug was exactly what Vicky needed; being reminded of Mike, wasn't. 'I know, Sweetie, but maybe now you understand why I can't stop being affectionate towards you, even in front of your friends.' Vicky drew away and grinned. 'Maybe, if they say anything, you could tell your friends they are jealous of you but I promise to do my best to keep sappy words to myself when we're in public. Deal?'

'Deal.' They high fived before Gina resettled into her chair with one leg under her backside and her arms draped across the table.

Vicky couldn't help but smile at their breakfast after they discovered someone, probably the same good fairy who had disposed of the bedsheets, had rid the refrigerator of all perishable foods, and even washed the shelves. They spooned down cornflakes, moistened with the fruit and sweet-smelling juice from a can of peaches. It wasn't so bad, in fact it tasted better than Vicky expected. Who needed milk? The black tea wasn't a problem since both always drank it without milk although she wasn't so fond of the cheap brand of tea which tasted as though it was made from the scrapings from the floor of a cardboard factory. Sometime soon she would have to hunt down the kind person to thank them, or maybe they would call in once they noticed Vicky was here.

After she rinsed their few dishes and wiped her hands on a tea-towel, Vicky spun around a slow 360 degrees, took in the kitchen and its contents. Solid wooden cupboards had been painted a sunshine yellow only a few years back. The bright colour reflected light from the large window over the sink, which gave cheery brightness to the room. The gas stove was newish, the refrigerator ancient but it had never missed a beat so had never needed to be replaced. It is a pity they don't make whitegoods to last, these days, she thought while she continued her scan. The benches were covered in dated 70's Formica, still in good condition if you took into consideration the age but she was certain it wasn't what modern-day buyers wanted in their kitchen. This kitchen was not going to bring in potential purchasers and the house would be sold for Vicky didn't want or need the hassle of renters. She would much prefer to invest the money for her old age and Gina's university education. Now being able to pay up-front for Gina's chosen career would be a welcome bonus. It would give her a head start when she started working, with no debt to pay off like so many graduates ended up with these days.

Regina had been house-proud, declaring her house clean enough to be healthy but dirty enough to be a home. Even when the onset of arthritis slowed her down, she dusted, swept, mopped and vacuumed every week while the kitchen and bathroom had been cleaned every day. It was a habit Vicky tried to maintain but work seemed to get in the way more often than not and Gina was a typical teenager who had to be coerced, bullied or threatened with dire consequences to keep her room respectable and help out with regular household chores. But at least she ended up doing them, not like some of her friends' children who never lifted a finger.

Regina's kitchen cupboards were stuffed full which meant

it was going to take forever to clean them out; something Vicky wasn't sure she wanted to tackle first. 'Why don't we do a walk through to see if there's anything we want to keep.'

'Sure thing.' Gina dropped the cutlery she had dried, into the drawer and fed the folded tea-towel over the rail screwed to the end of the cupboard.

Time had stood still in the sitting room except for a leather recliner-rocker and the latest flat-screen TV. It was whopping big – too big for the small room. Vicky recalled the shopping expedition to replace the old set when the old analogue system of broadcasting had been switched off, making the set defunct. When digital was required, Regina had spent two hours asking questions while she compared clarity, colour and size of every darn set in the store, until she pointed to this humungous and expensive flat-screen, which had stunned Vicky for her mother had always been frugal. "Since I'm going to gradually become housebound I might as well be able to enjoy the best," she had insisted after Vicky voiced her concerns. Regina had been right so the TV had come home, wriggled with much care into the back of Vicky's SUV after the rear seats had been lowered.

'What about the TV?' Gina asked.

'Too big for our place.'

'Pity.'

'Yes but we could sell it and put the money towards updating ours.'

'I could advertise it on the internet along with anything else you want to sell. What about Granny's chair?' Gina ran her hand over the blue leather before sinking into the cushioned comfort, rocking backwards and forwards several times before she pulled the lever to lift the footrest. She wriggled back. 'It's so comfy. Better than our lounge chairs.'

Vicky laughed. 'Where would we fit it?' she asked at the same time she pictured it in front of their TV. Maybe if she shifted things around. It was one thing she would like to keep even though it didn't match her furniture but a nice throw-rug tossed over the back in the right colour would tie it in with her green décor.

'Put it in my room.' Gina returned the chair to its upright position; the grinding click echoing.

At the vision of the large chair being squished into Gina's room, Vicky laughed. 'We would have to toss out your study desk and chair as well as your bed.'

'Yeah, well but it's too nice to sell.'

'I agree, we'll make it fit. The only other thing I want from this room is this.' Vicky laid her hand on the cover which hid the chest Regina used as a side-table. Vicky lifted off three books with markers in various places to indicate where Regina had got to in each. After piling them on the floor, Vicky added the notebook, pencil and pen. Amused, she picked up a used toothpick, held it in the air, grinning at Gina.

'Gross,' Gina said with an exaggerated grimace.

The only other item was the TV remote. She swept the long cover from the top of a cedar-wood chest and ran her fingers over the exquisite carvings. The polished wood was still in excellent condition despite the patina of age.

'Oh, wow, I've never seen this before.' Gina squatted in front of the chest where she mimicked Vicky by running her fingertips over the carvings which adorned the top and sides. 'What's in it?'

'Nothing, it has always been empty because Granny lost the key years ago.'

'Why did she always keep it covered?' Gina picked up and folded the discarded woven bedspread which had covered the chest since Vicky could remember.

'To protect it. Granny used it as a side table because it was large enough and high enough to hold the lamp, magazines, books and dinner plate. How about we get this into the back of my car? I am sure it will fit if we drop the rear seats down. We can pack smaller stuff around it.'

'Okay.' Gina tugged but the chest didn't budge. 'Are you sure it's empty?'

'Yes.' Vicky side-stepped to the other end, wriggled between chest and wall. 'It's carved from solid cedar. Smells wonderful when you open the lid. They were used as glory boxes way back.'

'What's a glory box?'

'Young women, your age, would buy linen and knick-knacks in preparation for married life. Wages were low and marriage was expected with the husband being the breadwinner and wife caring for the house and a busload of kids. Pre-contraceptive days. The cedar-wood keeps bugs, like clothes-moths and silverfish at bay. I think the Americans called them hope chests.' Vicky curled her fingertips into the carved handles. 'On three: one… two… three.' She hoisted.

'Hooley-dooly, it sure is heavy,' Gina groaned while she shuffled backwards.

'Heavier than I remember but it's been a few years since I've had to help shift it.'

By the time they inched the box to the front door, Vicky's fingers protested, along with her back. 'Okay, ease it down, I need car-keys. Watch out for toes.' The box landed with a thud, despite dropping only a couple of centimetres. 'Why don't you get dressed while I set up the car?'

After a quick search to find the keys, Vicky went outside to prepare the car. The bleak weather from yesterday had dissipated, leaving crystal blue sky, with the glint of sunlight ricocheting off still damp foliage. A bank of dark clouds hovered on the horizon. The bitumen had patches of light grey where the water had dried but puddles still nestled against the concrete kerb. A stab of brightness into her retinas jiggled her headache back to life. Soon she would need to search the bathroom cabinet for a painkiller but not keen on using too much medication she would put it off as long as she could.

Car ready, she returned to the house, eyeing the outside as she meandered along the cracked concrete footpath. Salmon bricks looked sad against faded peeling brown woodwork. It surprised her how neglected the house looked and wondered why she hadn't noticed before. The old adage, familiarity breeds contempt, came to the forefront of her mind. Now she could see it was true. How many times had she walked this path and not noticed the poor state of the paintwork but a coat in modern colours would cheer the old but solid house and make it more welcoming.

Gina, still tugging a sweater over blue jeans, met Vicky at the door. 'Ready?'

'Yes.' Vicky wedged the screen security door open and stepped inside. 'I'll go backwards until we get it out.' She waited until Gina was in position. Again she counted to three and hoisted, straightening her arms while she leant backwards. The chest was so heavy Vicky could only shuffle while she kept an eye out for the edge of the veranda. The last thing she needed was to topple down two steps and get flattened by a heavy hunk of wood.

'Got to put it down,' Gina gasped on a groan at the same time she let go.

The sudden weight caused Vicky's fingers to straighten and scrape free. The loud thud was followed by a strange tinkle. 'What...' Vicky stuttered at the same time she jumped down the steps and knelt so she could peer under the chest. 'There's something there... your end.' She reached under and scrabbled around with outstretched fingers.

'Got it,' Gina called.

Vicky peered over the top of the chest. 'Oh, my it's the key.'

'Funny looking key.'

'It's Asian. You slip the bent end in the slot and push. It releases the inside catch.'

'Can I try?'

'When we get home.' Vicky peered skywards and wavered her arm upwards. 'Clouds are closing in. Might rain again so let's get the chest in the car. I would hate for it to get wet.'

Exhaustion, accompanied by strained arm muscles, had set in by the time they managed to heave the box onto the tailgate and shove with their backs and shoulders to manoeuvre it far enough in they were able to shut the door. When it ground to a halt, Vicky noticed how one foot had become stuck hanging over the edge. She shoved the fingers of one hand under the leg to get a grip but paused when she felt a wad of something sticky stuck under the corner. She hunkered down until she could see what it was. Several layers of modern masking tape had kept the key stuck on the inside of one of the legs. Regret and hurt niggled. It was obvious her mother had lied to her. The number of layers and newness of the top ones told her the chest had been opened on a regular basis. A grimace broke out at the tacky tape as she scraped the wad free and tossed it into the boot. It took a mammoth effort to lift and shove at the same time but finally they managed to slide the box in far enough so the door could be closed.

A loud sigh escaped Vicky's lips. 'I'd kill for a decent coffee.'

'No milk.' Gina tugged her crumpled sweater into place. 'I could get us a take-away from the deli.'

Vicky tossed the keys to Gina. 'Best idea you've come up with this week. How about asking old Joe if he has any cardboard boxes? We're going to need heaps.'

As Vicky turned, a large plop of water landed on her forehead. She glanced up only to be smacked in the eye by another. She ran towards the house while Gina drove off. Inside, she went no further than the sitting room. The single waist-high cupboard against the far wall would be the easiest and quickest to empty. She knelt on the carpet, reached out with both hands, wrapped her fingers around the knobs and yanked the doors wide, groaning at the sight of jam-packed shelves. A loud knock at the door echoed her groan.

After easing up on a sigh, she hurried to the door she had shut only two minutes ago and opened it again.

'Who are you?' A uniformed police officer asked while his shorter partner peered around his shoulder.

'Vicky Saunders.'

'What are you doing here?' The tone was demanding and not in the least friendly.

'Sorting things.' It was difficult to maintain an air of nonchalance when everything inside her was screaming... beware!

'Why?' The second officer stepped beside his partner.

Vicky wasn't sure what to say or how much, when she could see no reason why these men were even here. 'Because it has to be sorted and the house cleaned out.'

'You have to leave.' When words are accompanied by a hand moving to a holster, something isn't right.

'Why?'

'This is a crime scene.'

Vicky reeled back two steps. Her lungs filled to bursting point on a sucked in breath. 'Excuse me?' It took a moment for her lungs to figure out how to work. 'This is my mother's house. She died in her sleep. No crime has been committed. The house, according to the lawyer I spoke to early yesterday morning, is now mine, including everything in it.' Vicky didn't like the way the two men glanced at each other. What should have been a simple look held a whole heap of meaning: a meaning which sent alarm bells clanging in Vicky's head.

'Regina Wakefield doesn't have a daughter.'

Before Gina brought the car to a standstill, Vicky yanked the passenger door open. 'Drive,' she mumbled while she scrambled inside.

'Why, what's wrong?'

'Just drive.' Vicky dragged her foot in, straightened, slammed the door and swung the safety belt into place.

'Mum.'

'Shut up and drive.' Everything inside her was strung tighter than a piano wire, ready to ping apart the moment someone dared to touch her. Even though Gina was driving, Vicky could feel the pressure of glances headed in her direction. She figured it wasn't the smartest thing to do, to tell police officers she was going to call the white-coat people to take the officers away because they thought it was normal to have a conversation with a ghost, since she couldn't have been born if her mother never had a child. Calling them idiots had not helped. But hell, she was a living, breathing human, daughter of Regina Wakefield: Vicky had the birth certificate to prove it. And what about the crime scene? She had asked. They said nothing – even drew their mouths into thin lines to prevent any information from slipping out. When she informed them she had spent the night there and had touched things in the kitchen... and bathroom... and two bedrooms... and sitting room, they had threatened arrest for interfering with crucial evidence.

'Mum?'

'Not now.' Vicky brushed her daughter's hand away. 'Drive home.'

'Coffee is in the console.'

'Okay. Thank you. Give me a minute to think.' But logical thought was beyond her. The picture of the pistol or maybe it was a taser, aimed at her body when she had laughed after she called them idiots, would not go away. Not good. Worse than bad, but heck, how was she supposed to react? The only plus was how they had given her both their handbags, but not before Shortie had rifled through them, taken out their driver's licences and written down all the details. Well, maybe this was a good thing for now they could log the details into their super-duper computers to prove how wrong they are. Idiots.

Vicky reached for the coffee, took a tentative sip. Not too hot so she sipped deeper while she stared through the side window and forced her concentration on the scenery. Now on the main road they passed the shopping centre and library, the houses in the next block, down the incline, across the bridge over the railway line, up the other side. Turn right to avoid the light industrial area. Vicky closed her eyes, sipped the coffee, opened her eyes, looked towards Gina.

'The police threw me out. Said it was a crime scene but not why. Threatened to arrest us for interfering with evidence. Said I wasn't Granny's daughter.'

'Shit.'

'Exactly.' Although Vicky never allowed Gina to swear,

this time she didn't pull her up because it was exactly how Vicky felt... and more. Deep down she wanted to shout out every foul word she could think of, again and again. It was only Gina's presence which kept her mouth shut.

'What are you going to do?' asked Gina.

'Don't have a clue except go home.'

For the next half hour Vicky's thoughts were a jumble of what ifs, maybes and don't be so utterly ridiculous. The appearance of her drive before her eyes brought her back to the present. Gina slowed, bounced over the low kerb and crawled to a stop in front of the garage.

'What now? Gina asked.

Vicky thought. 'Open the garage door. I'll reverse in so we don't have to carry the chest so far.' Since Gina had only had her licence for a few months, Vicky wasn't so sure Gina would have the confidence to reverse into such a confined space. Heck, she wasn't so confident herself since it wasn't something she did very often but she reversed out every day so how hard could it be?

She felt chuffed when the car went in straight, no hassles, no bingles, no scrapes on the wall shelves. Fifteen minutes later she watched as Gina slid the key into one end of the long lock of the chest. She jiggled, something clicked and the two pieces of the lock parted company. Gina unlatched the brass hinge and lifted. The pungent smell of cedar hit as the lid opened.

'Oh, my goodness,' slipped from Vicky's mouth.

'No wonder it was so heavy.' Gina dropped to her knees and stared at the boxes, files and piles of paper held together by large elastic bands. Amongst them were various objects, some of which Vicky recognised. Others looked vaguely familiar but most were old things she didn't recall ever having seen before.

'I don't know what to say. Granny always swore the chest was empty but…' Air escaped through her teeth in a long hiss. The surprises kept coming, disconcerting her more each day. It felt as though she had been transported to some alternate world.

'Why would she lie to me?' Her legs gave way. Vicky sank to the floor, bewildered. She reached into the chest, withdrew a stuffed toy: a lion, mane bedraggled. 'Oh, God, this was mine. I remember it. We went to the zoo. I must have been only three or four. I can't believe Granny would keep it.' A film of moisture washed across her eyes. To hide the unbidden tears, Vicky studied the lion, turned it over and over.

A thought came to her. 'I think it would be a good idea to empty the chest.'

'Why?'

'It left marks on the carpet. The police will know something has been removed. They might come here to look for it but I can't give them this,' she swept her arm over the contents, 'until I have been through it all.' Vicky scrambled upright. 'Quick, get those papers out.'

Gina joined her, grabbed a pile of papers. 'Where do you want them?'

'Papers and files in the filing cabinet closest to the desk – bottom drawer at the back has plenty of spare space. Boxes… in the bottom of my wardrobe. They are shoe boxes so won't look out of place. This other stuff... I'll get a rubbish bag – sort it later.'

It was as though the hounds of hell were after them the way they grabbed, raced and returned for another armful. Elastic bands snapped, papers scattered and were scraped back into bundles. Things fell out of boxes, were shoved back in, lids on askew. Vicky didn't bother to examine objects she lifted from the bottom of the chest but shoved them into a green plastic garbage bag until nothing remained but three rusty paperclips, the stub of an old pencil and grains of dirt; the type of dirt which collects in all drawers over time but seems to come from nowhere. As a final hurrah, she closed the lid, set the lock into place, which left her holding the key and wondering what to do with it.

'I need to hide this.' She held the key up in the air.

'Why?'

'If the police come and I produce a key, you can be sure they will want to know what I did with the contents. No key, no contents.'

'Don't you think you're over-reacting a bit?'

Vicky blew out her cheeks and slumped into the soft cushions of the nearest lounge chair. 'Maybe, probably but you weren't there. They scared me witless, especially when one drew his gun out.'

'Gun!' Gina shrieked.

'Sorry, I didn't mean to mention it but I'm scared, Sweetie. I need time to think, to sort things in my mind. The police hinted at things but wouldn't elaborate, it gave me the heebie-jeebies. Maybe I am panicking and they won't even come here but let us assume they do. I want to be prepared, so... key?' Vicky waved the 10cm piece of folded brass in the air.

'It looks like a metal tool. Why not in the garage with Dad's trays of nails, screws and junk.'

'Brilliant, although Dad would cringe if he heard you calling his things, junk.'

The key didn't look out of place in a tray of old brass bolts and catches. Vicky dumped the plastic bag half-full of objects from the chest, into the recycle garbage bin which lived against the wall of the garage. It looked like junk so wasn't out of place. If the police searched she could claim she had cleaned out old stuff to make way for things from her mother's house. It was logical. Even after they manoeuvred the chest between two lounge chairs, her heart still threatened to thump right out of her body.

While they sat at the kitchen bench with a fresh mug of coffee, she thought of her mother, still overwhelmed about the revelations and innuendos of the past two days. Life as she knew it, had been turned upside down in little more than twenty-four hours. It didn't matter how she interpreted the things she had heard; from Stan, from other mourners, from the police officers: none of them made much sense. There had to be some simple explanation. Stan, she could understand. Her mother had numerous relationships over the years. The fact she never told Vicky about them all - well, why would she? It was none of Vicky's business. It might have been if marriage had been on the cards but from what Stan said, Mum didn't want marriage.

But there were the yoga classes her mother had attended

which Vicky knew nothing about. Every Tuesday morning for several years, Vera had told her. Vera was a revelation as well. And line-dancing at the over-60s club on a Thursday. Why hadn't Mum mentioned them? Vicky sipped at the coffee but enjoyed the aroma more than the taste, while she thought of logical explanations. She scoffed. Why would Regina talk about what she did on weekdays? Vicky was at work, Gina at school. Vicky didn't relate her everyday incidents to her mother, nor did Gina. Nor did she tell Mum about her social activities unless she had to cancel a regular visit with her mum. Vicky enjoyed her privacy so why shouldn't Mum have the same rights to her private life? Neither was the other's keeper. Okay, this all made sense but what didn't, was the arrival of the police. Hmm, I wonder if Mum had ever gone through the process of getting a divorce. Vicky scoffed, another thing she didn't know but what the hell did it matter in any case?

Even though she was anxious to sort through the contents of the chest, Vicky was more anxious to avoid a confrontation with the police. It was ridiculous to be so uptight but no matter how hard she tried to relax and dismiss bad thoughts, they wouldn't go away, leaving her nerves tied into permanent knots. With a desperate need to get out, she persuaded Gina to spend the rest of the day out somewhere, anywhere. She didn't care where.

This time Vicky drove through the suburbs to avoid the city, towards the coast. With dark clouds and an increase in wind strength there was a threat of more rain which meant the beaches would be deserted and not the best place to visit.

But it was still a pleasant drive so she continued to the port of Fremantle, when she remembered the week-end markets. Why not?

A car pulled out of a road-side parking bay so Vicky filled the space, to-ing and fro-ing until the car was centred. Light rain began to fall as they alighted. With no umbrella in the car, they ran, down the footpath, across the intersection but paused to catch their breath under the canopy at the entrance to the popular indoor markets. Perfect. It had been years since she last visited here so what better way to clear the mind.

As they stepped inside, delicious aromas hit. Curry and coffee were pleasant and dominant, which set gastric juices flowing, reminding Vicky of the meagre breakfast they had eaten. The odour of cooking grease from fried food was not so pleasant. Side-by-side they wandered, scanned items, picked some up, replaced them and said little. It felt so darn good to be in sync with her daughter, doing normal everyday things. As they roamed, her tension began to ease as nerves relaxed. At the coffee bar, Vicky paused and tugged Gina to a standstill.

'Let's eat. What would you like?'

'You choose. I'll grab a table.'

Vicky raised her eyebrows at Gina's response. For once there was no smart riposte as only teenagers could do. Maybe her daughter could sense Vicky's unease. Or maybe Gina felt the same. It had been an awkward two weeks. The initial police call informing her of her mother's sudden death, the coroner's insistence on an autopsy, necessary for any unexplained sudden death, two separate meetings with her mother's lawyer, planning a funeral and now she had mysterious revelations from Regina's associates and the police.

At the thought of the men in blue, her nerves re-knotted themselves. A long sigh escaped. Vicky ordered coffee and chose two different rich cakes, asking for each to be cut in half so they could share. The snack was eaten in silence but a cacophony of background noises made it a comfortable silence. People chatted, passing feet scuffled, china chinked, the coffee machine hissed and groaned – all gave a sense or ordinariness, which went a long way to settle Vicky's agitation even more.

After several hours of slow mingling, Vicky felt more like her normal self as she drove them home.

A marked police car stood at her gate.

Four

Two officers, the same two, she noticed, unfolded from the front seats and were standing along the edge of the driveway by the time Vicky drove onto her property. It was a habit to press the button on the remote to open the garage the second she drove over the low kerb but she didn't realise she had automatically done it until she noticed the garage door rising. She slowed, waited for the roller-door to rise high enough to crawl in. The officers beat her and stood tall and rigid each side of the car front doors with eyes on them as she and Gina alighted.

Dread raced through her innards which caused them to tighten so much she felt like she wanted to throw up. The entire situation felt ominous with the officer's actions definitely of a threatening nature. Vicky eyed the holstered gun of the man closest to her. He was the one who had drawn his weapon earlier but so far his hand wasn't near it. Too scared to open her mouth, she eased from the car, not caring when the door nudged the officer enough to force him to sidle forwards to allow her room to exit. Too bad – he was the one crowding her and she had no doubt it was meant to intimidate.

'Can I help you?' she asked as she slammed the door and eyed Gina over the car roof. Poor girl looked as scared as Vicky felt.

'We have a few questions.' One arm unfolded and indicated towards the inter-connecting door which led into her kitchen.

'Fine.' She rushed ahead, pausing only long enough to let Gina go in front of her. An innate protective surge demanded she keep Gina safe; shield her from anything unsavoury. The moment she reached the kitchen, she plonked her handbag on the bench and gave Gina a surreptitious shove to keep going. Only when Gina was out of sight did Vicky turn, hands on hips, to stare down the larger of the two men who stood in front of his counterpart – no doubt using his size as another means to frighten her which worked better than she was game to let on. Man, they were good at this.

'Ask away.'

'Can we sit?'

'No, say what you have to say then I would appreciate it if you left. My daughter does not need any more stress. She is already overwhelmed emotionally.'

'You removed furniture from Mrs Wakefield's home.'

'Now my house, as is every piece of furniture contained therein, so no crime has been committed.'

'What did you take?' The tone had softened, thank goodness.

'A carved cedar chest.'

'Why?'

'It's one of only two items I want to keep.'

'Why take only the one item when you wanted two?' This time it was Shortie who asked as he stepped around his mate. Vicky didn't like the aggressive tone one little bit, nor his peacock-like stance.

'Because I could only fit one item in the back of my car.'

'What's in it?'

Vicky jerked around to find the taller officer had moved behind her, jamming her against the bench, between the two men. Oh, yes, intimidation tactics 101. The tension from earlier shot back with a vengeance. To take time, she sucked in a long breath and eased it back out again. 'Nothing, Mum lost the key years ago.'

'I don't believe you,' came from behind. She figured it was an attempt to put the wind up her, which worked but no way was she going to show how petrified she felt. She took her time to turn and stared at the shorter man. It was a small triumph when he looked away first. 'I get the feeling that no matter how honest I am, and I am being honest, you aren't going to believe me.'

'Where is it?' Oh, yes, they were playing the tag team game to keep her rattled. One followed by the other, front and back, to and fro.

'In the sitting room.' She indicated towards the archway. 'Feel free to see for yourselves.' Determined to not let these bullies get their own way, Vicky shoved past Shortie, stormed through the arch and pointed. 'One chest. Locked. Empty.'

'Open it.' Shortie dropped his right hand to his side in another obvious threat.

The smile she bestowed on each man in turn was supercilious and slow. 'Bit hard with no key.'

'Then we will.' He leant over and yanked on the brass lock. 'What the hell kind of lock is this?'

Fed up with the attitudes, Vicky decided these two had

gone too far in their game of intimidation, especially Shortie. The taller one, she could handle. He appeared more reasonable. 'If you damage it, I will sue you.' The man jerked upright. 'The chest is antique.'

'Gina,' she yelled. Poor girl must have been eavesdropping for there was a thump before Gina stepped into the room with an ashen face and in so short a time it was obvious she had been standing directly behind the passage door. 'Sweetie, can you please ring Granny's lawyer? The number is in my mobile phone. Graeme Hunt. Ask him to come here ASAP. Tell him we are being treated unfairly by police. No, better still, ring Uncle Marty.' She turned to the taller officer, mainly because she detested Shortie's attitude. 'I am going to sit in the chair over there.' She pointed to a single lounge chair set under the picture window. 'I will wait there until Martin St James arrives when I will inform him how you have acted with untoward aggression, demanding I answer questions without my lawyer present and how you refused to identify yourselves. I invited you into my home and gave you permission to sight the chest. I have not given you permission to wreck it and you do not have a search warrant so have no right to demand it be opened. You can do whatever you like but I suggest you do it outside since you don't have a search warrant, nor any evidence I have committed a crime for I haven't, so there can't be any evidence.' Terrified of some kind of retribution, Vicky stalked across the room, perched on the edge of the chair and folded her arms. 'You two should have done your homework before coming here thinking you could get away with your bully boy tactics.'

'What do you mean?' The taller man, damn but she hated thinking of these two as tall and short but still they hadn't shown their badges nor introduced themselves. He edged away as he straightened. The flash of fear in his eyes delighted Vicky. Maybe now he understood Vicky knew something about legal rights.

'You will find out when Martin arrives. He was my husband's partner. You might want to look him up on your computer when you get back to your squad car out there.' Her pointed finger was deliberate.

Every ounce of air whooshed out of her lungs when she heard the kitchen door close on the backs of the two men. With her body buzzing with adrenalin, Vicky was not sure what she wanted to do but sitting for however long it was going to take for Marty to arrive was not an option. A vicious workout on gym machines would be the perfect way to rid her body of intense angst but leaving was probably not a good idea.

'Uncle Marty can't get here until around eight. He says to not answer any questions and don't let them search without a warrant.' When Gina leant against the door jamb it looked as though she needed the support to keep upright. An ashen face along with trembling fingers were huge clues to how she was feeling.

'You okay, Sweetie?'

'Yes, of course.' Her face crumpled. A second later she ran and threw herself against Vicky's chest. 'I'm scared, Mum.'

'I know, Sweetie, because I feel the same.'

'What's going on?' The words stuttered out between sobs. Gina's tears followed, soaking Vicky's cotton top.

'I wish I knew but Uncle Marty will sort things,' she whispered in Gina's ear. 'The police were wrong to barge in here the way they did. They were wrong to not give their names or show their badges.' Vicky held on tight, wrapping her arms around Gina's heaving shoulders, giving needed comfort until Gina drew away on a long, loud sniff.

'Oh, sorry,' she said but grinned at the less than ladylike snort. Both her hands brushed away the moisture from her eyes and cheeks before she lifted the bottom edge of her T-shirt and swiped away the rest.

'Nothing to be sorry about. You hungry?'

'Not really.'

'Nor am I but I need something to do so why don't we create a fantastic toastie to share? Hmm?' She held out one hand. 'Come on.' It was the last thing Vicky felt like doing but doing nothing for the next three hours would drive her nuts.

Even though the toastie was filled with avocado, tomato, sliced red onion, cheese and cranberry sauce, Vicky struggled to get it down a throat which felt like it was stuffed with corrugated cardboard. When she stood to make hot tea, she glanced out of the window and her eyes boggled. The spot where the police car had stood, was now empty. Stunned but overjoyed, she raced to the sitting room to get a better view, suspecting they might have moved to a different spot, one where they could keep an eye on her movements. From the large picture window the street looked empty apart from normal neighbours' cars and a row of garbage bins which waited to be emptied, except for the spot in front of her house. Damn, she had forgotten it was garbage collection night but maybe it would be a brilliant way to check the street for hidden police vehicles.

She felt like a stalker the way she peered in all directions while placing the garbage bin, moving it a few centimetres one way, wriggling it backwards and forwards until it was in its designated spot one metre from the kerb. There was no police car in sight but she wasn't game to walk the street. It was a good job it wasn't recycle bin week, she thought as she returned to the house. The bag of objects will still be safe for another seven days, which would give her enough time to study each object and maybe keep what she wanted.

To fill in more time, Vicky lingered under a hot shower, willing the tension away. So she could massage her scalp to get rid of the still hovering headache, she shampooed her hair, dug her fingers in, rubbed, rinsed and conditioned. Dressed in clean jeans and jumper, she returned to the kitchen to find Marty perched on a stool at the kitchen bench, a mug of coffee in one hand. Gina sat next to him and joy of joys, there was a smile curling the corners of Gina's mouth upwards.

'Evening, Vicky. Seems like you have a problem or two. Young Gina has filled me in. How are you doing?' He stood, moved around the bench and gave her a much-needed warm hug.

'Could be better and quite frankly I don't have a clue what is going on.'

'Tell me all you know.'

Vicky settled on a stool and related the last two days in detail, including the two guys in sunglasses.

'They didn't tell you why Regina's house is considered a crime scene?'

'No, I asked. The only answer I got was to see their lips clamped together as though they had been super-glued.'

'Sounds like the coroner's report has been released but since you are the daughter, you should have been told as well.'

'I know but these same two officers said Mum didn't have a daughter.' Vicky cocked one eye at Marty's stunned look.

'So who were you living with until you went to university? Who raised you?' His grin had a definite supercilious sway to it.

'Beats me. They weren't impressed when I referred to myself as a ghost and figment of their imagination.'

Marty laughed. 'Not sure what I can find out tonight but let me make a few calls. I will go out the back. This could take a while. Why don't you start on those papers from the chest? Might be some answers.'

'You think what they said was true?'

Marty reached out and gave Vicky a loose hug. 'No, but there must be a reason for your mum to have stashed them away and not ever tell you. There might be some information on your mysterious missing father.'

'Oh, I never thought of that.' A tremor did a good job of snaking downwards from the top of her head to the ends of her toes. 'Not sure if I want to find out.'

In the fourth bedroom, set up as an office, Vicky settled onto the comfy office chair, swung around to face the nearest tall four-drawer metal filing cabinet and tugged out the bottom drawer. Gina had done a great job of stacking the papers neatly, which was a surprise given the speed with which they had emptied the chest. Not sure she really wanted to do this, Vicky hesitated before she reached over and lifted the first elastic band bound pile. Before removing the blue strip of rubber, she flicked through the top edges. Logic told her the papers in each pile would be related. These were but were all receipts. Dates indicated they were from the last three years: the years Regina had not worked. Worsening arthritis had forced retirement much to her mother's chagrin but standing long hours to manage her section of a department store had become impossible.

A more thorough scan revealed how pernickety her mother had been. She had no idea Mum had been industrious in keeping every single shopping receipt, even weekly grocery dockets were Sellotaped in rows onto separate A4 sheets of paper. On a long sigh, Vicky withdrew such sheets, dropped them into the small recycle bin she nudged closer with one foot. Why, oh, why would you keep grocery dockets? The pile was soon reduced by half but the bin was almost full.

On a second cleansing, Vicky recycled receipts for clothes and household goods, but retained the one for the TV to check for warranty dates. A few pages needed more thorough examination for they didn't seem to make much sense, so she added them to the TV docket to be studied in detail once she had turfed the junk.

By the time she had gone through the second pile, which contained receipts for the last two years of Regina's working life, Vicky's back ached and the paper bin had overflown onto the carpet. The loud knock at the front door was a relief.

Vicky paused to stuff in the few pages which fell to the floor before she picked up the bin. At the second more insistent knock, she wrapped her arms around the bin, using her chin to keep the papers in while she strode along the passage, past Gina's closed door from where rock music emanated at the reasonable level Vicky insisted on, past the family bathroom, her bedroom and into the sitting room.

'Coming,' she yelled at the third, even louder thump. When she opened the door, she swore under her breath. The same two police officers stood there, badges held out and open, to make an issue but she didn't read them for her eyes stalled on the folded paper the taller man held in his fist. She bet it was a hastily gained search warrant.

'Mrs Victoria Saunders, we are arresting you on suspicion of murder.'

The bin dropped with a resounding bang, scattering most of the papers at her feet.

Five

'Not good enough, fellas.'

Vicky squealed at the deep voice from behind. A hand settled on her shoulder, gave a slight squeeze but it wasn't enough to ease her thrumming tension. Having Marty here was a blessing but nowhere near as good as having Mike. Heavens but she missed her husband.

'Sorry, I didn't mean to frighten you,' Marty whispered in her ear.

'Who are you?' asked one of the men but with her head turned towards Marty, Vicky didn't see which one had made the officious demand. Shortie, she assumed, because he seemed to be the one with an attitude problem, the sort who gave police a bad name. With her heart doing a darn good job of threatening to thump right out of her chest, Vicky eyed Shortie at the same time Marty brushed against her side and stilled.

'Martin St James, Vicky is my client.'

It was only a look which passed between the two officers after it swung between Marty and her and lingered on the arm Marty still had on her shoulder, but the look said so much. It was as if Vicky could read their minds, which, she guessed, were in the gutter. Marty dropped his hand by his side, which only made it appear more probable there was something sexual going on between the two of them. As if. Even though

Vicky knew it was for the best, she felt bereft at the loss of human contact. To hide her face, she crouched down to retrieve the scattered papers, piling them in an untidy heap before she managed to roll them into a tube. She threaded the tube through the rubbish still in the bin where they sprang right back out of the roll.

'Keep your minds above your belts. I have known Vicky for years. Her late husband was my best friend and partner.' The words were meant to negate improper suggestions but somehow they sounded worse. Tough, let them think what they like, she thought as she stood.

It felt weird when Marty voiced her thoughts but it meant he had read the look the same way, so she hadn't misinterpreted, which was a good thing because these past few days had been so out of the ordinary she was beginning to feel she'd been transported to some alternate world. Everything was way out of whack.

'Let's get down to business,' said Marty. 'Why don't you outline the facts which have led you to believe Vicky has committed murder?'

'Mrs Saunders was present when Regina Wakefield was poisoned.'

'Poisoned!' shot out of Vicky's mouth on a gasp of shock. 'What do you mean? Mum died in her sleep.' A surge of adrenalin increased her heart rate to something which felt off the charts. Surely a body couldn't withstand such a rate. Hoping Marty had some answers she shot a glance in his direction.

'There was poison in her system,' Marty said so quietly, it sounded as though he was simply stating a regular fact when in reality he was sending massive shock waves through her body. 'I've just spoken to the coroner.'

Vicky spun her entire body around to face him. 'Poison!' Far out, she couldn't keep the shriek at bay. 'Sorry, I didn't mean to yell but this is... Lord, I can't believe this. Why? Why would anyone want to poison Mum?' She spun back and glared at the officer. 'I did not kill my mother.'

'Mum, what's happening?' Gina barrelled into her. 'Uncle Marty?' Gina's wet eyes peered at her godfather.

'It's okay, Gina. We both know your mother has not committed any crime.' He tugged Gina against his chest. 'Let's clear this up right now. First, gentlemen, you need some sort of proof about a crime before you can make an arrest.'

'We have proof. We found Mrs Wakefield's diary. The entry for Wednesday 7th April has 7pm, dinner, Vicky. Mrs Wakefield died sometime between 6pm and 10pm that night.'

Vicky laughed - she couldn't help it. The laughter gurgled up her throat and kept coming. She laughed so much, tears leaked and she had to lean against Marty and grasp his shoulder to keep from tumbling over. 'There's...' she choked out before laughter erupted again. 'There's the same entry for every Wednesday...' she gasped on a swallowed laugh. 'Every Wednesday of the entire year and the year before and the year before.' She managed to gulp in a long sobering breath. Eyeing the officers she sucked in another long breath. 'It doesn't mean Gina and I had dinner with Mum every single Wednesday. It was simply a day we tried to keep free of commitments so we could have family time whenever we could manage it. More so since my husband died. Many times one or other of us cancelled. Gina sometimes had school events scheduled on a Wednesday. Mum often cancelled for similar reasons, as did I. We cancelled on the 7th. The Wednesday before we dined with Marty and his family to celebrate his wife's birthday. Mum came as well.' When she glanced at Marty it was obvious he was trying to keep a straight face.

'Why did you cancel on the 7th?' Marty asked, his eyes crinkling.

'I filled in for Fiona at work. Her little boy had a high fever.'

A great guffaw burst from Marty's mouth. Unable to contain herself, Vicky joined in.

'What the hell is so funny?' The words were yelled so loud, Vicky jerked, her laughter ceasing in an instant.

'Do you want to tell them or should I?' Marty asked, his humour still simmering with the corners of his eyes crinkled.

'Better be you. These two men don't seem to want to believe anything I say.' Somehow Vicky managed to sober, stiffened her spine and eyed each officer in turn, desperate to watch their faces.

'Vicky manages the legal side of The Citizen's Advice Bureau. If she was working after hours, she would have been manning the phone for urgent cases. She had two years studying law before young Gina was born. Vicky gave up her studies to care for the baby while her husband, Mike, completed his degree. Mike and I were three years ahead of Vicky. Instead of returning to university, Vicky became a legal secretary, working for our firm. She knows the law inside out and if a request is for something more technical beyond her knowledge, she knows who to ask. Is that piece of paper a warrant for her arrest?' Marty pointed to the lengthways folded paper, which now wore creases where it had been gripped too hard against the tall officer's chest.

The man squirmed. 'Umm, no, it's a search warrant to search these premises.'

'On what grounds?' Marty asked, now sounding lawyer-like.

'Umm...'

'Let me look at your warrant.' Marty held out one hand but the man was hesitant.

Vicky knew he had no choice but to hand it over. Her breath held while Marty tugged the paper out of the officer's hand and scanned the two pages. He folded it before handing it back.

'Well since there is no suspect here, I can't see how this warrant has any relevance.'

'What about her?' Shortie stepped forward with one finger pointed to Gina, who still stood tucked under Marty's left arm.

'Mum!' Gina's face changed in an instant.

Beyond angry at the unfounded implication, Vicky stepped in front of her daughter in protective mode. 'Gina went straight from school to a girlfriend's house. She dined with them and I picked her up on my way home from work around 9.45pm. I cannot be certain of the exact minute for at the time mere minutes were not relevant. Here, I will give you the number so you can ring them now to check. That way you will know for certain I haven't contacted them and created some skulduggery by asking them to lie for me.' Without waiting, she spun around on one foot, raced back inside, along the passage, into the kitchen, grabbed her mobile phone from the bench and raced back. She stood slap bang in front of the men, made a show of scrolling through the numbers, until she found the one she wanted. She pressed call and held out the phone to Shortie, only because he was such a pain in the rear end. 'Go on, ask away. Joanne Lister. You can also check both of our phones and Joanne's as well, for the SMS messages we sent each other to organise the evening.'

The poor man had no choice but to talk. Vicky was delighted at his fluster with neck and cheeks turning a glorious shade of pink. Well, she thought it was glorious but he didn't, for he turned away, strode across the porch and down the path. This minor triumph felt so damn good. Gina slid from Marty's arm and sidled over to Vicky, nestling against her side. Vicky lifted one arm, slung it around Gina's shoulders to give her a gentle squeeze. 'Relax, Sweetie.'

'Yeah, right,' Gina mumbled. 'Easy to say, impossible to do,' she added.

Vicky looked down and smiled at Gina's upturned face. 'We can prove where we were. Again they didn't do their homework but jumped to conclusions because it was easier than doing real legwork to find real evidence.'

'Unfounded conclusions,' Marty added.

Shortie returned, nodded to his partner and handed Vicky her phone. The displeasure on his face told the story.

'Are you satisfied?' Vicky dared to ask.

'About your daughter, yes. We'll need to verify your presence at the Bureau so we can eliminate you from our list of suspects.' It delighted her how the tall officer had modulated his tone to something which sounded a lot more reasonable. This man, Vicky could deal with.

'I am stifled by privacy laws. It will require a court order for me to reveal the names of clients with whom I spoke on that night. There is nothing I can do about it. I am duty-bound to uphold the laws I work under but the security guard will be able to verify my presence and the time I left for he always walks after-hours' workers to their cars. Brendan McCawley.'

'There's still the matter of interfering with evidence.' Shortie hadn't yet lost his belligerent tone.

Fed up with his manner, Vicky stepped closer to him, right into his personal space. 'I still don't know your name,' she took her time to eyeball both men, 'either of your names but had you or the coroner's representative had the decency to inform me,' she stressed the word, 'The next of kin, about a possible crime scene, we wouldn't have gone to her house. Mum's lawyer told me things were cleared and gave us the go-ahead. We did not arrive at Mum's house until around ten, Friday night. Since we were both exhausted we went to bed. When I woke, I showered. We ate breakfast in the kitchen, washed the few dishes, put them away before we wandered through the house to decide which room would be the easiest to clean. When we reached the sitting room we decided to keep the chest and leather rocker. We managed to get the chest into the back of my car, Gina drove to the nearby delicatessen to buy coffee. You arrived, I left when Gina came back. End of story. Oh, and we moved the stuff off the bed Gina slept in. If we inadvertently interfered with possible evidence, I am sorry but no-one,' she paused to glare at both officers, 'bothered to tell us otherwise.'

Spent after her tirade, Vicky stepped back again, desperate for the security of Marty's presence but careful not to touch him.

'Doesn't explain the evidence you removed,' said the tall man.

'The chest?' Vicky asked while straightening her spine into a rigid rod. 'I fail to see how a solid wooden chest can be a weapon for murder, especially one involving poison. It is freaking heavy. No-one, not even you,' she indicated to the taller of the two men, 'would be able to lift it without assistance.'

'Not the chest *per se* but the items you stashed in the chest.'

'Excuse me? The chest is empty. Has been for years, my mother always insisted. If you can open it, feel free but don't even dare to think you can damage it.' Vicky turned away on a huff of released frustration, stormed back into the house. Frustration wasn't a good enough word to describe how she felt. Nor was angry. Furious sounded much better and there were a few more unsavoury words she wanted to add.

The shuffle of footsteps accompanied by the mumble of men's voices were an unwelcome intrusion. Vicky turned back, retraced her steps, followed the sounds. The only thing she spied was Gina's back disappearing into the sitting room. Damn cheek, she thought but another thought chased away the first. Let them see for themselves. She hadn't lied about

there being nothing in the chest and the bit about the key...
well she was only relaying her mother's edict: the key wasn't
there. When she reached the sitting room door, she paused at
the sight of three men shaking the chest from side-to-side.

'There is something there,' one muttered but she couldn't
figure out who.

Amused, Vicky watched them upturn the chest with a few
grunts before they grappled it hand-over-hand to get it upside down, one man with his ears against the solid wood. She
wanted to laugh at their antics for they looked ridiculous but
common sense shouted at her to let them go.

'Got a skewer?' Marty asked with amusement tickling the
corners of his mouth. 'Let them open it. Sounds like something small in there.'

A snigger escaped before Vicky swallowed on a choke.
'Fine, I'll get you a skewer.' Marty shadowed her through to
the kitchen. She tugged open the long drawer stuffed with
every kitchen gadget and cooking implement known to
mankind, rummaged around, pulled out a packet of wooden
satay sticks which had been there so long she didn't recall ever
buying them. 'I am desperate to see their faces when they see
what's in there.'

'What is it?' Marty whispered after a quick glance over his
shoulder toward the opening to ensure they were not being
observed.

'Three paper clips – rusty and one ancient pencil stub.'
She choked in her laughter which threatened to bubble out
but still had to jam her fist over her mouth and pinch her nose
shut.

'Oh, I'm going to enjoy this,' Marty said as he returned to the sitting room.

It took fifteen minutes of whispered curses, snapped satay sticks and macho man-power take-overs before the men managed to release the lock. While eager hands lifted the lid, Vicky swung her eyes between the two officers.

'Shit,' blew from Shortie's mouth.

'There are women present,' his superior admonished in an undertone.

'Sorry,' was mumbled but Vicky bet he didn't mean it as she ambled over to the chest and peered in.

'Oops, I lied. There *is* something in there. A relic of a pencil and three itty-bitty rusted paperclips. You'd better make sure you don't leave your fingerprints on them as you put them in evidence bags. Oh, and don't forget the dust. It could be the poison you were talking about.'

Discretion played a huge part in her hiding in the toilet after the vicious glares speared at her.

Six

Her forehead rested in outstretched fingers while she scanned the old-fashioned type-written words on the single sheet of paper. The edges were yellow, the creases deep and the words indecipherable. Greek was her first thought but she wasn't certain. Something about the way the words were set out gave the impression the letter was official but who knew? Written missives from way back were formally set out but she guessed friend-to-friend letters would have been handwritten with pen and ink. To her, type-written would have been for more formal business-like correspondence. There was no date to give a clue as to when it had been written.

Even after she wracked her brain to sift through bits and pieces of old memories, she could not recall her mother ever mentioning someone from Greece, if the letter was written in Greek. Maybe the letter was older than she imagined. A grandparent, maybe, or great-grandparent but they were as mysterious as her non-existent father. Mum never mentioned them. *All dead,* she repeated every time Vicky asked until she got sick of asking and asked no more. *No point in dredging up the dead.* How many times had she heard the words?

Vicky turned back to the letter as her mind churned, seeking what she knew about Greek modern history. Didn't the British fight in that region during WW1? They fought in

Turkey. Close enough, but the receiver of this letter would have been able to read Greek. Defeated, Vicky moved the letter onto a small pile of other such mysterious insights into her mother's life.

Reading through the first file slowed to a pace less than a snail would make unless it was in the last throes of dying. After an hour, she had six documents of mystery, all of which needed further scrutiny, and an empty recycle bin. On a long sigh she leant back, slid her eyes shut and rubbed at temples which had started to ache. The day had been traumatic and long. She hadn't dared leave the safety of the bathroom until Marty had rid her home of police officers but only after he had been able to convince them neither she nor Gina were responsible for Regina's death.

But they still wanted to question her. At the station. Soon. Written statements were required. She knew this but it still rankled. And she wasn't so sure Shortie, Constable Aiden Bishop, she later learned, didn't have her pegged for some other heinous crime. For some reason he didn't seem to want to believe her but Sergeant Phil Rogers had eased his stance and become more human and understanding. It was a good job he was the senior officer. Vicky sent a request skywards for the sergeant to be the one who took her statement.

Too tired to think straight, Vicky shoved the papers back into the thin black cardboard file and replaced it in the drawer of the filing cabinet. There was no light or noise creeping from underneath Gina's door as she passed. Two-minute ablutions were all she could be bothered with before she changed into fleecy pyjamas and fell into bed.

* * *

There was a rumble in her ears, which caused her body to tremble. Vicky fought in her sleep to figure out what it was.

'Mum, Mum, wake up, Mum.'

'Huh?' Her eyelids shot apart. A shaft of light lasered in, stabbing her to awareness. 'What's wrong. Why is the light on?'

'Mum, are you okay?'

With a fuzzy brain, Vicky fought to get upright as she tugged arms from twisted bedding and winced at the brightness. It took a few quick shakes of her head to align her brain cells and recognise her daughter who crouched by the side of the bed. 'Why are you waking me in the middle of the night?'

'Mum, it's ten o'clock in the morning.'

'Huh?' A quick glance at the bedside clock confirmed it was indeed ten and an equally quick glance towards the window told her Sunday had arrived. ANZAC Day, she remembered. Her bed was a mess, confirming the dream she'd had was an active one, with her being chased by two men wearing trench coats, Akubra hats and sunglasses. It was difficult to figure out if the tangled bedclothes occurred when she had run between tall trees which had drenched her with dripping water, or when the men caught her and she struggled to free herself from bound wrists and ankles. It was a huge relief to discover she was in her own bedroom, unbound and the only person after her, was Gina.

'Sorry, Sweetie, looks like I overslept.'

Gina leant forwards, gave Vicky a hug then sat back on her

heels. 'Looks like you've had a fight with Jeff Fenech. Are you okay?'

'Didn't know you even knew who Jeff Fenech is.' To tell Gina the truth would be a mistake. Letting her know of the intense nightmare would only increase the girl's level of worry. Vicky forced a smile. 'I'm fine but it looks like I had a restless night after the happenings of yesterday. Sorry I slept in but maybe my body was telling me I needed it.' She managed to tug her feet free and stood. 'Have you had breakfast?'

'Yeah, ages ago. Can I go to Sarah's place?' Gina hesitated. 'I figured you wouldn't need me at Granny's.'

'Homework?'

'Done. There was only the book critique.'

'About the dumb book you hated?'

A coy grin crept from the corners of Gina's mouth. 'Yeah, that one but it wasn't so bad at the end. Once you explained what it meant I sort of got it.'

'Enough to answer questions in your exams?' It had taken two readings of the set novel, plus studying several internet reviews for Vicky to figure out why the book was chosen as an English Literature novel. It certainly wouldn't have been her choice to give to 17-year-old kids but it was required reading. Gina was a good student, always conscientious about handing in every assignment on time and to a high standard. Her aspirations were to follow in her father's footsteps and take up law. Her study habits were good enough for Vicky to know Gina would be able to hack the work requirements.

'When I pass you'll know the answer.' This time Gina's

grin was of the cheekier kind. 'So, can I go to Sarah's? She said it was fine.'

After the past two days, it would be good for Gina to experience some normalcy: to be a teenage girl hanging out with her best friend, doing girl stuff, chatting, laughing, listening to music. 'Okay but take your mobile so I can contact you if I need you. Be back by five but if they've got an outing planned, make sure you come home.'

Gina's grin widened as she pounced upright. 'Thanks.' After a quick hug she ran. Sarah only lived a block down and around the corner, close enough the girls could safely walk the distance but not so close they lived in each other's homes.

Vicky took things slower. She wallowed under a hot shower where she undertook the full beauty routine of hair shampoo, shaving legs and exfoliating after which she massaged in her favourite body lotion before she blow-dried her shoulder length dark brown hair. A leisurely breakfast of mashed avocado and poached egg on toast was eaten on the covered back patio while she appreciated the sounds of birds flittering amongst the mature shrubs of her large backyard.

Dishes done, it was an easy decision to retrieve the garbage bag of objects from the chest and spill them onto the kitchen table for a thorough examination.

Something hidden under a small box, glinted, begging her to pick it up first. Shoving the box to one side, Vicky stalled before picking up the glass beads strung on a thin piece of common brown kitchen string. Oh, my. She had made the bracelet for Mum, way back. Heavens, she must have only been six. At school. Memories surged. Year one. All the kids in the class had threaded beads to make their mother a Christmas present. Tears welled. Mum had kept it all these years but why had she never said? Why had she kept these things hidden? Had it been treasured the same way Vicky treasured hand-made bits and pieces Gina had given her? Had Mum loved Vicky? A tear dropped onto the beads.

But Gina knew what Vicky had kept, knew where they were stored in a box in the bottom of the sitting room cupboard, next to the box of special Christmas ornaments. Every year, they had fun going through the box with Gina embarrassed by her crude drawings and soppy words in various cards. When Gina had been a toddler, Mike had guided her tiny hand to write those words. Once she had learned to write she had scrawled her own words, many misspelt but to Vicky they were precious: never to be discarded. Was it possible her own mother had felt the same way? A crack opened in her heart, allowing a flow of gooey warmth to ease in.

She took care to place the fragile bracelet to one side, then poked around some more, homing in on another bracelet, this one a gold chain with a metal name tag. She lifted it with two fingers, dropped it into the palm of her hand. The tag was engraved but she didn't have to read the name. *Mummy.* Oh, God. Vicky had saved her pocket money and done odd jobs all year to buy this for her mother's 40th birthday. Memories shot to the forefront. Age about nine, she had wanted to get something meaningful, something precious. Mum had worn it for... she couldn't recall but it must have been a few years. But Mum had said she'd lost it when the catch had broken. Vicky studied the catch, noticed the broken loop. Oh, Lord.

She wrapped her fingers tight around the chain while fighting back tears. 'Damn it, Mum, why didn't you ever tell me?' she yelled towards the ceiling.

The next item to catch her eye was a small box measuring about 10 x 5cm. Made of stiff cardboard, it was covered in bright paper featuring Chinese or Japanese motifs; Vicky wasn't certain which and didn't recognise the box. She was sure she had never seen it before. It rattled when lifted, intriguing her. Taking care, she eased the lid, wriggling it from side-to-side, corner-to-corner until it freed itself from years of un-use. A soft *plop* and the lid came off, exposing a handful of shells. Vicky picked one up, a shiny cowrie, perfect condition, with dark circles of brown on the smooth rounded top. It was beautiful. The second shell was like a fan with pale oyster pink stripes. The third, a spiral in white, brought back the memory.

A holiday, the first she could recall, when they had actually gone away for an entire week, staying in a motel one street back from the beach. Esperance. Yes, it was the first time she went to Esperance. Now, she knew how back then, raising a child as a single mother was beyond difficult, especially when there was no man to provide much needed child support. It was even more difficult on the basic wage her mother earned as a check-out chick. It had taken years in the same department store for Regina to move through the ranks to managerial level with better pay.

Early the first morning, she and her mum had gone for a walk along the beach. It had been cold to start with but once the sun rose, so did the temperature. By the time they reached the caravan-type café at the other end, past the small jetty, it had been warm enough to take off her jacket and tie it around her waist. They had breakfast of toasted bacon sandwiches, a real treat for her, sitting at a portable table in front of the caravan with only a wide strip of glinting white sand between them and the Great Southern Ocean. Vicky had taken off her sandals and waded in the water, which, she recalled now, had been warmer than she had expected and it had been crystal clear. It was under the water where she had spied this shell.

A smile hovered as she studied the shell, ran her finger over the rough spirals, turned it over, marvelling at the smoothness of the inside and the perfect mathematical ratio of the spirals. She sat back, forcing the memories from the dark recesses.

The week had been magical with Mum making sure they filled each day with fun activities. Hmm, there was the museum with the humungous train engine in the wooden building across the road from the beach. They had gone fishing twice, using hand-held lines while they stood in ankle-deep water on the wet sand of the beach one night and the end of the jetty on another. She pictured the fish and chips they had eaten while they sat cross-legged on towels spread out on the sand, tugging the food from a torn end of the white paper which kept the food warm. And the pizza, delivered to the door on the night it rained. Pizza had been such a luxury for until then Mum had never been able to afford take-away but always cooked plain but healthy food at home.

They drove somewhere one day but the destination eluded her. Couldn't have been memorable if she couldn't recall. But the drive to and from Esperance had been long – all day long, not getting home until late at night. Somehow, she knew she had hated the drive, eager to reach Esperance and equally as eager to get home, despite the week having been fabulous.

Now she recalled the holiday a new realisation hit, her mother had gone out of her way to ensure they enjoyed every second of their time together for Mum only ever had four weeks off work each year and many of Vicky's holidays were spent being palmed off to friends. There were no relatives to babysit her when she was a youngster. Why hadn't she been able to see, way back then, how her mother had given her full attention, showed Vicky how important their time together was? Didn't that indicate a form of love and caring? A sudden wave of sadness swept through her for not understanding,

Vicky fingered all eight different shells in the box, now certain they had all come from the same place. And Mum had kept them which surely must mean they had been important to her as well. Why else would she have stored them away? 'Oh, Mum, I'm sorry,' Vicky whispered as she added the box to the two bracelets and the crack in her heart widened to let in even more warmth.

The ring of her phone was an intrusion she didn't appreciate. Ignoring it didn't work for as soon as the familiar tune rang out, it began again. She huffed out a long breath, reached for the phone and jammed it against her ear. The message was short and welcome in one sense while unwelcome in another.

The police had finished with Mum's house. She was free to resume her activities. Such formal words: resume her activities – they held an innuendo she wasn't sure she liked.

Seven

While she sat in her car parked in the driveway of 28 Siesta Lane, Vicky stared at the drawn curtains. They had been open before so who could have closed them and why? Must have been the police, but why would they unless they didn't want neighbours to see? Fiddlesticks, she shouldn't let her mind think dark thoughts. Just because Constable Aiden Bishop was an upstart, full of his own self-importance and didn't have a clue how to relate to people, didn't mean they were up to some sort of funny business. He was not the only police officer she had met who was arrogant but most were genuine friendly, helpful people with a difficult job to do: a job she wouldn't be able to handle.

The tension which simmered low in her gut wasn't welcome but Vicky couldn't seem to shove it away while she walked along the path, up the two steps onto the portico. Her right hand grasped the front door key, slid it into the lock and twisted. There was an audible *snick* as the barrel released. Vicky gave the door a gentle shove, holding her breath as it swung open. Her eyes boggled on a sharp indrawn breath. 'Oh, my goodness.' Her hands flew to her face and gripped each side. The passage looked as though a massive wrecking ball had taken a swipe from front to back, knocking pictures off walls, flinging the two narrow hall tables onto the floor. Table drawers had parted company with their keepers and treasured ornaments were nothing but broken shards on the floor.

The sort of anger she had never felt before, surged and exploded. She picked her way over debris, zigzagged from door to door to check in each room as she went. A wrecking ball was too mild. It was more like a war zone after being strafed by bombs. Beyond furious, she used the camera on her mobile phone to snap photo after photo of the destruction before storming to her car, her breathing so hard she had to pause at the door and will her anger to abate before daring to drive. The way she churned inside she figured she would cause an accident before she reached the police station.

'Damn, damn, damn,' exploded from her mouth, to accompany the thumps of a clenched fist on the roof of her car. 'Why?' she yelled while staring at the sky, which now contained clouds as dark as her anger. She blew out her cheeks, three times, closed her eyes while counting to ten ever so slow. It helped – a little – but enough to get in the car and drive without cleaning up every other car, bicycle and pedestrian who dared to be on the road.

While she drove, various thoughts tumbled through her brain, too fast to make any logical sense. Marty – she should send the photos to Marty but she knew how precious weekends were for busy lawyers, how down-time with partners and children was so important and she had already encroached on his precious time by dragging him away from his wife and three young children for several hours last night. No, not going to do it. She knew the law; knew that not ever did the police have the right to destroy belongings the way they had.

Maybe if they were searching for a stash of drugs they could search in hidden crevices, take apart furniture but to smash pictures, ornaments, china and glassware was beyond the pale. 'No right, no damn right,' she chanted in time to the windscreen wipers swinging from side-to-side when the heavens opened with a deluge.

Only when she arrived at her local police station did she realise she didn't have a clue if this was where the officers were stationed. Too bad, she thought, they would be able to find out. It was why they had computers; ones which were interconnected throughout the state. Even though it looked as if the sky was about to deliver a repeat of the forty-day flood, Vicky parked, shoved the door open and ran, getting soaked through within seconds. When she reached the front door, she grabbed the handle and tugged, almost wrenching her arm out of its socket when the door didn't budge and the surrounding plate glass panels shuddered and rattled.

Vicky stared at the offending door before swinging her eyes to the right where she read the prominent, easy-to-read sign indicating opening hours. Closed to the public all day Sunday. Just dandy. Furious with herself for not even recalling it was Sunday she cursed the world, spun around and splashed her way through puddles and streaming gutters back to her car. By the time she was seated she was wet – wetter than a shag who had been floundering in the water for an hour and had nowhere to perch to hang out her wings to dry. She was also mad – madder than the Mad Hatter. No, not such a good analogy. He was crazy mad, not angry mad. Then again maybe she was on the verge of crazy mad for her life seemed to have taken a turn towards insanity at the moment.

Her grin widened. She turned the key, the engine rumbled to life. As she reached over she pressed the button for the radio but winced at the loud rock music which blasted through the speakers. She used one hand to switch to her favourite classical station, turned the volume down to a barely audible level and reversed from the parking bay. Determined to calm, she took her sweet time to check the road was clear before turning left, headed for the central city police station. They would be open: they were always open and were going to regret being open once she arrived.

The Chopin waltz was pleasant, soothing her ire as she passed the small shopping centre, the 24-hour gym and nearby medical centre. She didn't even mind the wait for the lights to change from red to green at the major intersection. By the time she reached the flashing red lights and barrier at the railway crossing she was feeling cool, calm and collected despite the discomfort of saturated clothing, which had begun to steam from the blast of the heater.

It was unfortunate Tchaikovsky's Concerto in B flat minor began while she crossed the river for every thump of the piano chords moving up the keyboard seemed to increase her heartbeat with the same intensity. By the time she parked in front of the main police station, her tension pumped as hard as Gina's rock music. Water still leaked from the sky but had reduced to a steady stream instead of a deluge as Vicky ran towards the main door, this time taking a lot more care to tug on the handle.

The door swung open with ease to reveal a room humming with activity. Half a dozen frazzled looking people were standing at the front counter. An equal number sat hunched in a row of seats. None wore smiles. Two police officers crowded a man against the end of the counter. The dishevelled man, who looked as though he had slept in his clothes for an entire week, did not look overjoyed to be there. Three uniformed officers behind the counter fielded questions while they scribbled notes or punched computer keys each time they glanced down. Phones rang, voices hummed, seats creaked and feet shuffled, along with sighs of people who sounded fed up.

This was going to take a while so Vicky settled into a vinyl chair and picked up a magazine so tatty, she wondered what disease she would come away with.

Two hours later, Vicky felt like she wanted to commit the murder she was originally charged with. An interview, interspersed with several phone calls and her pictures being emailed, had resulted in vehement denials from the forensic team. No way did they leave Regina Wakefield's house in such a state but now she was right back where she had started - denied access to her mother's house while another forensics crew searched for clues as to who had made a midnight marauding of 28 Siesta Lane, the street name now such an anomaly it was ridiculous.

Her clothes had continued to steam from the warmth of the heated interview room Vicky had been ensconced in for almost two hours. Not only did they feel uncomfortable, but her slacks chafed at each step and a less than pleasant aroma emanated from her direction. Fed up with everything, she returned home, scrubbed her body clean, dropped damp clothes into a bucket of soaker, dressed in smart warm slacks, a blouse and pretty sweater and left again, in search of good food in a noisy atmosphere and a glass of red – maybe two glasses. The level of noise was important for silence would force her brain to think and she didn't want ideas to rampage through her mind to allow a wild imagination to germinate ludicrous suggestions. For once, noise would be preferable.

A crowd of cars at a suburban hotel drew her like a magnet. It was a popular watering hole with the pub fare having a good reputation, hence the packed car park. Perfect, exactly what she needed. It took two slow circles of the car park before she noticed a car leaving but so did another arrival. Vicky wasn't usually an aggressive driver but today she revved the engine, shoved on the indicator and nosed forwards, barely giving the departing driver enough room to manoeuvre out.

'Not going to happen,' she muttered to the new arrival who replicated her actions from the opposite direction. Departing car edged out, Vicky edged in, glared at the other driver and ignored the single finger salute aimed at her. 'First in, first served,' she gloated while straightening her vehicle from the skewed entry she had managed, which had left her absolutely no room to alight. Not in the space to hear words of abuse, she waited, pretending to take a phone call until the loser moved on and crawled around the corner of the lane. The very second the car was out of sight Vicky grabbed her small tote bag and departed, jogging through various vehicles to the footpath where she slowed to a more sedate power-walk around to the front entry, through the open doorway into the public bar.

She had wanted noise but not this much. The stench of beer was overwhelming as was the level of voices, each person shouting to be heard over the ruckus. A television blared a horse race which added to the hubbub. It was difficult to wind a path through the crowd, most of whom were standing since every bar stool was occupied, some with the edges of two backsides fighting for space where only one should fit. It was a relief to reach the slightly quieter lounge bar with people crammed around beer and chip laden tables. Again, it was crowded, this time with sports' fans eyeing two separate programmes which blared on large flat screens on opposite walls: soccer on one with Aussie Rules Football on the other.

Through a set of wooden swing doors, Vicky found what she was looking for - the restaurant. Here there was a far more acceptable level of noise consisting of chinking cutlery against china dishes, a rumble of quieter voices chatting, the hiss of steam from a coffee machine. Instead of the overpowering yeasty stench of spilled beer, fried food and coffee dominated. A waitperson arrived with a pile of menus balanced on one bent arm.

'How many?'

'Only me but I don't mind sharing if tables are at a premium.'

'No, it's fine. I have just cleared a table for two. This way.' The young lass dressed in traditional server garb of black slacks and white blouse, turned away. Vicky followed to a table under the front window. Perfect.

Settled in with a glass of wine, Vicky sat back and sighed long and deep. After a detailed study of the menu she decided on Chicken Kiev, with salad on the side, despite having ordered red wine and not white. She wasn't a wine snob so who cared? Kiev was a dish she wouldn't cook at home. It was a habit she had created; when dining out she never ordered what she cooked at home. Couldn't see the point. She always ordered more complicated dishes, the ones she never had time to prepare. Depending on the size of the meal, she might have a slice of decadent cheesecake as afters. Something decadent sounded darn good. Calorie counting and weight watching could go take a flying leap.

To keep her mind away from topics she didn't want to think about, Vicky made up stories about groups at other tables. A group to her right, of four adults, didn't once look up from their mobile phones the entire time they sat there. Food was consumed by blind stabs with a fork and shovelling whatever landed on the tines, into mouths. The same hand padded around for a glass, gripped, lifted, sipped then replaced; all without looking while the other hand held the phone with the thumb tap-tapping. Why even come to share a meal if you weren't going to communicate? Ha, she imagined an argument about where to go. All had disagreed on the venue, arguing vehemently. The driver had turned into this venue to shut everyone up. Now they texted other friends or maybe the entire world, with slanderous comments about each other. Could even be plotting how to get rid of them. No, let's not go down the track of murder.

The aroma of garlic preceded her plate being lowered.

Melted butter oozed from a tiny crack in the side of the crispy, golden-crumbed coating on the chicken. A huge pile of various greens, topped with halved cherry tomatoes, sliced cucumber with grated beetroot and carrot strands on top, filled the plate. Yum. Sighing in pleasure, Vicky hoed in, sliced off the end of the chicken and smiled at the gush of melted butter which sent up an even stronger smell of roasted garlic.

While she savoured each bite, she turned her head to the left. Ah, much better. Two tables joined together to fit ten. Looked like grandpa at the end, grandma to his right, two other sets of adults – possibly children with spouses and four youngsters. A birthday, maybe. She imagined one of significance, so studied the older man with thin white hair, deep wrinkles and a few skin lesion scars marring a still handsome face and settled on 80. They all wore happy faces, mouths moved, hopefully with genial repartee. And not an electronic gadget in sight. She liked this family and could only think of joyful scenarios as the plot to their story.

More joyful than her own story. Fiddlesticks, why did she allow her mind to wander back to her own life, which hadn't been all bad. Most years were happy, delightfully so. She had loved school, found it easy, even though she had worked hard to gain above average marks. Early on, finances were limited but Regina had ensured Vicky never went without the necessities. The frugal life had an upside, teaching Vicky to appreciate the small things and the value of saving to buy a desired object, which made it far more precious because it had been worked so hard for. It had been a triumph to gain a hard-fought place to study law at university. Meeting and falling head over heels for Mike had been one of the highlights of her life. They simply fitted together like two sides of a chocolate mould. Gina had been an accident but a treasured one, especially after the massive haemorrhage at Gina's birth which could only be contained with a hysterectomy. It had been either lose her reproductive organs or her life. Vicky had chosen to live and devoted half her life to raising the only child she would ever have, to the best of her ability. The other half of her life went to Mike, the husband she adored.

They had been happy. Mike was the kind of man every woman dreamed of marrying; sweet-natured, funny, adoring and as handsome as sin. He had been a brilliant prosecution lawyer until he took on a case against a bikie-gang leader. To this day, Vicky didn't believe the car smash which resulted in Mike's untimely death, had been an accident. Nor did Marty but to find proof had been impossible. Mike's loss had devastated her. Still, she mourned his loss, missed him every second of every day and even though the pain of the loss was not so acute, she was not ready to move on. Friends kept telling her to get out, meet someone else, she was still young enough. Easy for them to say. Well, she went out, look at her now, in a restaurant, all alone but a new man's company would be an intrusion; feeling like she was being unfaithful. One day, she knew, she would reach the stage where she would feel comfortable with a new man, but not yet.

After the meal had been demolished, Vicky felt so replete, cheesecake was not going to happen. She slugged down the dregs of her single glass of red, paid her bill and drove home with time to spare before Gina was due.

Eight

It was a good job she had organised a week off, Vicky thought as she waved Gina off for school. Which task did she want to undertake first? It was difficult to decide. There were still papers to sort, shoe boxes to search and more items hidden in the recycle bin. A time had been agreed to meet Marty at the police station to write her statement, something she was not looking forward to. No-one had rung to say she could go back to Mum's place, which was a pain for it was the reason she had taken a week off. Two hours, what could she do in less than two hours? Shoe boxes would be easiest for it only required a single lid to be taken off, a glance inside, lid back on, box back in the wardrobe. Easy.

In her bedroom, she knelt in front of the wardrobe, slid the mirrored door to the left, eyed the six shoe boxes and scoffed. No-one seeing these, would believe they were hers. Even the design on the outside indicated an age before Vicky had even been born. A laugh escaped at the small sketch on the end of the top box. Men's old-fashioned brogues, size 11. As if. But her eyes stalled on the price: 22 pounds, so they were either pre-1966 or from the U.K. Had to be British because Regina didn't emigrate to Australia until 1982. Interesting. Why would Mum have brought out an old shoe box?

'One way to find out,' Vicky muttered as she reached forward to wrap both hands around the box. After it was settled on her lap, her breath stalled while she thumbed the lid off. It slid to the floor in front of her knees to reveal photographs, most of the black and white variety. A musty smell rose as she got more comfortable by unfolding her legs and wriggling backwards to lean against the side of the bed. Her knees were bent, feet flat on the ground allowing the box to nestle in the V. Taking her time, she lifted photographs, one at a time to study the image in each. The only way she could figure out when the photos were taken was by the style of dress.

A cane pram beside a woman who wore a summer dress with the hem hovering below the knees looked to be from the 50's. The fitted top had wide straps revealing the skin of her arms, a square neckline and gathered skirt – definitely 50's. The woman held a baby wrapped loosely in a shawl. Could this be her mum as a baby? And Vicky's grandmother? At the thought, Vicky's heart began to thump. The photo was small, too small to make out features despite bringing it closer to her eyes. She turned it over. Surprise hit. The words were in the same language as the letter in the file. Where does Greece fit?

Going back to the picture, she studied the background. It looked like the woman stood on a pier or jetty with a row of village-type shops aligned along the side of the road in the background and low hills behind the town. Where was it? It didn't look English. Regina. She thought about the name. To her it didn't sound like a Greek name but more European. French? German? Maybe but Mum came from the U.K. It was ridiculous the way her disappointment was so strong as she put the photo on the ground to her left before she delved further into the box and lifted out a few more. Amongst them were some in colour. She filtered them out, placed them to her other side in a rough pile before she sorted the black and whites into separate piles according to size. When the box was empty she lifted the coloured images, fingered through them with a shockwave quivering up her spine. Most were of her at various ages. Stunned, she scrambled upright, spread the photos out on her bed and re-arranged them into a rough timeline.

Memories flicked through her mind as fast as she put each picture down. Interspersed with each thought were questions. Why? Why had Mum kept these hidden away? Why weren't they in albums kept in a bookcase within easy access? Why did Mum never bring them out? In the back of her mind she recalled how she posed in so many different ways for some of these photos, recalled seeing them after they were processed. Maybe they had hung around on the coffee table for a while, in yellow Kodak folders but they had disappeared when the next roll of film came back from the pharmacy. A few individual shots had made it into frames which had been displayed on the mantelpiece or cabinets for several months but they were updated every now and again. Vicky hadn't asked what had happened to the old photo when a new one took its place. At the time it hadn't mattered. The sensation of being important enough to her mother to want a picture on display in the house had over-ridden the need to know about the old photo. In her immature mind as a child, Vicky had imagined it as a sign of being loved, being important to her Mum – that Mum cared about her. Now, being older and wiser, she wasn't so sure.

Finished sorting the photos, Vicky stacked them in order, earliest on top. It wasn't a huge pile, about fifty she guessed, but Mum had kept them – there had to be a reason. While she searched for an envelope to put them in, she noticed the time.

Fiddlesticks, she needed to hurry. She dropped the photos of herself in the drawer of her bedside table, took care to stack the other piles side-by-side in the box, which she slid on top of the other boxes before she closed the wardrobe door.

* * *

To see Marty rise from a chair when she pushed the heavy glass door open was a huge relief, although why she needed his presence was an enigma when she was here to only give a written statement about what she had already said. Tension simmered when he led the way past the end of the reception counter, down a passage into the inner sanctum, past a tangle of computer and paper-strewn desks into a separate room which had the appearance of an interview room. Two chairs on either side of a wide table sent the tension to boiling point.

'I don't understand, what's going on?'

'Your statement has to be recorded for accuracy.'

'Why? I thought this was about me writing everything down.'

'Relax, things have to be done by the book.'

'You have to be kidding. So far none of their actions have been done by the book.' Vicky sat in the chair Marty pulled out. Only then did she notice the recording set up, which should not have shocked her for it was standard practice, something she had explained to desperate members of the public numerous times. Now she understood how different words of encouragement were to actually being in the position.

'Which is why I insisted correct protocol be carried out from now on. I've lodged a complaint on your behalf.'

A rush of footsteps grew louder. A thud on the heavy door and squeak of a hinge followed within a split second. Vicky drew in a breath but couldn't find the gumption to turn her head. Even knowing the law, sitting on this side of the table was downright scary.

'Morning all. Are we ready?' The voice from behind was unfamiliar, which was sort of a relief.

'Yes,' Marty answered but with a hard lump jammed in her throat, words eluded Vicky.

With her head down, she noticed tan trousers rounding her end and dark grey on the other end. So, not uniforms which meant detectives. Good or bad? She couldn't make up her mind but at least supercilious Shortie wasn't here. The scraping of chair legs across industrial strength linoleum caused her to wince while her breath stalled. She couldn't figure out why she felt like she was about to walk to the gallows with an overwhelming urge to flee and keep running. Imagine how she would feel if she were actually guilty of some crime. She could handle being not guilty.

'Mrs Saunders?'

Vicky dared to look up. The men opposite wore open-necked business shirts with sleeves rolled up. Somehow, her nerves sky-rocketed into the stratosphere.

'Yes.'

'I'm Detective Sergeant Mark Simpson. This is Detective Constable Ben Jackson. Homicide squad.'

Vicky shot a glance to Marty. 'Homicide?' She turned back to eyeball the sergeant. 'You think Mum was murdered? Why? She had no enemies. She was nothing more than an ordinary everyday woman enjoying retirement.'

'We have a few questions.'

The something hard and uncomfortable which had been lodged in her throat, bounced down to her toes and back up to settle in her gut. She gulped, shook her head, opened her mouth but no words formed. 'Marty...' finally squeaked out.

'Everything is all right, Vicky. Okay, guys, let's get this done.'

'Fine,' said the sergeant as one hand reached out and fiddled with the recording paraphernalia set up on the end of the table. They did the rounds of each stating their names and the correct time to the minute. Vicky was anything but fine.

'Apparently, Mrs Saunders, you gave details of your and your daughter's whereabouts on the night in question. Could you please repeat those details for the record?'

This, Vicky could handle. After a long sigh of relief, she retold her story, added in as many minute details as she could recall, not caring a damn about how long it took. She even told them what programme she had listened to on the car radio during the drive home from work, what she had for her meagre supper before going to bed. Done, she sat back with arms folded and huffed out a long breath.

'Why did it take so long for Mrs Wakefield's body to be discovered?' asked the constable.

Vicky glared at him. 'What are you inferring?'

'According to you, she was your mother, one you visited regularly, one you had a loving relationship with.'

Vicky was not stupid and knew where this was leading. 'Do you have a mother?' she asked while holding his stare.

'Yes, of course.'

'Do you ring her every single day?' It was difficult biting back her grin at the man's pink flush. 'Nor do I. I work full time. I have a daughter who attends school weekdays. When I get home from work, often after six at night, I cook our evening meal, we eat together, we do dishes after which I carry out other household chores like washing or folding laundry or cleaning while my daughter buries her head in her studies. This is her final year at school, with important exams in a few months. She is a top student so studies hard.

'I am not my mother's keeper and she isn't... err... wasn't mine. We phoned each other or met up a couple of times a week. Often it might be a simple SMS message, as I'm sure you have already checked by obtaining our phone records.' A quick guilty-looking glance between the two officers told her she was correct.

'Mum had her own life with a host of social engagements. Even though she was close to seventy she had all her faculties and was wise enough to not need me to keep tabs on her every minute of every day and vice versa.'

'A simple answer will suffice,' said the sergeant.

Vicky laughed before quickly sobering. 'I don't think so.'

'What do you mean?' asked the same man.

'Simple answers without qualifying background can be twisted to suit. I've worked with the law for twenty years.'

This man had more control than his offsider, not letting a flush of guilt escape but a muscle tightened along his jaw indicating she had touched a nerve.

'Can you explain how it was a neighbour who found the body?'

Another laugh slipped out. 'I am certain you have already spoken to Meg. Mum missed a regular coffee date without explanation, something which was unusual. They have keys to each other's places for when either is away, to water plants, take in mail from the letterbox and check on things. Meg went to investigate, noticed Mum's car was there, couldn't rouse her so went inside. She rang the police; the police rang me.'

'What did you do with the evidence?' Stunned at the blatant innuendo, Vicky straightened as she spun her head towards the constable.

'I beg your pardon? I have no idea what you mean.'

'Oh, come on, you removed the bedclothes and cleaned out the fridge to dispose of evidence.'

Vicky stood and shoved the chair back, ensuring it made a lot of noise. 'I'm done here. Your accusations are unfounded and insulting. I have already said, more than once, I had nothing to do with Mum's death. I have no idea who did those things but I assumed it was Meg but have not asked her yet as I haven't had a chance to visit with her. I didn't even know the fridge had been cleaned out until Saturday morning when I opened it looking for something to eat for breakfast.'

'Surely you went to Mrs Wakefield's house before last Saturday. She died two weeks ago.' The constable stood and wagged his finger at her before pointing at her chair. 'Please sit.'

Marty tugged her back down into the chair. If he hadn't she would have left.

'No, I didn't.' Fiddlesticks, she was so darn angry at the blatant innuendo.

'Why not?' The constable resat.

Vicky blew out her cheeks. If she didn't tell all she would probably be arrested despite these guys not having a skerrick of evidence. To her, they were looking for an easy way out. Most crimes against a person are committed by someone familiar to them. She knew the statistics. 'After the police contacted me, at work, I rang Mum's lawyer. I couldn't leave work at the time for I was the only one on duty to field calls from distressed members of the public. Graeme Hunt, Mum's lawyer, spoke with the police to get details. He mentioned there would be a post-mortem because of the suddenness of the death and suggested I not go to Mum's house until the coroner's report was released. Knowing how the law works, I abided by his suggestion. I met him the next day when he handed me a letter, written by my mother, which outlined what she wanted as a funeral. Last Friday morning before the funeral, Mr Hunt gave me the go-ahead to begin cleaning out Mum's house. He detailed the contents of the will at the same time.'

'I think Vicky has explained things logically and in detail, gentlemen. There is no evidence at all that my client has committed any sort of crime. She has done things by the book, acted not only on Graeme Hunt's advice but also mine.' Marty stood. 'Let's go, Vicky.' He grasped her elbow to assist her up. 'Might I suggest you stop wasting your time by trying to pin this on an innocent woman and begin to search for the real criminal, if, in fact, some real crime has been committed. Any further questions are to be fielded through me.'

As Vicky preceded Marty to the door, a comment which had niggled, came to the forefront of her mind. On a sucked in breath, she paused, turned to face the officers who were taking tapes out of the machine. 'There's something I would like you to explain.'

'What? The sergeant straightened while pocketing the tape.

'You said, according to me, Regina was my mother. What did you mean?'

'We've checked all Australian birth records. No-one by the name of Regina Wakefield gave birth to a son or daughter on or near the date you were born.'

'Which means I don't exist and yet here I am.' She took one step forward, raised her hands and opened out her arms. 'Could be because I wasn't born in Australia.' Joy flooded through her at the stunned looks before Vicky spun back around and strode outside as fast as she could without seeming to run.

'I didn't know you're not an Aussie,' Marty panted in her ear as he caught up with her.

'Technically I am but I have dual passports. Pity they didn't check.' She turned her head to catch his eye and grinned at his stunned look. 'Mum emigrated from the U.K.

when I was two months old. She is a naturalised Australian citizen, has been since the year after she arrived. I came out on a British passport, which has always been maintained. As soon as Mum was naturalised she applied for Australian passports for us both but even though she kept it up to date, Mum never left her adopted country again.'

'I wonder how long it will take before they track your mum's history down.' Marty paused at the corner. 'I have to go. Got a court case to prepare for.'

'Now I feel guilty. Sorry to take you away from your work.'

'No need, I will always be here for you, you know that but I'll be in court for the rest of the week so try to stay out of trouble.'

'Funny man, Martin St James.'

She heard his laughter all the way while she crossed the road. Time to search more shoe boxes.

Nine

Excitement thrummed through her body by the time Vicky reached home. The entire trip she racked her brain for the name of any person she knew who came from a Greek background when a sudden thought had sent a jolt to her brain. Surely the internet had some sort of translation ability. Nowadays you could find almost anything given the right words being logged in.

With the idea gelling, she didn't concentrate until she bumped over the lower driveway kerb. She pressed the remote as she headed towards the garage, frustrated when she had to wait a few seconds for the door to rise far enough. 'Come on, hurry up,' she muttered, leaning forward to watch the door rise. High enough, she pressed her foot on the accelerator, shot forward. Her heart stalled before racing to catch up the missed beats when she had to slam her foot on the brake to prevent hurtling through the end wall. 'Damn, damn, damn,' hissed out as the brakes jammed. Her body kept going with the momentum until the seatbelt caught and jerked her back into the seat, forcing all the breath from her lungs. It took more than one gasp to re-inflate her lungs. She sat, hands gripped along the top of the steering wheel until her thundering pulse evened out and she could take in a another long breath to calm tense nerves.

Not game to rush any longer, Vicky decided tea and a

snack were needed to gain equilibrium and fill the empty hole in her stomach. The silence inside the house was welcome, the presence of no other person – peaceful. To maintain serenity, she took her time to create a small plate of crackers, cheese with a variety of toppings and a mug of hot, strong black tea. Even though eagerness almost overwhelmed her, she kept her pace slow while she carried plate and mug along the passage to the fourth bedroom Mike had set up as his home office. The way her nerves were zinging she would drop the lot if she didn't keep calm.

This room had remained the way Mike had set it up when they first moved into their home. It still held his magnificent roll-top desk, leather office chair and twin four-drawer metal filing cabinets. Vicky never could face getting rid of the furnishings but instead used them, feeling close to the man she still adored. She sat, placed the snack on a magazine and ran her fingers over the smooth patina of the polished wood of the desk top. Whenever she sat here she felt close to Mike, felt his arms surround her, keeping her safe. Apart from her meal, laptop and a printer, the desk was clear. Mike's paperwork had gone after Marty had undertaken the difficult task of sorting them, returning work related items to the office. He had sorted remaining papers, ditched irrelevant junk, filed papers he figured Vicky would need for tax purposes and a separate file for important papers like insurance, licences, guarantees. Vicky would be forever grateful for it had been a task she had not been able to face. The pain of losing Mike had now eased from crippling to acceptance but she doubted it would ever go away entirely.

'Oh, Mike, I miss you so darn much,' she whispered. When her heart gave a little tumble-turn she spun the chair around and reached down to the bottom drawer, tugged it open to see what her mother had hidden. Not the time for reflection.

Vicky ate while she searched, surprised how easy it was to find translation services. It took longer than she would like to figure out how to translate from Greek to English since she didn't have a Greek keyboard to punch in the symbols.

The names on the photo were easy but didn't help much because once she figured the scrawl on the back said *Helena with Sophia* it meant little since she didn't have a clue which was which. It was more of a mystery when she figured out the first sentence of the letter. *My darling Sophia.*

Maybe it was a love letter.

My heart is breaking.

Oh, heavens, a sad letter.

It is impossible for us to marry for my parents will not allow me to break the arrangement I mentioned to you.

Vicky paused, head in her hands while the grief stabbed even though she didn't know these people.

We were seen by my father's minders so you will be in danger should they find you, especially in your condition.

Condition? Oh, my, she must be pregnant.

I urge you to leave the country. I beg you to leave so I know you will be safe. Enclosed are train tickets to Paris and 10,000 drachmas. This will cover the cost of the journey back home to London, food and rent until you can find a new position. It will also pay for the surgery we agreed was for the best to abort the child. The address enclosed is a reputable medico who carries out the procedure for society women.

Oh, how cruel can a man be? Who the hell are you to force a woman to abort the living being snuggled in her womb? You might not want your child but a mother loves her child the very second she is aware of its presence. Vicky shook her head vigorously to rid it of negative thoughts and read on.

This necklace is a safety net. Take it apart so it will not be recognised for it is a family piece left to me by my maternal grandmother to give to my wife. In my heart you are the only wife I want. Sell the separate jewels to different gem dealers. Break up the gold setting.
My forced marriage can never be a happy one for my heart lives with you. You will never know how sorry I am. All my love, K.

Vicky hadn't realised she was crying until a tear plopped onto her hand. She sniffed back the leaking moisture and forced a grin. She didn't even know these people for goodness sake, so why should she let the letter affect her? And it wasn't even related to the photo. All she really had were two names of people she had never heard of and the first letter of a man's name. Oh, and one heartbreaking letter. Sophia was mentioned on both but was she the mother or the baby? Oh, maybe the baby was the one K talked about. Oh, please let the baby have survived.

In case it was important or had some relevance later when she ploughed through other papers, Vicky pressed the print button. After all the work she had gone through to get a proper translation, not much point in having to do it again. She set the letter aside with its translation underneath to study the other papers in the same file. Please let them be related since they were together, she thought as excitement gripped when she saw the next letter was written in English and joy of joys, she recognised the name at the bottom.

> *My dear sister, Georgia,*
> *I am desperate for your help.*
> *Please, please, please can you meet me in Paris?*

Oh, Paris, Vicky thought. She went back to the name at the bottom. Sophia. So Sophia and Georgia are sisters. Anticipation mounted as her eyes sought out the next sentence.

> *I am sure I have been followed by bad people. If they find me I know I will come to harm. I am too scared to go outside. A friend is posting this for me. Attached is the card for this pension where I am staying.*

Adrenalin spurted as she placed the letter on the desk, flicked through the other pages, about ten, she guessed. When she found nothing, she searched again, lifting each page with care but the card wasn't there. Fiddlesticks, an address would be a starting point – much better than the entire city of Paris.

When you see me, you will know the reason for my distress.
Please, Georgia, please come immediately.
Sophia.

It felt weird knowing why this woman was so desperate, yet without a single clue who these people were. It was like being a voyeur, peeking through a window into someone's privacy.

After she read through all the other letters, she could see no relevance to the first two nor any obvious importance but she slid them all back into the folder before replacing it in the drawer and taking out the next file. She didn't know what to expect but was disappointed when it contained only normal household papers. There was the Title Deed to the house. Yes, it was important but certainly not as exciting. House insurance, car insurance, car licence, bank statements for... she filtered through... two years. Boring, boring, boring. The file went back with the thought she would need them for probate purposes and putting things in her name. A second thought chased away the first. The papers were recent so Mum must have opened the chest on a regular basis but never when Vicky had been around. She sent thanks skywards for finding the key so the chest could be opened or she would have spent hours searching for these papers and it's possible she never would have found them, which would have been a pain.

The car wasn't new but was in excellent condition so would suit Gina. It will be in better condition when it comes back from her mechanic, after he gives it a thorough mechanical and safety check. Vicky had ordered new tyres and insisted on the brakes being overhauled. It should be easy to transfer the licence into Gina's name. A car would be useful when Gina went to university in the new year. The money Vicky had saved to go towards a car could now be used to pay enrolment expenses. Good things always seemed to follow bad but she would have preferred Regina to still be alive.

Vicky's eyes widened at the next file which contained... she counted... twelve yellowed certificates, none of which she had seen before. With her hand flat on the top paper, she wasn't sure if she wanted to read them. Her heart was doing a fabulous job of trying to break her ribs, so she huffed out a long breath, picked up the first. Her lungs deflated. It was in Greek with a date of 1947. She studied the names, thought she recognised one. Going back to the translations, she compared them. Georgia. Could it be a birth certificate?

A similar, red-framed certificate caught her eye. The first glance at the bottom found the date, 1951. Her breath hissed out. The year of Regina's birth. Could it be a co-incidence? Surely not. No way. Overcome, Vicky searched for the name, found it and her stomach lurched. To ensure it said what she thought, she went back to the translations to check the Greek symbols. Oh, my, certainly not her mother but it was Sophia's birth certificate, which meant – she scrabbled around for the photograph and read: Helena with Sophia. Now things were coming together. The photo must be from the same year and Sophia is the baby. Which meant Sophia didn't have her baby. Darn, too sad to contemplate.

Frantic with excitement, she studied the Greek word for Helena and compared it to where she thought the names were on all the certificates. Using her forefinger, she ran down the hand- written words, There, on what looked like a birth certificate, the date at the bottom, 1928. A different certificate had Helena and the date 1945, while a third had 1981. Calculating the years between the dates, she guessed these were the birth, marriage and death certificates for Helena but poor girl was married at 17 and gave birth only a year later. Way too young. A picture centred in her mind of Gina in a wedding dress - today. No way – far too young but Vicky guessed it was probably an arranged marriage like the one Sophia's mystery beau was forced into. Vicky couldn't imagine being forced to marry a man her mother had chosen. A shudder wove across her shoulders at the thought. Mum hadn't taken to Mike at first, yet he turned out to be the best man any woman could hope for and her mother ended up always citing his many virtues.

To get everything clear in her mind, Vicky grabbed a sheet of clean paper from the printer tray and jotted down all she now knew with a continual thought nibbling away at her grey matter. These people had to be important to her mum, otherwise why would she have kept them? And Greece was predominant.

'Mum, where are you?'

Annoyed at the interruption, Vicky's glance went from door to her watch and back towards the office door. Time had raced away from her. With the mystery of her life only beginning to unravel she really wanted to continue researching, get more translations, find out where her mum fitted in. A long sigh slipped out as she bundled the scattered papers back into the folder.

'Mum?'

'Coming.'

A wispy tendril of memory teased Vicky's grey matter. There was something she should recall about the small rubber toy egg but as the tendril tickled, it pulled away, refusing to release its information. Never mind, it will come, probably in the early hours of the morning when she was in desperate need of sleep. Right now sleep was impossible with her anxiety levels sky-high. It had been a difficult few hours spending mother/daughter time with Gina which was of utmost importance for during the week it was a rare occurrence with her work hours. They chatted over an afternoon snack about normal everyday activities. She cooked a decent meal filled with good brain food, being on hand to assist with the maths homework Gina was far better at than Vicky. Vicky had sipped on wine while idly flicking over pages of a magazine until Gina had bathed and gone to bed. Only then did Vicky dare to continue delving into her past, deciding the bag of objects from the chest would be the easiest.

Vicky put the egg aside, picked it up again and laughed when the memory surfaced. Easter, when she was about ten. The Easter Bunny, aka Mum, had given her a common old papier-mache egg carton filled with a variety of eggs. A caramel fill chocolate egg had been her favourite. Other holes were filled with tiny chocolate eggs, some wrapped in foil, others coated with a layer of lolly. There had been marshmallow eggs and small hollow chocolate eggs. A few were real eggs, two painted with food colouring on the shells. One had been hard boiled but another, she found when she cracked the shell on her head, had been raw. Her mother's raucous laughter at the mess, surfaced, bringing a grin to her own face. Hmm, something to do for Gina next Easter, if she remembered a year from now.

Still smiling at the memory, Vicky burrowed into the garbage bag, felt around, pulled out the next item, inspected it, puzzled as to what it was. Obviously made of metal, it wore a coat of rough, white oxide. The long, tapered end had to fit into a hole. The quarter circle swung on a swivel but a rough edge indicated the rest had snapped off. Memory surged. Oh, my dear heaven. She knew what it was. A thole from a rowboat - with a broken rowlock. Her face heated to incineration level. How did Mum even know about this? How on earth did she get it and why keep it?

Stunned, Vicky ran her fingers along the metal, the oxidisation rough on her skin. Kane. Good grief. How could she have forgotten such a night? Fourteen. Yes, she had not long turned fourteen, thought she was so grown up, was smitten with Kane, the boy from down the road who went to an elite private school while she attended the local government high school. Kane had asked her out. Ecstatic, Vicky had asked Mum if she could meet up with Kane. Mum said no, Vicky was too young to be going anywhere alone with a boy, especially one who was three years older. But typical teenager who knew better than stuffy old-fashioned mothers, Vicky had snuck out. Climbed through the window dressed in… oh,

Lord, the heat in Vicky's face erupted like the magma from a volcano. Short, shorts, which left nothing to the imagination and a skimpy top revealing several centimetres of her midriff and sandals on her feet because they were meeting at the edge of the river. Down near the Garratt Rd Bridge.

Vicky recalled how she had run the three blocks. Remembered standing at the top of the embankment, searching with her eyes. Spied Kane next to a thick wooden pylon where a couple of boats had been moored. Now, she could still feel the thrum of her nerves while she scampered down the steep incline. Her first date: an illicit, forbidden date. For a while they sat on the clumpy grass, sharing a bag of potato crisps between sips on a can of cola which Kane had brought. Even the snack had given her conscience a serve for sugary sodas were forbidden by Mum except for a rare special occasion. Now, she recalled how she eased her conscience by telling herself a first date with the local hunk was an extra special occasion. How she enjoyed defying Mum while she had savoured every sip of the forbidden drink.

After Kane had tugged the boat to shore, they both climbed into the old metal rowboat, slipped the oars in the rowlocks and rowed to the end of the mooring rope attached to a buoy while she was squashed right up next to Kane's hard, warm side. Their thighs had rubbed together sending squishy feelings through her innards. She had been scared witless but at the same time overcome with the wonder of being this close to a boy, one from a classy private school. At the time it had felt out of this world amazing such a handsome older boy would want to date little old Vicky.

It had been fine until she had felt Kane's fingers creeping under the leg of her shorts, under the fine fabric of her knickers until they found their way into her private spot where she knew it was wrong. Despite being terrified, she had stilled with her breath held. Even though it was so wrong and scary, it was also way beyond thrilling. When his fingers crept in further she had panicked, fought him off but he was a lot stronger, pushed her onto her knees in the bottom of the boat where he tussled with her while he tried to rip her top off. She recalled his hands on her breasts and the way he squeezed so tight, it hurt. She recalled being so frightened she grabbed an oar and twisted it around as hard as she could. She heard the *snap* of the rowlock when it broke, the *whack* of the oar when it caught Kane on the side of the head, the *grunt* from Kane which had been instantly followed by a stupendous *splash* when Kane hit the water, leaving the boat on a wild ride from side-to-side.

Vicky had lost her balance and fallen, scraping skin from the side of her face on the rough top edge of the boat. Petrified, she had scrambled upright and snatched out the broken thole, ready to fight Kane off when he grabbed the side of the boat, almost tumbling her into the water. She had lashed out at his hands until he let go and began swimming towards shore, cursing and calling her all sorts of filthy names. It had taken too long to realise she needed to get the hell out of there. Petrified, she leapt from the boat into waist-deep water, scrambled to shore and ran full pelt all the way home. It had been difficult to climb back in the window. A shiver raced across her shoulders when she recalled how hard it had been to clean up the weeping bloody gashes on her face without alerting Mum. It had been even more difficult to explain the injury the next morning. Now she scoffed at the ridiculous excuse she had given; fell out of bed in her sleep and hit the side table. No way would Mum have believed her.

Vicky stared at the broken thole. She didn't want to think about how Mum had got the darn thing. Maybe, in her fright, Vicky had carried it home but she couldn't recall ever seeing it again. Better to never know the how or why because the only logical explanation she could come up with was that Mum had followed her. What she does recall is how she never saw Kane again. Had Mum intervened on the quiet? Dear God, how embarrassing.

After this revelation Vicky wasn't sure if she wanted to delve further but figured nothing could be as bad so she plunged her hand into the opening of the plastic, felt around, grabbed what felt like paper. She drew it out, unfolded the small rectangle to reveal a childlike pencil sketch of an insect. The large round head had two stick feelers going off at skewed angles. Big boggle eyes dominated the face with a grim looking mouth underneath. This poor ant was not a happy one. The thorax was sausage-like with three stick legs each side and a small round tail tacked on the end was blackened like the eyes.

Tears welled. Gina had drawn this as a toddler and given it to Granny as a present. It had been attached to the fridge by four insect magnets for months, the entire length of time Gina had been fascinated with the creepy-crawlies she found in the garden. Oh, yes, many had come inside to live in lidded shoe boxes with holes punched for air. Snails had escaped their unwelcome home and been squished underfoot which resulted in unstoppable tears. So had caterpillars, none of which survived long enough to turn into beautiful butterflies. Vicky's long sad tale of a queen dying because her workers couldn't get home with the precious pollen to feed all her babies had freed the three bees within hours of being caught. The ladybirds were placed on rose bushes to feast on greedy aphids which had been devouring the buds and Vicky had drawn the line when an enormous stick insect was found on the kitchen bench after escaping little hands intent on turning it upside down to examine the tiny feet.

With a grin, Vicky rose, took the sketch with her. It took a bit of re-arranging of bills and memos but she managed to find a magnet for each corner and stuck it slap bang in the middle of the fridge door. It would be interesting to see if Gina remembered.

The next item pulled from the bag of memories was a doll of the Barbie variety wearing nothing but a pair of knickers and a scary short hairstyle sticking out every which way. Vicky laughed. This had been hers. When Vicky had her hair cropped in a new, short style for summer, she figured the doll had to be the same but hair made of stiff thick nylon strands didn't sit down so well. It was difficult to believe this had meant something to her mother but these first edition Barbies were worth a bit of money. Vicky eyed the doll, maybe not worth a cracker looking like a freak – a naked freak. She tossed it into the garbage bin next to her.

When a small scruffy koala emerged next, Vicky smiled and her heart turned to mush. The grey fur had worn away from the hands and feet and the black rubber nose was missing but for the number of times this had gone to bed with her, it was a wonder it was in such good condition. Even after thinking hard, Vicky couldn't remember who had given her the koala. She must have been very young but she could recall insisting this one soft toy be tucked in with her every night. No different to the floppy super-soft monkey Gina had adopted as her bed buddy until she began primary school. This, Vicky would keep in the same box holding the monkey. She wondered if other mothers had a box of treasures hidden away – most of which would embarrass their children – like the broken thole. Maybe she should go through her box of Gina's things she had kept and re-think what was worth keeping.

A gasp of disgust flew from her mouth when Vicky felt something gross and slimy at the next lucky dip. She drew out a mass of disgusting lime green rubbery stuff which had petrified with age. It took a minute of inspection before she figured out it was one of those sticky hands which you threw at a surface onto which it would adhere and you could draw out the arm to ridiculous lengths before the hand would release its grip and ping backwards. A gurgle of laughter bubbled up her throat. She had won this at the Royal Agricultural Show. Or rather Mum had. In side-show alley, Vicky had dared her mother to shoot at a row of metal ducks with an air rifle. The first attempt resulted in Mum missing the lot but Vicky had pestered her to have another go. Five shots, one duck and this ridiculous toy had been the prize since the sign had said, "Every hit wins a prize."

'Oh, Mum,' Vicky laughed while she balled up the goop before tossing it in the bin to keep poor macerated Barbie company. She leant back against the chair, let the memories surface of the day at the show. How old had she been? Eight or nine, she guessed. Going to the annual show had not been affordable until then but after the kids at school had expounded the fun they had, Vicky had begged, promising to save every cent of her pocket money so she could pay her own way. It had been a magical day. They had wandered for hours, ducked into every single exhibit, eaten fairy floss, hotdogs for lunch and a hamburger with chips for the late evening meal while they sat on wooden benches to watch the fireworks.

She had been allowed to choose a single ride and after they had traipsed around the area to inspect each magical contraption she had opted for the Mighty Mouse. The kids seemed to be having so much fun, with loud squeals and wide grins but once she sat strapped into the little car, hurtling around on inadequate rails, it had scared the pants off her. At the time, she recalled, nothing would have induced her to set foot on any other ride, which Mum had thought was hilarious.

It was then she remembered the two show bags she had agonised over, trying to decide which ones she most wanted, for two was the limit to her savings. Liquorice: yes she had bought a sample bag of liquorice and one containing a variety of bite-sized chocolate bars. The agony had been carrying them all day after she insisted she buy them early in the day despite Mum's arguments to wait. The ecstasy had been eating the contents over the next two weeks for too much sugar in one hit had never been allowed but she had wanted them to last as long as she could.

Since that first time, Vicky had been to the show many times but it had never held the same sense of enchantment except for the day she and Mike had taken Gina to her first show. There was an animal nursery which had enthralled Gina for over an hour. The magic had been in seeing the delight on Gina's face.

A sense of disappointment settled into her gut when she plunged her hand back into the bag, wriggled her fingers to the very bottom and scrounged around. Only three items remained so she up-ended the metre of green rustling plastic and shook hard to dislodge them. Out fell two tiny shoes and a small square of fabric. The shoes were unfamiliar but by their size Vicky figured they might have been her very first pair from when she was still a baby. The fabric was a mystery until she opened it out and spread it on the carpet, ran her hand over it to smooth out the creases. Oh, my, this doyley had been her first attempt at embroidery. Mum had taught her basic lazy-daisy and stem stitch before she bought a transfer printed piece of linen for Vicky to practise. Giving the stitches a close scrutiny, Vicky thought she hadn't done too bad a job but it was possible Mum had re-done a few bits. The crocheted edge certainly wasn't of Vicky's doing for she could visualise how Mum had spent a few nights with a crochet hook and ball of shiny ecru thread.

While she cast her eyes over the little pile of objects, something again shifted in her chest region. A mother who didn't love her child would not have kept such trivial but significant objects.

Eleven

The phone jolting her awake, was not welcome. While she reached for the offending instrument, Vicky opened one eye to peer at the window and groaned. Barely light. The other eye opened to look at the time - 7am. With a sigh she jammed the receiver against her ear.

'H'lo,' she slurred.

A masculine laugh answered. 'You okay?' asked Marty.

Vicky struggled upright. 'Yes, sorry, my brain isn't fully awake yet.'

'What did you think of my email?'

'What email?'

'I sent you a copy of the Coroner's report. Makes interesting reading. And you can continue cleaning out your mother's house. The police have completed their investigation.'

It was ridiculous the way Vicky's heart rate increased at the last sentence. 'Did they find anything?'

A chuckle preceded a lengthy silence, which did nothing to alleviate her racing heart. 'Whoever did the house over was incredibly careful.'

'You call destroying every single item being careful?'

Marty's laugh echoed. How dare he be so cheerful at this ungodly hour? Although, she thought, it wasn't really so early. Vicky just hadn't had enough sleep after she spent too many hours reminiscing with her bag of lucky dips.

'Careful about leaving DNA. Personally, I think there is nothing to find. I have to go, got court today.'

He hung up, leaving Vicky stunned for a few seconds before scrambled brain cells aligned. She freed her limbs from the bedding, grabbed her dressing gown, shoved arms into sleeves while she strode along the passage to the office. She pressed the button on the computer, stood back to wrap the belt around her waist and tie it in a loose bow before she settled into the chair.

Waiting for the computer to spring to life was like sitting on a bed of singeing hot needles. The number of emails she had missed since last Thursday night surprised her but she was interested in only one. She ran the cursor down to the one from Marty, clicked, waited with her breath held and pressed on the attachment. The few seconds it took for the attachment to open felt like forever.

Since she expected nothing more than she had already heard, she made a quick scan, but stalled on the word cancer and began reading again, much slower, doing her best to absorb words into a shocked brain. Even after she had re-read every word she sat back in disbelief, convinced the report belonged to someone else and had been sent in error. It couldn't be the correct report for Regina Wakefield.

She read it again, pressed print. While she waited for the pages to spit out of the slot in the printer she relaxed back in the chair, thinking over the past months to see if there had ever been any indication her mother showed signs of being so ill. She must have been suffering agonising pain for months but definitely not the arthritis she said she had. For the cancer to have spread so far it would have grown and spread for months and months. 'Oh, dear God, Mum, why didn't you say anything?'

'Say anything about what?' Gina asked from behind.

Vicky squealed, jumped and spun in the seat at the same time. 'Don't scare me like that.'

'Sorry.' As Gina neared, she peered over Vicky's shoulder. 'What didn't Granny tell you?'

'The coroner's report. Her body was riddled with cancer, so bad it's a probable cause of death.'

'Cancer!' Gina dropped to her knees, lifted the pages from the printer and read the words as she leant back on her heels.

Still unable to believe it was true, Vicky re-read the words over Gina's shoulder but they hadn't changed, still said the same thing.

'Oh, wow,' Gina said when she had finished reading. She glanced at Vicky. 'But why would the police accuse you of poisoning her?'

'There's mention of barbiturates in her blood.'

'Wasn't Granny on medication for her arthritis?'

'Yes. Now I wonder if it was arthritis. Maybe she only said it was arthritis to cover up her real illness.'

'Why would she?'

'So we didn't worry and make a fuss. Who knows, maybe I need to have a chat with her doctor, find out what was prescribed?' Vicky scoffed. 'Amongst other things, like when she was diagnosed, how long she had known and why she didn't have treatment. Anyway, enough talk of sad things. You've got school and I've been told I can resume cleaning out Granny's home.' Vicky closed down the computer and stood. 'Cheesy scrambled eggs do for breakfast?'

'Hmm, sounds good. Why don't you get a skip bin in at Granny's?'

Vicky held out her hand to hoist Gina up. 'Brilliant idea. Breakfast in fifteen.'

* * *

All the while she drove, Vicky had sent silent messages skywards, praying the mess wasn't as bad as she remembered. But it was and she hadn't gone any further than standing in the front doorway. In fact it looked worse than she recalled. If whoever had done this had been looking for a particular item, they certainly searched not only every nook and cranny but also every minute crack and even inside the objects by smashing them apart. If they found what they searched for, Vicky would never know what was no longer here. Now she was glad she had taken Gina's advice and booked a skip bin which was promised within the hour. There was little in the hallway that could be saved. The two small tables looked to be solid despite lying dead with stiff legs pointed skywards but the drawers were nothing but kindle. She tracked a jagged path, avoided the worst of the mess, to the laundry where she picked the broom from the floor, put the brush end down and made figure eight swirls, collecting shrapnel as she went, sweeping from laundry door, along the passage where she left the mound against one wall near the front door. China shards mixed with snapped picture frames, broken glass and smashed wood. She supposed the small stationery items which had resided in one drawer could be saved but weren't worth the time to pick them out from the detritus. She carried the larger pieces of wood out to the porch, spun around and eyed the hallway. At least she now had a clear path.

By the time she heard the clangs and bangs of a truck unloading the metal skip, there were several piles of rubbish in four different rooms. All she had to do now was pick up the piles and transport them to the front verge. Transport, now there's an idea. Grinning at her brilliance, she made her way outside, around to the back where the garden shed resided, door bent almost in half and gaping. It appeared to have been in receipt of several hefty kicks. Looks like the mystery interlopers weren't content with destroying the house, which could mean they didn't find what they were looking for. Hmm, something to think about. Vicky was almost too afraid to go closer. With her heart jammed in her throat, she stilled for a few seconds before striding with false bravado along the crazy paving to the shed door where she stopped dead and swore under her breath. Mum only possessed basic household and garden tools but an atomic bomb would not have left such a mess. The only good thing she could see was the wheelbarrow which stood upright and intact, already full of stuff which had been flung from the shelves and benches, probably after an inspection of each item. She wheeled it outside. It took a few minutes gagging at the acrid aroma, to free the long-handled shovel from its coating of potting mix, spilled paint and fertilizer. After she balanced the shovel across the barrow, Vicky pushed the barrow to the skip which she eyed, now regretting she had ordered the largest they had for it was going to be almost impossible to lift a houseful of rubbish over the tall sides. Trying to figure what to do, she circled the bin. Delight blossomed when she spied the heavy latches at one end with a hinge across the entire length about two-thirds of the way down. A ramp would be created when they were lowered. Logical.

After struggling in vain to pull the pins from the latches, Vicky returned to the shed, used a rake handle to filter through the mess until she found a hammer. Several hearty whacks with the hammer freed the bolts which shot out all of a sudden and clanged against the sides on the end of short thick chains. She grasped the top rim, tugged and almost wrenched her arms from their sockets when the heavy metal dropped and caught her on the hip as she jumped out of the way. A loud metallic clang echoed and drowned out her cussed words as dust eddied up from the ground.

Sore and with sweat dripping, she eyed the full wheelbarrow, picked out a trowel, three decent plant pots, a can of rose spray, which she shook to ensure it was worth saving, and a strong plastic bucket which looked almost new. After putting the items aside, she managed to push the barrow up the ramp to the edge where she tipped it up to let the contents fall into the bottom, ignoring the echoing racket. With this much noise it was a wonder the neighbours weren't pouring out to investigate. It was at that moment she recalled some inkling memory about fertiliser being mixed with something to create nasty explosives.

Stepping back, she glanced around for any signs of neighbours before she wheeled the barrow inside where she shovelled up the piles of rubbish and transported them back to the skip. Four journeys to and fro left her smudged in dust-laden sweat but it was a darn sight easier than using a much smaller bucket or box which she would have to carry and make ten times as many trips. A tick for ingenuity she thought while wheeling the barrow back inside. So far the liquid paint hadn't caused a chain reaction with the fertiliser so maybe there wouldn't be some mighty explosion.

Determined to clear the floor of the smaller smashed items, she kept going without a break until all she had left were the larger pieces of furniture. Exhausted, she flopped into a kitchen chair to catch her breath, thankful it was a cool overcast day with rain having the decency to threaten but not fall. It was a relief to take a break while she ate the sandwich she had brought with her and downed three glasses of cold water. Sated, she scanned the kitchen, noticed the patches of grey graphite covering most smooth surfaces and shuddered. The forensics team must have had a field day.

Pots and pans were still in one piece. She packed them in cardboard boxes retrieved from the car. Most would go to charity. Cutlery and cooking utensils filled the voids. Tea towels protected the few china and glass items which had escaped destruction. Another box was filled with canned and packaged food items retrieved from the larder and the floor. Those she could use would go home. The ones, like canned chickpeas, which she detested, would go to charity. In the larder, she found three bottles of wine – definitely going home, the first of which would be opened tonight.

When it neared the time Gina would reach home after school, Vicky packed the boxes in the car, locked up the house and drove home, dog-tired but overjoyed by the amount she had achieved. It was going to take another full day to rid the house of wrecked items before she could sort her mother's clothes and personal belongings and begin cleaning.

The traffic on the route Vicky used, was clogged, slowing her down to a crawl in places. She realised since it was near school finishing time, a lot of these cars would be picking up children. Her frustration rose as exhaustion settled in. She wanted to blast the horn to clear the road but didn't. Instead, she turned on the radio, switched to CD and instantly regretted it when the heavy rock blasted from one of Gina's CDs. She blew out her cheeks and turned the machine off before flicking the indicator to turn left into her street which was devoid of any other moving vehicle. Thank goodness. Serenity swapped places with the tension. It always felt good to come home. It hadn't for two years after Mike's death when coming home had meant intense loneliness and heartbreak. Now, it was better after her anger, grief and hurt had turned to acceptance.

Vicky turned into her drive, pressed the remote and slowed to drift into the two-car garage. Now there was only one car – she had sold Mike's but soon Regina's car would live in Mike's spot. She was not sure how she would feel to see his space filled with an interloper but no doubt acceptance would soon override the initial discomfort.

A shadow hovered as she straightened from alighting. She turned and huffed out her breath at the sight of the two detectives. Ah, fiddlesticks, what now?

'Gentlemen,' she acknowledged as she grasped her handbag against her chest.

'Mrs Saunders, could we have a word?' The tone from the sergeant sounded less confrontational than he had before but didn't alleviate her fear.

'Certainly, please come inside.' Without waiting, she turned and led the way inside. She indicated kitchen chairs before turning to fill the kettle, switch it on, taking her time. 'Tea, coffee?' She pointed to each caddy.

'No, thank you, we won't be long.'

Unable to face the two seated men, Vicky busied herself. She took her time to lift down a mug, drop in a tea bag while wild thoughts fought to take precedence in her mind. Scared, she thought, she was plain scared. Tea made, she lifted the mug and turned, forced a breath and a smile before sitting.

'How can I help you?'

'You and your daughter are no longer suspects in the murder of your mother.'

She should have felt relief but didn't. Vicky flicked a glance at each man. 'You still think she was murdered despite the coroner's finding.' The look which passed between the two men was one of amazement. 'I've read the report, no thanks to the police department.' Her insult hit the mark for both men squirmed. 'I am next of kin. It is my right to be informed.' The constable opened his mouth but Vicky was not finished so held up her hand to stop him. 'Or do you still maintain

Regina is not my mother. I do have a British birth certificate, one which has been accepted as genuine on numerous occasions over the years when I have applied for various things where legal proof of identity is required. My birth has never, in almost 37 years, been questioned.'

'The validity of your birth certificate is not in question.'

Relief surged on a long huff of breath.

'But we haven't yet been able to trace your mother.'

Vicky felt her mouth gape at the same time the mug slipped from her fingers. A large splotch of hot tea spilled onto the table and soon spread. Since she was already filthy, she used the bottom edge of her blouse to mop it up.

'Do you have copies of your mother's birth or marriage certificates?' came from the constable.

Vicky stared at him. 'No, why would I? She was a normal adult with full control of her faculties, perfectly capable of keeping her own personal papers. Your people went through her belongings, even took her medication from the bathroom cabinet.' Seeing the flush of red on the sergeant was a small triumph. 'I presume they are being tested to compare with the so-called poison traces found in her body.'

'Where is your father?' came from the constable. Vicky was not sure if the suddenness of the question was to take her off a track they did not want to discuss.

'I have no idea. I never met him… have never seen a photo of him. He departed on announcement of my conception.'

'Don't you think that strange?' The same man fielded the question as he leant forwards with a gleam in his eye.

'I was a normal child, inquisitive, needy, wanted answers.

Yes, I asked, many times. When I was old enough to understand, I got the impression Mum was seriously hurt when he did a bunk and refused to face up to his responsibilities. She never wanted to discuss the subject so I gave up asking.' Disgruntled with the level of personal interrogation, she stood and leant over the table, determined to outstare the constable by not even blinking until he looked away first. 'Who or where my absent father is has no relevance to my mother dying from cancer, nor does where my mother came from. I am done with this intrusion into my birth and family history. You are overstepping the bounds.'

'I don't think so.' Vicky twisted her head towards the sergeant. 'When you consider the two men who searched your mother's home were private investigators from a foreign country.'

Her legs gave way. She plopped back into the chair, the scrape of legs on tiles, spine-tingling. 'You caught them? How?'

'A young lad from across the road saw them around two in the morning. Apparently he has trouble sleeping. He wrote down detailed descriptions of the men, their vehicle and the number plate.'

Despite her shock, a grin escaped. 'Toby Jones. He has autism. Sleeping is difficult for him. But he is super-intelligent. Spends a lot of time writing down detailed descriptions of what he sees and hears outside. He will talk if you know how to approach him. Never look at him but sit by his side and keep your voice low.'

'Yes, his mother said.'

'You've arrested these men?'

'No, we traced the number plate to a car hire company. The car had been returned to the Perth Airport depot. The men had tickets for yesterday's flight on Singapore Airlines back to their country.'

The answer came to her before she asked the question. 'What country?'

'Greece.'

It was a blessing when Gina appeared at that moment until Vicky saw the tortured look on her daughter's face. The corners of Gina's eyes crinkled a split second before tears dripped from the bottom edges.

'Mum,' Gina shrieked at the same time she barged across the room.

Vicky spread her arms wide to catch her but they remained empty when Gina spun around with hands planted on her hips to face the two detectives.

'My mum never killed anyone. You cannot arrest her. I don't have anyone else,' she yelled, her back rigid as she reached up to her full height between Vicky and the man as though determined to protect Vicky whose insides managed to turn to mush.

'Gina,' Vicky said, 'it's okay.'

'You can't take her away,' Gina added with a catch in her throat, but since she didn't turn around Vicky guessed Gina hadn't heard her.

'Gina,' Vicky said louder to break through the fear barrier as she rose and put one hand on Gina's shoulder. 'I'm not being arrested, Sweetie.'

'Ugh?' Gina turned. 'You're not? Then why are they here?'

Vicky placed a hand each side of Gina's upper arms and gripped tight. The poor girl looked distraught, as though she was barely holding onto her sanity. 'They came to tell us we are both in the clear.'

'Both of us?' In an instant, fury replaced the fear in Gina's eyes. She spun around again. 'You thought I would kill my own Granny?' she spat.

It amused Vicky when both detectives took a step back, hands in the air to show submission. She cocked one eyebrow at them. Let them make the apology.

'We have to check everyone to eliminate possible suspects.' At least the sergeant had the good sense to moderate his tone towards someone so young. 'I'm sorry but it is our job. You wouldn't like it if we missed catching a killer because we didn't follow up every single lead to verify the facts now, would you?'

The very second the sergeant started the sentence Vicky knew there was going to be trouble. He ignored her frantic handwave to stop him.

'You sure as hell didn't follow all your leads to catch the bastard who killed my dad.' After the bold statement Gina turned and ran. Her heavy footsteps echoed along the passage. Vicky spied her tears as Gina turned; tears Gina would be too embarrassed to let fall in front of anyone other than Vicky.

'I think you should leave. You have managed to open up very raw wounds. I do recall asking you to not upset my daughter.'

'I'm sorry, we didn't know.' The sergeant had the decency to look stricken.

Fury erupted. 'Maybe you should follow your own advice and do background checks before you jump to conclusions.

You have delved into sections of my private life which have no relevance to my mother's death from cancer, yet you did not bother to delve into the reason for the absence of a much-loved husband and father before you came with your brutal insensitivity. Now go.' She pointed to the door. 'If you wish to speak to me again, you contact my lawyer first.' The pointed finger didn't drop until the door closed on their backsides.

Vicky ran. She crawled onto the bed next to her grief-stricken daughter, wrapped her arms around her, tugged her close. Together, they sobbed out the agony.

* * *

Only when she was certain Gina slept, did Vicky dare leave the bed. It was like a ginormous vacuum cleaner had sucked out all traces of emotion. An all-pervasive emptiness had replaced her innards as she staggered to her en-suite, dropped clothes on the floor at her feet and stood under water as hot as she could bear. She leant up against the tiles, let the full-force water pummel into the skin on her back as she swayed, ducked and stretched slowly so it reached every single taut muscle and sinew. She turned around for the water to massage the front the same way. Too drained to bother with food, she dragged on clean pyjamas and fell into bed.

The sleep she was desperate for didn't come, even after she had counted backwards from a thousand and carried out her yoga relaxation routine – twice. Her body was exhausted but her brain was relentless with pictures, ideas, unanswered questions and re-runs. The end of a person's life should be the closing of a Chapter but this time, Vicky thought... this time, by opening the chest, she had literally opened Pandora's box with a single revelation, which led to another mystery followed by another and another but with not a single answer.

Vicky flopped onto her back, switched on the bedside light and reached into the drawer to take out the pile of photos. One by one, she studied each, recalled each moment in vivid detail and manage to relive each experience. Halfway through the pile, she realised there was only one for each, roughly, six months of her life until about a year after Gina had been born. There were also a lot missing. She could recall several at the same occasion when the printed photos had come home from being processed. She wasn't sure what she felt about her mother keeping only a few and discarding the others. But at least she had kept the best. Which was a good thing. Or was it? But her examination of the photos had settled a small piece of her mind; her mother had cared, much more than she had been able to verbalise. One mystery down – many to go.

She slid from bed to the floor, leant over on her knees and opened the wardrobe door. Since she now knew what was in the top box, she eased out the second, opened it on a held breath and smiled as the breath gushed out. The contents were familiar to her but she'd had no idea Mum had kept every single one of her school reports. Oh, wow.

Overawed, she upended the contents into the lid, lifted off the first sheet, turned it over. Year one – half-year report. She read the comments and laughed. If it hadn't been a report about her, she would have thought it to be cute. Before reaching the final report for the year, she found several small certificates for various achievements. *Beautiful Printing* brought a sense of pride; *Staying in her seat all day,* gave her food for thought. Had she been hyper-active or plain naughty? The memory eluded her so probably the latter although a teasing niggle told her she had often been bored at school because she found the work too easy. Until year four when Mr Stewart had set her harder challenges, taught her how to research interesting topics but only after she had completed the set work the rest of the class had to do each day. There was a lot to thank Mr Stewart for and she wasn't the only bright student he had actively encouraged. Now her mind was back in year four, she pictured a group of eight students seated in a cluster of desks towards the back of the room. There were races amongst the eight of them to see who could finish first, competitions in spelling and maths, pride in high test marks, disappointment when errors had appeared on their page but those disappointments did not affect any of them in a negative way. It only made them determined to do better next time. The competition among the group spurred each to do better. There was never any pandering to avoid disappointment the way they do these days. This modern way of never letting a child fail was not something Vicky agreed with. If a person never had the opportunity to feel the pain of failure as a child, how on earth would they cope once they turned eighteen and met up with the real world, away from school, where making blunders and learning from them was a fact of life. It would be better to teach children how to accept mistakes as learning opportunities and make it okay.

Vicky flipped the pages until she found the year four reports. Ooh, she didn't remember such glowing comments. A pain lanced her heart when she couldn't recall if Mum ever said she was proud of Vicky at the time. But Mum kept every single report as well as all of Vicky's various certificates so in her own way, Regina must have felt some sort of pride.

A crack of thunder was followed by the patter of raindrops on the corrugated iron roof. The sound, as always, was pleasurable. She glanced at the window, smiled at the streaks of water lashing against the glass. A flash of blue light forked from leaden clouds in the distance. She waited for the echoing roll of thunder, counted the seconds between light and sound – a habit she'd had since childhood, when she believed the theory of each second being a mile from the flash. Except now we used kilometres to complicate the old theory, making the calculation a little more difficult. Thunder rumbled, less intense than the first.

A knock on the bedroom door came seconds later. Vicky turned her head, smiled as Gina settled on the floor next to her. It didn't surprise her for they had both gone to bed before six, which was way too early.

'What are you doing?' Gina asked, as she snuggled closer.

'Reading these. Found them in one of those shoe boxes.' She held out a single report.

Gina read it, glanced up with a grin. 'Granny kept this?'

'She kept every single one.'

'Which means she loved you or she wouldn't have.'

'I know – now but I never knew she still had them. The hard thing for me is how she never verbalised her love, never said she was proud of me. I was always present when she read my reports but I never heard the words, *good job,* or *well done.*

When Gina dropped her head on Vicky's shoulder it felt as though her daughter was attempting to make up for Regina's shortcomings. 'Oh, Mum, I'm sorry and I'm sorry I lost my cool earlier.

'It's okay, I understand. You were scared and hurt. Are you hungry?'

'Yeah, starving.'

'Bring those with you. You can read while I cook.'

It amused Vicky when Gina noticed the crude drawing on the refrigerator and headed straight for it. 'Do you remember drawing the ant?'

'I did this?'

'You sure did. Your creepy crawly faze. You gave it to Granny and it appears she must love you for she kept it. I found it in the bag of goodies we took from the chest.' Vicky laughed when Gina snatched the picture from the fridge door, screwed it up and tossed it into the recycle bin.

They read while they ate and laughed together at some of the comments. Gina teased her at the less than complimentary comments but it felt so darn good to be doing normal things.

After they had cleaned away all traces of their meal, Gina settled down to homework while Vicky returned the reports to their home and took out the third box of keepsakes. A faded red velvet pouch held four worn gold rings. Two were plain wedding bands. Hopeful for clues, Vicky inspected the insides for inscriptions. Disappointment replaced hope when they bore nothing but worn smoothness. The third ring looked to be an engagement ring with a flower-shaped cluster of diamonds, again unmarked. To Gina, the fourth ring appeared to be more of a gold dress ring with three sapphires set in what she guessed was platinum for it wasn't tarnished as silver would be. Neither setting looked to be modern.

While she held the rings in the palm of one hand, she fingered them with the other hand, turning each over and over. She lifted them one at a time to inspect the settings. Who had they belonged to? What stories could they tell? Could any of them have been Mum's? But Mum had never worn either a wedding or engagement ring and these had been worn a long time. Maybe they were from Regina's mother. It made sense. To Vicky, they didn't mean much but were worth having valued, maybe re-set the gems. She slid them back into the pouch, drew the strings tight and dropped it on the floor.

Two identical silver serviette rings caught her eye. She lifted them out, rubbed at the inside surface to take off a small patch of black oxidisation over the stamp, recognised the British sterling silver mark indicating solid silver. Her eyes widened the moment she turned it over and recognised the engraved Greek name: Sophia. Excited, she turned the other one over and read: Georgia. Now she was absolutely certain these names were important to Mum. Vicky now had a couple of distinct clues: two Greek names on British silver, another name and a rough date in the early 1950's. It was possible sterling silver items could be purchased in Greece but conversely it was equally possible people from Greece could have migrated to England or visited on a holiday and bought them as mementos. Sophia's letter had been written in perfect English but the one Sophia received was in Greek so she must have been able to understand the language.

A marcasite brooch was nestled in one corner. When she picked it up Vicky saw it was shaped like a butterfly with wings spread. It was pretty but, she guessed, of little value. She inspected both sides but found no markings to indicate to whom it had belonged. There would be no harm in getting it valued so she slid it into the bag with the rings. Nothing about the brooch tugged at Vicky's innards to tell her it was something she wanted to keep.

The intricate inlay on the top of a small wooden box was something Vicky recognised. She had a similar but larger one, bought for her by Mike when they holidayed in Italy. When she turned the box over, it confirmed her thoughts – Sorrento. She turned the wind-up key, opened the lid but was disappointed to hear no music. The music-box mechanism didn't work, even after a gentle shake. Inside was a small carving, yellow with age. She used the pads of her thumb and forefinger to lift it out and hold it up. She wasn't sure but it looked like ivory, delicately carved. About six centimetres long, it depicted an Asian woman draped in a long flowing gown and covered with miniscule intricate flowers. Of all the things she had found so far, this was the most beautiful and the one item she knew she would keep. If it was of ivory, she thought, it would be old and possibly valuable but the delicate perfection would far outweigh any value. To carve something so small, this well, would require great skill and patience. To ensure its safety, Vicky took utmost care as she laid the carving back in the box, closed the lid and set it to one side.

The next item to catch her eye was wrapped in tissue paper. She picked it up, unravelled two separate layers of tissue to reveal a small Chinese cloisonné dish. Unlike normal cloisonné ware, the dish was almost transparent. She held it up to the light. Oh, so pretty. It would look gorgeous against a window with the sunlight shining through the delicate pale greens, blues and pinks.

After re-wrapping it she picked out the next item and grinned. Now this definitely looked like something from Greece. Made of wood, the small donkey carried a pair of panniers on its back. The tail was a short length of floppy black string. Again, the workmanship was exquisite. The donkey was not carved from a single piece of wood but was constructed from minute pieces, each cut to shape and smoothed off before being glued together. The face had an intriguing, cute look at which Vicky couldn't help but smile.

There were only two items left in the box. She plucked out a small crystal vase, which was probably old but meant little to her. There was nothing about it to give her emotions a little tug so she set it aside. But the square of embroidered fabric was far more intriguing. The moment she touched the threads, Vicky knew it was special for it felt incredibly soft and lustrous. She ran her fingers over the embroidery which had a certain sheen which told her it was not the normal cotton embroidery thread but pure silk. A close inspection confirmed her suspicions but amongst the mass of embroidered flowers and garden creatures was a name in Greek; one she recognised from her research. Helena.

When the edges of the fabric parted, Vicky sucked in a

breath of dismay until she realised she hadn't torn it but it was meant to come apart. She opened it out to find four flannel pages inside, each with a few pins and needles threaded through the fabric. 'An old-fashioned needle case,' slipped from her mouth as she examined it. 'So beautiful,' she added while closing it up to give closer scrutiny to the gorgeous embroidery. If Helena made this, Vicky thought, it had to be at least fifty years old, probably closer to seventy or eighty. She must have been a skilful embroiderer. No, seamstress, she corrected when she figured the entire thing had been hand sewn with stitches so fine they were barely visible.

Content with the night's finds, Vicky packed everything away, keeping out the couple of items worth getting valued, put the box back in the wardrobe and slid back into bed. She would never know where these things had come from, who they had belonged to or why her mother had kept them hidden away but there was a sensation of knowing, in her gut, they somehow related to her past. It was the first time in her life she had something tangible from a past she never knew she had. There were names and items. It would take a great deal of time to research but maybe, from these clues, she could find out more, even find out who she really is because it had become obvious what she knew about herself was far from the truth.

Thirteen

I t was raining and had been for most of the night. The road was slick with leaves and debris left in rills as the water subsided bit by bit, leaving puddles in low spots and against the kerbs. In some areas the storm-water drains had worked well, in others muddy water still swirled over clogged grilles, making the act of driving suicidal. It took all of Vicky's concentration to navigate the five kilometres from home to the jeweller she had found on-line. When she finally turned off the engine in the parking bay, her nerves were strung tight like a finely tuned piano wire.

With her stiff fingers still gripped around the steering wheel, she dropped her head to her chin on a hissed-out breath. This was crazy. There was no need to get the items valued today. She could have waited. But she was here now, she thought as she straightened, so now is as good a time as any.

The run from car to front door was short but long enough to catch more drops of water than she wanted. While tugging the velvet bag from her purse, she strode to the end counter towards the only other human in the shop, who took the five items into a back room to be examined by a mystery jeweller, who, she gathered by the brief conversation, was a man but no names were exchanged.

While she waited, Vicky wandered and glanced into various display cabinets, admiring a few pieces but not being a jewellery fanatic, nothing said, *take me home.* She visualised the few elegant pieces Mike had given her over the years of her marriage; pieces she enjoyed wearing for the right occasion but she had never had an urge to buy glitz just for the sake of owning it. She was the same about handbags, which was kind of amusing to some of her friends who had shelves full of expensive name-brand handbags and were always on the lookout for the latest and greatest but handbags never appealed to Vicky. She owned one for which she received a lot of teasing. It was tan leather, smallish and serviceable; only big enough to hold the basic essentials of comb, tissues, money purse, sunglasses, keys and phone. With a grin, she patted her faithful friend held against her side by a long shoulder strap.

She was the same with shoes, buying the best she could afford, for style and comfort but at least no-one ever commented on what she had on her feet. Maybe her friends never noticed, which was possible for she never studied what they wore on their feet. At a guess, she figured she had nine or ten pairs, each for different occasions, from flip-flops to walkers to work shoes and sparkly heeled sandals. She only replaced a pair when they wore out. Her policy was to throw a pair in the bin whenever she brought a new pair home. If she couldn't bear to part with a pair, she didn't buy replacements. Her money, especially since Mike had died, was too hard earned to waste on unnecessary frivolities.

When she heard her name called, Vicky spun around and returned to the counter. An elderly man with a jeweller's magnifying loupe in one hand used his other hand to spread out her items on the glass countertop.

'This brooch, 1940's. Has little value. It's well made but hardly worth selling.' He set aside the marcasite butterfly. It was as she had thought.

'These two rings,' he tapped each wedding band, 'are worth gold value only.' He caught her eye. 'But at today's rates there's about a thousand dollars here. I would buy them if you were in the mind to sell them.'

He picked up the sapphire ring. 'This was made in the early 1900's. The sapphires are of excellent quality – great colour, set in platinum with 18 carat gold band. The face of the gems show a bit of wear but can be polished back to an excellent finish. I would value this ring at about $1500. As for this ring,' he exchanged the two and held the diamond ring high. 'These diamonds are of the best quality. No flaws, finest colour grading. It is hard to get stones of this quality nowadays. I wouldn't ask anything less than $10,000 for this ring.'

'Ten thousand...' Vicky's jaw gaped. 'Oh, wow. I had no idea... would never have thought... are you sure?'

'Absolutely. You have six perfectly matched diamonds, each at least a half a carat. Made in the late 1920's or early 30's. Gold is 18 carat, platinum setting. It is a mighty fine ring. Where did you get it?'

'My mother recently passed away. It was amongst the things she left to me but I don't know the history.'

'I can tell you one more thing. It was made by a first-class jeweller, a master. The workmanship is exquisite, the diamonds of the finest quality. If it were mine I would never sell it.'

Stunned, Vicky took the ring and studied it a little more

closely. Maybe she would keep it. Might even try to research its history; if it was even possible to trace pieces of jewellery. At least she had a rough date and a niggle in her gut which hinted that whatever the history, it was also her history. Otherwise, why else would Mum have kept it? She certainly didn't keep it for its value for she would have sold it early on when things were so tough financially.

'Would you consider selling me the two gold bands?'

Vicky glanced at the man. 'Maybe but not today. There are quite a few papers I need to go through. There might be some clues so I will keep them until I am sure the rings have no significance. I'll bring them back if I find nothing.' She smiled at him. 'I promise.' She gathered the pieces together and plopped them back into the velvet bag. 'Thank you for your help. I appreciate it.' She paused as a thought came to mind.

'I found a couple of small antique pieces. Ivory and cloisonné. Do you know anyone reputable I could take them to, who would be able to date and value them?'

'Hmm.' The man ran one hand through his still thick iron-grey hair. 'There is an antique dealer who has a good name. Give me a minute to find his details.' The man retreated to his hidden back room but was back in less than two minutes. He held out a small scrap of paper torn from a notebook.

'Try this man. I've used him myself and found him to be honest.'

'Thank you.' Vicky took the paper, glanced at it and folded it over before she slid it into the bag with the jewellery. It was something she could do later, after everything else was cleared away. 'If I find anything else, could I bring it to you?'

'Of course, it would be my pleasure especially if I have the joy of handling such fine pieces. A hint though.' He lifted one finger and pressed it against the bag. 'I'd say European – one of the better jewellery houses.'

'You can tell?' Vicky asked, surprised at the words.

'Between the wars, such quality, it would be a sound guess. If it were in its original box the maker's name would be in the lid. I don't suppose...' He had a hopeful look on his face.

'No, or at least not yet. Who knows? I have still got a few boxes to go through. If I find a ring box, I'll bring it in.' Vicky gathered her things together. 'Thank you again. Please, can I pay you for your time?'

'No need, it was my pleasure.'

Outside, the showers had passed. There were now large gaps of blue between broken clouds. In order to collect herself, Vicky sucked in a deep breath, enjoying the freshness despite the chill which seemed to sear her lungs. Now the rain had gone the temperature had dropped. A shiver wove its way down her spine in response to the cold after the warmth of the shop.

The drive to Siesta Lane was much easier now the rain had ceased, the drains had caught up with the backlog of water and the morning rush-hour traffic had reduced to a trickle in comparison to earlier. For the entire thirty-minute drive, Vicky couldn't stop the quick glances at the little velvet bag on the seat next to her, nor stop the thoughts and questions from racing through her brain. Those thoughts kept centring back to one major point. Why would Mum keep these things from her? Why did she hide all these objects and information away? What was so bad about her past?

It was a relief to arrive at the house for it meant she had to concentrate on other things. First, it was the mess in the garden from the night's storm. Leaves, twigs and small branches had been torn from their anchors, flung about and drowned in places they didn't belong. Vicky sighed as she spun around, absorbing the mess. She winced at the sight of the trickle of sludge leaking from the bottom of the skip-bin. It not only looked rank but smelt acrid. The only good thing was there had been no explosion. A snort of *so what,* escaped. There was nothing she could do about it but she didn't dare peek into the bin as she passed it on the way to the front door where she swept a pile of sodden leaves away with the side of her shoe.

Once inside, she dropped her trusty handbag on the kitchen table, slid the jewellery in for safe-keeping and set the filled electric jug on to boil. Tea was needed and it was all she would get for in her haste to reach the jeweller she had forgotten to bring fresh milk for coffee. While she waited, she removed her warm jacket and set it to dry on the back of a kitchen chair. She rolled up the sleeves of her long-sleeved blouse. It was oldish so it didn't matter if it got torn or stained but was also presentable enough for her earlier task. The bottom button was missing but she didn't much care for when it was tucked into her jeans, nobody could see. Besides, it was lost and finding a match had been impossible.

The kitchen table and chairs with metal frames and legs, had survived the marauding but were old. Somehow, she didn't think anyone would want them unless they were into the 70's retro trend. Maybe a night on the verge with a *Free* sign might see them go to a new home. There were a few other things she could add to them. Not such a bad idea but not until the weather improved. Since at least one chair and the table would be useful until the end, Vicky decided to leave them be. Instead, she carried the filled mug of tea to the sitting room where she had piled the books from the cabinet she hadn't had a chance to clean out when the police had arrived. The emptying process had been done for her by the midnight marauders who had left the cabinet on its back with doors torn off. Such a pity but with shredded wood where hinges had been, it was irreparable. Ditto two small side tables. Good job they were as ancient as the house but not of quality antique status. Serviceable cheap furniture was all her mother could afford but she had taken pride in her possessions and by taking utmost care of every item with regular dusting and a coat of polish, they had lasted well. Vicky put the wheelbarrow to use, wheeled broken furniture from house to bin, up the ramp, hoist, tip and back again. Anything worth saving went into boxes which she stacked along one wall in the sitting room.

A close inspection of the up-turned leather recliner revealed no major damage but it was too awkward for her to manage moving into the car by herself. She pushed it to one side. It would be an evening task with Gina to help. After she had filled all the boxes she had brought with her, Vicky ventured to Old George's corner deli to see if he had more, making it an excuse for a coffee break with a decent mug of coffee.

The break was welcome but not as much as the caffeine hit. Back at the house, she managed to wrestle six empty cartons into the house, juggling the awkward slippery boxes as she walked.

'Yoo-hoo!'

Vicky jolted at the female voice. She dropped her load which scattered at her feet in the passage. She spun around to see a shadow waving from outside the screen door.

'Hello.' She stepped over a box but caught her foot on another, stumbled several steps, and hit the wall before she managed to regain her balance without spilling a drop of coffee.

The door opened.

Vicky's breath stalled.

'It's only me,' the voice continued but it was difficult to make out features against the glare of the background light.

'I've brought these back for you.'

A pile of bedding was thrust towards Vicky. It was an automatic reaction to grasp the folded items with one hand and her forearm while she tried to keep the coffee upright but now she knew who the woman was, especially since her vision cleared and the facial features formed into those of Meg.

'Meg, sorry, I tripped.'

'I'm so sorry about your mum. I'm going to miss her.'

'Me too and thank you. Come into the kitchen. I can only offer you black tea. No milk.' She felt like an idiot, blathering away but her heart was still trying to return to its normal pace.

'Not for me, thank you. I've not long had a cuppa. Thought I would try to catch you while your car is here.' Meg didn't take the proffered chair but stood behind it.

Vicky sat. She needed the stability of four secure legs while her heart ceased its frantic drum-roll. 'Thank you for these and for everything.' She dumped the sheets and blanket on the table. 'It couldn't have been easy finding Mum the way you did.'

'No but it wasn't such a shock. We knew she was near the end.'

'You knew?'

'Yes.'

'About her cancer?'

'Of course but she didn't want you to know... didn't want you to worry.' Meg reached out and placed a hand on Vicky's shoulder, giving it a gentle squeeze. 'More important, she didn't want to leave here. She wanted to stay in her home... to die here.'

'But why didn't she seek treatment?'

'The cancer was too far advanced when she received the diagnosis. They gave her strong medicine for the pain but it didn't work so well these past couple of months. I did my best to convince her to tell you.' Meg moved from behind, pulled out the chair, sat and grasped Vicky's hands. 'I'm sorry. You had a right to know but Regina can be one stubborn woman at times.' Meg scoffed on a grin. 'Why am I telling you this? You know exactly how stubborn she could be. So I did my best to give her the support she needed. I'm sorry.'

Vicky wriggled one hand free and placed it on top of Meg's. 'Not your fault but I wish I had known. I would have found the time to be with her more often, to talk more to... I don't know but we would have made it work.'

'Which is exactly why she didn't want you to know. You have an important job with long hours as well as your daughter to care for. You have had your own heartache and your Mum wanted to spare you. She was proud of you, always extolling your virtues.'

Vicky's jaw dropped, she couldn't help it but the words were a shock and they hurt with a pain lancing her heart. Why couldn't Mum have ever told Vicky to her face? But she couldn't say anything to Meg. 'Thank you,' was all she could think of to say but it felt so inadequate.

Meg stood. 'I have to go. We oldies are having a casserole night at the senior citizens tonight. Can't let mine burn or I'll be the butt of their teasing forever more or at least until someone makes the next blunder.' She moved to the door. 'I'll catch up next time you're here.'

And she was gone.

Not in the mood to do any more, Vicky followed suit.

Fourteen

'Oh, my goodness!' A pile of ancient newspaper cuttings spilled from the shoe box as Vicky lifted the lid. A waft of mustiness reached her nose. She sneezed, spilling even more and tipping the lid onto the carpet. To prevent another sneeze, she sniffed and squeezed her nostrils together. Happy there would be no more, she gathered the scattered pieces of yellowed paper in one hand. There must be hundreds, she thought while she sifted through the handful of collected pieces which appeared to have been carefully cut for the edges were straight with equal margins around the words. These hadn't been hastily torn articles, the way she occasionally tore a recipe from the daily paper or a magazine.

After she set her pile to one side and the box to the other, she picked off the top article to read, delighted to find it was written in English. It didn't take long before she was entrenched in reports of the hardship of Greek life during and after the civil war. She had to pause to drag dates from her memory. Somehow she thought there was more than one so which civil war were these cuttings about? She searched for dates but most were short articles cut from much larger pages, the headings and dates no longer present. The great thing was, she now had a much stronger link to Greece.

Even after she had studied several items she was still clueless about dates but guessed sometime after WW11 by the few clues mentioned. Churchill was predominant and she recognised the name of George Papandreou. Desperate to satisfy her curiosity and set a date and timeline in her mind, Vicky put the articles aside, unfolded from the floor and moved from bedroom to office. It took mere minutes before she was mesmerised by the conflict between communists, republicans, royalists, British and Russians which began in 1944 after Greece had been liberated from German occupation. After she devoured the entire document, she had to agree with the writer's assessment how the Civil war wasn't so much about good versus evil but more of opposing belief systems unable to co-exist. Unfortunately, the general Greek population who didn't want either, managed to get themselves caught in the middle and suffered the most. The strategic position of the country, at the head of the Mediterranean Sea, was an obvious incentive to prevent the communists from winning control. How different things might have been in this world if they had won.

Vicky shuddered when she reached the bit about how the communists kept records of all the three to fourteen-year-old children they stole from the more isolated Greek village families and sent across the northern borders in order to indoctrinate them as future soldiers for the communist cause.

'Oh, my God, more than 25,000 Greek children were stolen and only about 6,000 were ever returned,' she read aloud. 'Appalling,' she muttered. Those poor kids... and their families. Even though she knew what it felt like to lose someone you adored, she couldn't picture losing Gina in such a way and never hear from her again. Shocked at the thought, she leant back in her chair with her eyes closed. How awful for all of those poor families. No wonder so many Greek citizens fled to seek a better life in countries such as Australia, Britain, Canada and the USA. Now she understood the reason for the influx of Greek citizens into Australia in the early 1950's. Maybe this explained why Sophia and Georgia were so fluent in English and Greek. Had they been refugees? And Helena – Sophia's mother - had she taken the girls to England for a better life? It made sense and explained a lot but what about the father? What happened to him?

She read on about the death toll which was unbelievable with more people killed during the civil war than during the German occupation, which made it worse for it was Greek who killed fellow Greek and not invaders. Nausea rose by what she had read but at the same time she was satisfied she had found a tenuous link. She shut down the programme and returned to her bedroom to scour the rest of the newspaper articles. Some were nothing more than a few lines, hardly worth printing but maybe they filled a gap on a page during the print set-out which would have been a manual process back in the fifties. Others took up half a page but never more. Despite the number of reports, she learnt little more than what was in the computer features. A huge yawn made the decision for her - time for bed. She made a quick flick through the remaining small pile of un-read pieces but stopped short and flicked back when a sluggish brain recognised what looked to be a page of obituaries.

With a held breath, she drew the folded sheet out and scanned the names. Most were typical English surnames, ones she skipped over for none of them held any meaning to her. When she found nothing of interest she turned the page over, thinking maybe there would be the name Wakefield near the end. When she unfolded it she couldn't miss the reason the page had been kept for six entries, all with the same name, were high-lighted with asterisks.

LEBTOS – GEORGE.

Her heart raced. Careful not to damage the aged piece of newsprint, Vicky placed one finger on the first notice.

Beloved husband of Helena.

Vicky's heart stalled.

Adored Papa of Costas, Georgia, Lukas and baby Sophia.

'Oh, my goodness,' rushed out on a long breath. One hand covered her mouth in shock while the other stalled on words which had become bleary by a wash of moisture which flooded across her eyes. Vicky shook her head, feeling stupid for having such a reaction. 'For heaven's sake,' she chided to herself, 'I don't even know these people.' But deep down she felt as though she did. Gut instinct along with plain logic told her there must be some relevance or why would Mum have kept these items relating to the same people. This was important – it had to be. She now had a surname and two others, boys. An entire family. Her eyes shot back to the single word, baby. Sophia was still a baby when her papa died. Vicky glanced at the top of the page. A date: at long last she had a date. 19th November 1951.

Adrenalin surged as thoughts tumbled through her mind. November was almost winter in the northern hemisphere. The picture of Helena with Sophia was definitely taken in warmer weather. Maybe June or July which would have Sophia only five or six months old when her papa died. So sad.

Stunned, she sucked in a long, slow breath to still her racing heart before she dared go back to the death notice.

> *A kind, gentle and loving man, dedicated to his family and patients.*
> *I will always love you my darling George.*
> *Helena.*

This time, the breath she sucked in caused her to choke on a lump of emotion while she slid her eyes closed tight to prevent a leakage. It took a moment before she could read on. One notice was from his parents, Costas and Maria, one from his children which caused the threatened leak to overflow with salty tears running down her cheeks. The last entry stopped the tears in an instant.

> *Murdered in prison, a political prisoner for nothing more than treating injured patients under the Hippocratic oath he swore to dedicate his life. The Royal College of Surgeons.*

Oh, my. A doctor and political prisoner.

'Mum?'

Startled, Vicky glanced up to see Gina hovering half in the doorway as though too afraid to enter. 'Yes,' she mumbled while trying to bring her stupid emotions under control. She felt like an idiot to allow some stranger's obituaries to have this effect.

'You know Granny's rainbow jacket.'

'The long knitted one?'

'Yes... um... can I have it?'

Shock loosened Vicky's grip on the article. 'You want it?' Gina had forever maligned the bold, patchwork knitted jacket which had arrived on the scene from some craft market about two years previous.

'Yes.'

'Why? You've always been less than complimentary whenever Granny wore it.'

A sheepish grin crept from the corners of Gina's mouth. 'I know but only because... well... she kinda looked too old to be wearing something so... I don't know.'

Vicky laughed. 'Maybe you hoped she would discard it if you teased her enough so you could snaffle it up.'

A blush raced up Gina's face. 'Maybe.'

'Sure thing. I'll bring it home tomorrow. Granny loved it but I have to agree with you, she did look ridiculous especially when she teamed it with those godawful purple baggy pants. Would you like those as well?'

Gina straightened with a look of horror altering her face in an instant. 'No way.' At last, she found the courage to come out from behind the door frame and crept across the floor where she snuggled down next to Vicky. 'What are you do-ing?'

'I found these old newspaper articles in one of the boxes. Many are about the Greek Civil War which occurred after the end of WW11. I've printed off some details I found on the in-ternet about the war.' She retrieved the death notice. 'But this one has a few notices about the death of George Lebtos who was a doctor and was the father of the Sophia and Georgia I told you about. Helena was his wife and there were two other children – boys.' She passed the piece of paper to Gina, who studied the words before handing it back with a hitch to her breath.

'But why do you think Granny kept this?' She reached out and ran one finger down Vicky's cheek. 'Why have you been crying?'

A snort escaped Vicky's mouth. 'Silly, I know but the thought of Sophia losing her papa when she was such a young baby. He sounded like he was a good man.'

'Maybe she was too young to remember – a bit like you.' Gina's dark hair tickled Vicky's face when she nestled against Vicky's shoulder. 'It would be better than losing him when you're fourteen like I was.'

When her heart lurched, Vicky swung one arm around her daughter's shoulder and drew her close. 'It is never a good time to lose your dad. I can imagine how the other three chil-dren felt. They were older and would have suffered the same heartache you did. I am sorry, so sorry, you had to go through such agony. I know you still miss Dad as much as I do. I would give anything to be able to bring him back but I can't. I guess we need to be thankful we had him as part of our lives for as long as we did, even though it wasn't anywhere near long enough. I thank him every day for giving me you. Every time I look at you I see his eyes - his smile and I thank God. Dad still lives in you. You are very much like him in nature as well.' Overcome, she couldn't say any more, especially when she felt the warmth of Gina's silent tears soak through her top. Her own tears fell until they were spent. Like many nights over the past three years, they climbed into the big bed together and held hands, desperate for each other's touch until Mother nature sent her healing powers of sleep.

Fifteen

Already dust motes floated, stirred up by the mere act of opening the front door. To Vicky, the sight high-lighted the leaden sense of emptiness in the house she had always loved. Whenever something had gone wrong in her life, Mum had been behind this door to steady the rocking boat and give Vicky an anchoring point. It had always been her safe haven. She sighed as a wodge of emotion threatened to choke her. Gone – Mum was gone. She shook her head vigorously to dispel the gloom and stepped into the passage. This was where she grew up; a place where she always felt safe and secure.

Early on, she knew it was a struggle for Mum to scrape together the monthly loan repayments but by the time she was fifty, Mum owned the modest three-bedroom, one-bathroom home. Compared to the outlandish cost of property today, this house had been cheap and was able to be paid off over a reasonable length of time. The acquisition of property in the early eighties wasn't the huge hurdle it was today: an insurmountable hurdle for more and more people.

A smile crept out as the memory surfaced of the celebration after the final payment had been made. Regina had splurged, what would have been the next month's loan amount, on a slap-up dinner for the two of them in the classiest restaurant in the city. They really hammed it up, dressed in their best outfits, making out it was an everyday occurrence for them. After they had stuffed themselves with three haute-cuisine courses they laughed on the way home, mostly at the la-di-dah actions of other diners and their own social gaffes. It had been a fun night.

From then on, the same amount each month went into a new designated savings account. Regina used the money for special holidays she had never been able to afford before, or renovations, or the purchase of some item she really wanted but did not necessarily need, like the huge T.V. Life for Regina had become much easier and far more enjoyable with little financial stress. Never again did she take out a loan but saved to pay cash for anything she wanted: even her car. It was a habit Vicky did her best to follow but a loan for Gina's university fees had been on the cards. Not now. Vicky sighed as a wave of sadness swept over her.

Regina's death meant the sale of this house. Vicky glanced around as she strode along the passage to the kitchen. It would pay the required fees up front with enough left over for her own nest egg. An oversees holiday sounded good. Guilt swamped her: guilt at benefitting from her mother's death. She blew out her cheeks as she dropped her bag on the kitchen table. There wasn't a darn thing she could do about it but at least Regina's hard-earned money was going to a great cause – Gina's career. Vicky was certain her mum would be okay with the idea.

A thought came. Had anyone informed the pension people of Regina's death? Surely the lawyer had done it. Maybe not but it was something to add to her list. Monday, she would do it Monday when she was back at work. But now?

Vicky wasn't sure what to tackle first. A walk through decided her. Almost all the broken things now resided in the skip bin so she would empty each room of remaining furniture and stack the pieces in the one space. The living room was largest and closest to the front door for easy access but she would need help to move them outside.

Start with the easy bit first, her subconscious said. She carried feather duster, broom and vacuum cleaner into the third bedroom. It was the smallest and had been used for almost everything over the years as most spare rooms had in so many households. A single bed for guests had been rarely used, mostly for sleepovers with her friends until she had left home. The room had housed the much-used sewing machine, set up on a small table while the three-doored wardrobe had stored spare sheets, blankets, pillows and all those items needed only once in a while.

Vicky stood in the doorway, glanced around with raised shoulders and a long sigh. The bed was already dismantled, thanks to the intruders, who had stripped it and torn off the mattress, which now stood against the wall showing off its deep gashes and protruding stuffing. Since it was a single mattress, Vicky was able to manoeuvre it through the door and along the passage with ease. Once outside, she dragged it down the path and up the metal ramp. It felt good to let it fall on top of and hide the smashed remnants of her mother's life, still soggy from yesterday's storm. Now everything looked plain sad, even if it smelt gross. On another long sigh, she dusted off her hands by slapping them together before rubbing them down the side of her jeans on the way back inside where she studied the bed. It was ancient – or at least nearly as old as her but the wood ends and slatted base were in good condition. Maybe the kerbside recycle pile along with the kitchen table and chairs would see it gain a new home. And there were always charitable organisations she could ask. In the meantime she dragged the pieces, one by one, to the living room where she set them against the far wall. The neatly folded bedding joined it, along with the spare winter blankets and doonas from the wardrobe, all retrieved from the floor where they had been flung during the search for whatever it was the housebreakers had been looking for.

It was a surprise to find the sewing machine intact, still inside its plastic case. It was not so old and had been regularly serviced so maybe someone would have a use for it even though not many modern women actually sewed any longer since clothes nowadays were cheap and easily obtainable. Those who could afford luxury brand names probably wouldn't be caught dead in something home-made. Two hands were needed to carry the darn thing. It landed next to the bed with a thud and rattle. To make sure it wasn't hiding another surprise, Vicky lifted the lid and poked around, sighing when she found nothing except what should be there. She was not sure whether she was glad or disappointed.

When she returned to the bedroom it was with a large empty cardboard carton which she filled with all the other items from the wardrobe. There weren't many for most were already in the skip bin after being smashed or shredded. Since there was no way she would be able to move the free-standing wardrobe by herself, Vicky set to with the duster, swished at cornice, down the walls, across the top of the window and door, knowing there would be little dust due to Regina's fastidious housekeeping. The room was small so even a thorough vacuum took little time, far less than it took to wash and polish the window and painted woodwork.

Room clean, she decided coffee from the corner shop had been earned. Plus it was a great opportunity to ask Old George for any more cartons he might have. Since the weather had decided the city had received enough rain for a while and sent the sun to a now cloudless sky, Vicky walked the hundred metres, enjoying the fresh air while she reminisced about the people who had lived in each house she passed. Like her mother, a few families had been content to stay put, liking the proximity to the city and since it was only one street back from the main road there was easy access to public transport. As Vicky ambled, she wondered how long it would be before some big developer would buy up these older properties to build concrete monstrosities to house hundreds in units. It would be a sad day. Note to self, she thought, make sure a family buys Mum's house.

With one arm wrapped around three smallish boxes, stacked inside each other, Vicky sipped the strong white coffee while she strode back to the house. The constant rumble of vehicles didn't deter native birds from flitting and chirping in mature gardens. They were probably immune to the noise as much as Vicky had been as a child. She noticed it more now than she could remember while living here. Guildford Rd had been the main arterial road for as long as she had been around so traffic density would not really be much more than it had been twenty years ago yet now she noticed the noise.

A lump of emotion settled high in her chest while she gave her childhood bedroom the same treatment as the previous room, especially when she turned the mattress over to discover it also had been torn apart. Itchy eyes accompanied her journey to the skip bin, which was ridiculous, she thought when she paused on the top of the ramp to study the mattress. 'For goodness sake,' she scolded herself, 'it is only a mattress – an ancient mattress which needed replacing years ago.' She shoved, watched it fall and spun around.

A pile of clothes between bed and wall, greeted her in Regina's room. While she had ridden the room of broken items the day before she had given the pile only a cursory glance but now she had no choice but to sort through her mother's clothes. The lump of emotion returned as she knelt by the pile and laid one hand on the top item, Mum's dressing gown. A more recent purchase, it was in a modern soft, cuddly micro fibre – bright red to suit Regina. In two minds about keeping it, Vicky folded it and put it to one side. She caught sight of the rainbow jacket, tugged it free and shook out the creases. While dropping it on top of the gown, she spied something red and lacy which had been dragged out with the jacket.

When she tugged it free, her eyes popped. 'Oh, Mum,' Vicky gasped before laughter escaped at the sheer red lacy negligee. I didn't need to know about this, she thought while bundling it up, along with a version in black. The images which flew through her brain, along with pictures of the men she knew Regina had relationships with, were X-rated, causing her cheeks to heat. She knew it was a stupid reaction when sexual relationships were a normal part of life but when it was a parent – especially your mother, it felt kind of weird. It didn't surprise her to find much of her mother's underwear was equally as raunchy; clothes she shoved into a box for the bin. They might still be in good condition but they had hugged the most intimate parts of her mother's body. No way would she allow any other person to wear them.

It took almost an hour to sort the clothes into three piles. After much thought she decided to keep only three items, the dressing gown, rainbow jacket and a new thick jumper which had never been worn. The sweaters, coats, slacks, scarves, gloves which were still in top condition would go to charity. Someone in difficult circumstances could find them useful. It took two trips to the skip bin to get rid of the largest pile of underwear, shoes and clothes which were either outdated or too far gone to be of any use.

She eyed the half a dozen handbags she had stacked against the wall, still undecided what to do with them. Better check inside, she thought, reaching for the first. It took ten minutes to unzip zippers, search for hidden pockets and remove $32.45 in notes and coins along with several clean folded handkerchiefs, two opened packets of mints, five bobby pins, four biros and the remains of three tiny notepads which looked like they had been well used.

To ensure there was nothing left hidden away in the wardrobe, Vicky stood and slid the first door open. An ancient pair of leather walkers sat tucked in one corner. For the life of her she could not remember the last time she had seen Mum wear them but it had to have been before Vicky married. As she lifted them she gave both a vigorous shake to ensure there were no more surprises hidden in the toes. A brush inside with one hand confirmed their emptiness but it felt creepy, especially with the hardness of the lining which was brittle and cracked. 'Ugh,' she said in disgust as she tossed them towards the door.

Old lining paper still sat on the wardrobe floor. She picked at one corner, swept it up and screwed it into a ball. It joined the shoes, as did the paper from the other end of the hanging space. The middle section contained four shelves at the top, all empty, and three drawers underneath. Working from the top down, Vicky pulled out each drawer, removed the musty pink lining paper and screwed each before tossing. In the bottom drawer, the paper didn't come away with the same ease. It seemed to have had something spilt in the front, sticking the edge to the wood. Vicky knelt on the floor and eased her fingers under the back, slid them along while she jiggled her fingers up and down. It took a bit of effort but finally the paper came free. She lifted it out and stared. Two old studio photographs stared back at her.

Stunned, she reached out with a hand which had taken on a definite tremble. The first picture was of a young couple standing in a semi-embrace as though to get any closer would be frowned upon. The woman was beautiful, a head shorter than the man, who was not handsome but had rugged good looks with a long, strong face under hair which was slicked down with oil as per the fashion of the time. A twinge of familiarity stabbed. Vicky drew the picture closer to study it in more detail. Where had she seen this woman before? Unable to believe she would be so lucky she turned the photograph over and grinned. The grin turned to a frown when the names were not in English but she smiled again when she recognised the Greek for Helena.

So this was a younger Helena, and probably her husband, George, she thought while flipping it back over. Her eyes slid closed as thoughts tumbled. There were way too many clues to not figure her mother had close ties with this family. Tension thrummed while she put the photo down and picked up the other one. One glance and her heart stalled before racing to catch up on the missed beats. The same couple with three young children. This had to be Helena, George, Georgia, Costas and Lukas before Sophia was born. Which would make it pre-1951 but not much before. Vicky searched for a pregnancy bump on Helena but couldn't make one out, especially since the children were huddled in front of their parents with adult arms criss-crossed on various children's shoulders.

Vicky blew out her cheeks as she sat back on her heels. For Mum to keep these hidden away there had to be a lot more to the story. There had to be a solid reason and the idea which jabbed at her grey matter was how it was possible Mum could be Sophia. They were born the same year, well according to the documents she had, they were born the same year but not on the same day or even the same month. Could it be? Was it possible? If so, why all the secrecy? As quick as the idea came, she dismissed it. Regina didn't look anything like these people although with the photos being black and white it was difficult to tell eye and hair colour, except both looked to be darker rather than lighter.

While she disposed of the last of the rubbish items and put what she wanted to keep in the car, possibilities kept tumbling through her mind. If Mum was related to these people, why had there been no contact? Mum had consistently said all of her family members were dead. But were they? And if these people were family, what caused such an upheaval to split them apart permanently?

A creepy sensation sent the hairs on the nape of her neck standing to attention when her hand settled on the driver's door handle. Unnerved, she hesitated, too afraid to move. Somehow, she had an inkling someone was watching her. Up ahead, nothing seemed out of place, even after she made a thorough search with her eyes through the shrubs and shadows of the neighbouring gardens. Slowly she swung around to her left, scanned the properties as her head turned. There were no tell-tale twitch of curtains in windows, no householders in front gardens, no children playing. There wasn't even a dog or cat peering at her.

Nothing, nothing, nothing until she came to a grinding halt. Behind her, a man dressed in blue jeans, white shirt and dark jacket, stood leant up against the side of a silver sedan. He was tall and dark-haired. Vicky's heart did a tumble-turn when he turned all of a sudden and caught her eye. Her held breath rushed out when she realised he was talking on a mobile phone. Idiot, she thought, he had probably pulled over to take a phone call.

Embarrassed, she yanked the door open, folded into the

driver's seat and slid the key into the lock. Of course, the engine had to stall on a kangaroo hop when she tried to drive off. Her faced flamed as she hunched forward to attempt the simple process of starting a car engine, for the second time. She was overjoyed when she managed a sleek take-off but didn't dare peek in the rear-vision mirrors while she drove along the street to the corner.

By the time she reached home, her pulse rate was back to its normal pace but the ideas which surged and ebbed around in her brain began to sound ludicrous. Tonight, she was determined to spend time tonight doing a lot more research on the internet. What if she simply logged in each of these names to find out if any of them were still alive? And there was still a pile of certificates to get translated. Surely the answer would be amongst them.

Sixteen

The moment she heard a key rattle in the lock, Vicky grabbed the voluminous, coloured jacket and raced to meet Gina. As the door opened, she held out the folds to look as though it was waiting for Gina to step into it. Gina looked surprised for a split second before a wide grin broke out. She slid her school bag from her shoulders and replaced it with a flowing rainbow, spun around several times before she posed in a range of outrageous stances as a photographic model would.

'It suits you.' Vicky tugged the shoulders into place, ran her hands down the front then stood back to admire with one pointed finger against the side of her mouth. 'Hmm, not bad. Since it is Friday, how about we go out for burgers?'

Gina's face lit up. 'Alfred's Kitchen?'

The roadside café had been there for years, nestled between the highway and railway line in Guildford. Open only at night, it drew constant crowds from all walks of life. Vicky had seen them all, from business-suited men on their way home from a late night in the office, to on-duty police officers during their break, to homeless people warming cold bodies while enjoying a mug of soup, albeit the best pea and ham soup she had ever tasted, something for which the eatery was famous. An open fire in the cooler weather was a drawcard. When she and Mike had first gone there, they sat on the huge logs which surrounded the fire-pit but the weathered logs had recently been replaced by weather-friendly metal benches resulting in some of the charm now lost and cold backsides when brisk air snuck through the patterned holes designed to let water through. Equally as recent was the appearance of a dining car from an old steam train, which offered indoor seating, which was great during inclement weather but what could be better than standing around an open fire with a group of complete strangers who seemed to have no hesitation in chatting to each other? A smile broke out at the memories of their favourite haunt during their marriage and the last time they had been there... her smiled turned to a frown. It was only a week before he had been killed. Since then, the thought of going back had been too difficult. She eyed the hopeful look on Gina's face.

'Okay, why not?' Vicky had to force a grin but when it came it seemed to ease her trepidation. Time to let go, time to begin saying goodbye so why not start at Alfred's Kitchen? Something hard and uncomfortable lodged in her throat at the thought.

To catch up on her own home chores, Vicky threw a basket of clothes into the washer, waved a duster over the lounge furniture and swept the kitchen floor while Gina did what all teenage girls found necessary after school on a Friday afternoon – lie on her bed listening to music with the ever-present smart phone in her hand, catching up with friends via modern technology. Friday nights had always been a time for relaxation after a hard week for them all so Vicky didn't mind the few hours of letting go. Normally she would be doing the same but this past week had seen little housework on the home front.

After she bundled wet laundry into the clothes drier, it didn't surprise Vicky when Gina emerged from her room adorned in the multi-coloured jacket over blue jeans and a black skivvy. In comparison, Vicky felt dowdy in her old favourite navy blue fleece jacket and equally ancient red, long-sleeved cotton top. Maybe it was time to splurge on a few new clothes, she thought while she locked the kitchen door and folded into the car. Heaven's, why not? She could afford it but since Mike passed away she hadn't felt like prissy-ing up her wardrobe.

After she took care to reverse onto the front verge, Vicky checked in the side and rear-vision mirrors before pulling onto the road, surprised to see an unfamiliar car parked on the roadside a few houses down. It was not often a car was parked in the street for everyone had blocks large enough for garages and longish driveways but she dismissed it as a visitor to the occupants. With the road clear, she pulled onto the street and drove to the corner where she paused to check for clearance before turning into the next street. At Guildford Road she had to wait for a stream of traffic to pass before she was able to turn right across the double lanes and swing into the centre lane going east. At the major intersection green lights gave her a free passage through but the next set of lights flashed amber seconds before she arrived. It was touch and go whether to speed through but discretion won the indecision war in her head. She jammed on the brakes and managed to stop with the front end of the car hanging over the thick white line accompanied by a blast of a horn from behind.

'Oops, sorry,' she muttered under her breath but didn't appreciate the soft chortle from the passenger seat. With a raised hand, Vicky waved an apology to the driver behind while she shot a glance in the rear-vision mirror. But it was the car next to the one behind, which held her stare. Surely not, it couldn't be but somehow she was certain it was the car which had been parked in their street. A wave of apprehension managed to stall her breath before she dismissed the sudden thought of being followed. Co-incidence, it had to be co-incidence.

Even though she had convinced herself she wasn't being followed, her eyes kept glancing at the silver Mazda sedan which had now pulled into her lane three cars back, which made it impossible to make out the driver. It was still there when they reached the Guildford Road bridge and had to feed into a single lane. It was still there when they coasted past the antique shops in the old Guildford townsite and still behind when she turned into the car park of Alfred's Kitchen. A huff of breath rushed out when the car didn't follow her into the car park but turned left at the next corner, metres from the entry.

The spooky sensation didn't leave her until after they had ordered the large mug of soup to share, an Alfred's special hamburger and bag of fries, also to share. Going the whole hog by herself was not on. She had learnt years ago, to eat an entire burger was a struggle, same with the soup and fries and having all three was impossible and a waste of money but each item was so delicious in its own right, it was difficult to forego one. Vicky rarely ate fries but these ones had to be the best in the country.

Order made and paid for, and with their ticket tucked into her pocket, they moved to the flickering fire, wriggled in amongst the patrons, some of whom were enjoying their food while others warmed their backsides while they waited for their order. It always amazed her how people simply shuffled around and squeezed up to let newcomers in, without comment apart from mumbled, 'Hi and hello.' This was one place where everyone accepted everybody else regardless of what they wore or what they looked like. It was a melting pot of class and ethnicity. Never once had she seen or heard a rumble of discontent but it didn't mean disturbances and less than appropriate behaviour never occurred. Alcohol was not served but there was an hotel across the road.

Gina stood hunched up next to her, shoulders touching while Vicky stared into the orange flames. What was it about a fire that was so mesmerising? A quick glance around the circle of patrons told her all those staring faces were equally as absorbed.

Except for one.

Standing leant up against the corner of the brick building was a tall man dressed in jeans and a long trench coat and even though he glanced away when she caught his eye, Vicky was certain he had been watching her. Where had she seen him before? Some niggle of recognition stabbed into her grey matter but the recollection remained hidden in some dark recess. Vicky kept staring until the man looked her way. He quickly dropped his eyes before he moved from his position and slunk around the corner towards the service bar. It was far enough for her to not be able to see him but he had nowhere to go unless he forewent his order and walked away.

A shiver of unease caused the hairs on the back of her neck to stand at attention. Still she watched.

'What's up, Mum?'

Vicky jerked at Gina's words. 'Not sure but I had this strange feeling we were being watched.'

'Mum, really, anyone of these people are probably watching us.'

'I know but there's a man hidden behind the corner over there.' She indicated with her hand. 'Something about him seems familiar.'

'Number 134,' was shouted from the servery.

Gina nudged Vicky. 'That's us, Mum.'

'Oh, yes.' Vicky searched her pocket, withdrew the ticket and checked the number. 'Give me a hand.'

As they walked towards the servery, Vicky kept her eyes on the corner. When they rounded it, the man wasn't there. She searched around, spun on one foot until she spied the trench coat headed for the car park. While she crab-walked towards the servery, she kept one eye on the man but stopped dead when she saw him getting into a silver Mazda. He had no food in his hands.

'Mum, come on,' Gina whined.

Now certain this man had been watching her, Vicky flung the ticket on the counter, grabbed the mug of soup with two plastic spoons and handed them to Gina. She swept up the large brown paper bag containing their burger and fries. 'I want to eat this at home,' she said as she straightened in front of Gina.

'What, why?' Gina's mouth had a definite pout of displeasure.

'I remember where I have seen the man before... and his car. He was standing outside Granny's house this afternoon next to a silver Mazda, that silver Mazda,' she pointed to the car which was now on the opposite side of the road – headed west - towards home, 'was parked in our street when we left tonight and it followed us here.' She grabbed Gina's hand and tugged. 'Let's go. We are going home.'

'But, Mum, it's probably a co-incidence.'

Vicky tugged again. Gina stumbled but followed. 'Too many co-incidences make me nervous. I want to go home to be sure.'

The walk to the car was ungainly and rapid. Soup went in the console, the food at Gina's feet. Vicky was so unnerved she managed to stall the engine twice before she was able to reverse from her parking position, head to the road entry and pull onto the roadway, headed east instead of west, with a central island making it impossible to do a U-turn. It was 200 metres before she was able to turn the car onto the west bound lanes towards home. She planted her foot on the accelerator, dared an extra five kilometres over the speed limit with her heart in her mouth the entire journey home.

When she turned left off the main road, she darted her eyes in all directions, searched for a silver Mazda. By the time she turned into her street, her nerves were so tense she was afraid they would snap if she spied the car. Relief gushed from her mouth on a long huff of breath when the street was devoid of parked cars, silver or otherwise.

Something greasy slithered down her spine while they had to wait for the automatic garage door to rise. Vicky didn't dare drive in until she had eyed every object inside to check for some shape or shadow which should not be there. For the umpteenth time on the journey home, she peered in all three rear vision mirrors to ensure someone wasn't about to sneak inside behind them. She pressed the remote to close the garage doors before the car was completely inside.

'Told you, Mum. There's nothing but your wild imagination,' Gina mocked. Vicky couldn't blame her but didn't want to alarm her any more.

'Maybe you are right. Maybe, after Granny's house being trashed, I imagine even the slightest of things being out of whack is ominous. I am sorry. Let's go inside and enjoy this food. It's been too long since we had an Alfred's Special.'

'Three years.'

'I know.'

'Because of Dad.'

'Yes, but we will go back more often now I've broken the ice.'

'Soon?'

'Definitely.' Vicky grinned at her daughter.

Gina grinned back before she alighted. With a sly grin she snuck a golden chip from the bag, stuffed it into her mouth and moaned in delight while her eyes rolled.

Friday night television was not the most inspirational so

they watched the ABC national news while they sat either side of the sofa with the food between them. After they both cleared away the trash, Gina showered and settled in her room while Vicky decided to make a further foray into her mother's secret life. There had to be a reason why a man was watching her, especially since she had figured out who he was. She now remembered what was familiar about him. The same style trench coat had been worn by the two men at the funeral.

Seventeen

To make sure she hadn't missed anything of importance so far, Vicky revisited the four boxes she had already opened. The jewellery and antique items were not so valuable they would be worth tearing a house apart. Maybe ten thousand dollars plus a few more dollars for the other items would be a lot for some people, it was a lot for Vicky but not so valuable to risk getting arrested for. And who else knew what she had found? She hadn't told anyone, not even Gina. There might be some historical significance to the rings but without written facts, how was she supposed to know, or find out? When no logical answers came to mind, Vicky set the box aside.

The photographs? The ones of her certainly held no value and would never incriminate anyone but her. She dismissed them and flicked through the older black and whites. Some were so tiny it was hard to make out faces but they seemed to be no more than family snapshots. Maybe now she had a tiny bit of history, they held relevance but there was not a single photo which sent alarm bells clanging. No famous face stood out, not even a person she recognised although she might be able to pick out Helena if she studied each photo hard enough with the aid of a magnifying glass.

Almost at the end, a small, faded snapshot caught her attention. The face under what looked like a nun's veil, looked familiar but was fuzzy as though the camera moved at the very instant the shutter was pressed. A wave of pleasure spread through her when Vicky turned the photo over and read the words, *Georgia taking her vows – 1972*. Oh, wow, so Georgia was a nun. A mental calculation shot through her grey matter. Georgia would have been 25 at the time. Maybe she is still alive. Another calculation in her head told her Georgia would now be in her early seventies. It could be possible but how was she supposed to find out? Intrigued by another trail she could follow, Vicky set the photo apart before closing the lid on the box.

There was nothing in the box of her school achievements which could bear the slightest bit of importance to anyone other than her. She flicked through them again to make sure there was no hidden piece of paper with some major earth-shattering news written on it. Satisfied, she settled the box back in the cupboard and took out the one containing the old newspaper articles. It took ages to give each a thorough read. Apart from the obituaries, all were about the Greek conflict and since they were published articles, available to the entire world, there was no way they were worth stealing.

Trepidation simmered when she tugged out the fifth box and flipped off the lid to reveal what look to be letters and smallish but thick diaries. Vicki stacked the six diaries on the floor to one side and took out the pile of letters. Her fingers shook when she opened out the first. Disappointment hit. The words were in Greek, but the numbers in the date were understandable. 1992. Vicky would have been around ten. So this letter arrived when Regina was in Australia, which meant

Mum could read Greek, assuming, of course, the letter was sent to her mother. There was no other explanation, or at least, none she could think of. Vicky opened out the next letter. 2003. Greek.

Shaken, Vicky unfolded them all, one after the other and stacked them in order of year, stunned when she realised there were thirty-seven in total, one for each year Regina had been in Australia. Who had written them? And why? She studied the names of the sender on the latest but didn't recognise it. She went back to the earliest and realised it was in a different style of handwriting, on this one the letters sloped forwards while the later one was more backhand. Excitement mounted as she went through them again, splitting the pile into two definite hand-styles, the earlier pile had fewer in number. All the letters in one pile had the same Greek symbols at the end, which obviously denoted the sender's name while the other had a different name. So two people had written to Regina over the years. Vicky checked the beginning of the letters but there was nothing which looked like it would read *Dear Regina.* They all began with what appeared to be a full sentence. To get these translated would take forever if she used the same method she had done with the certificates. She glanced at her watch. With it getting so late there was no time to even start.

Frustrated, Vicky stacked one pile on top of the other and put them still opened out, back in the box. She picked up the top diary, opened it to the first page and sighed. Greek. She flicked through the pages and groaned. Greek, Greek, Greek. Ditto the rest of the diaries. Well, she thought on a long sigh, she was definitely not going to get any more clues from this box, at least, not tonight.

One shoe box to go. She wriggled it free, piled the others on top of each other on the wardrobe floor. With a huge huff of breath she nestled the remaining box into her lap and settled back against the side of the bed. Please let there be some answers here, she thought as she flicked off the lid.

The only item in the shoe box was a large flat red case which took up almost the entire bottom of the box. It was difficult to get her fingers in far enough to wrestle it up. By wriggling, she managed to ease the object up and out. It could only be a jewellery case and if she were not mistaken, covered in fine leather. She ran her hand over the top, lifted it to her nose, sniffed. Had to be leather, which meant it was expensive.

Vicky sucked in a breath, almost too afraid to unhook the two gold catches. With a single fingernail, she unhooked the first, huffed out her breath, unhooked the second and slowly lifted the lid. Her breath stalled at the magnificence of the diamonds and rubies sparkling back at her.

'Oh, my goodness, this is unbelievable.' The triangular shaped necklace had diamonds from the catch on one end to the hook at the other end. In the centre it dropped about ten centimetres to point down into the crevice between the breasts. A huge central ruby was oblong shaped with rounded corners. It was surrounded by large, faceted diamonds which created a radiating star. Smaller rubies graduated in size, pointed outwards between the points of the star. Spaces were filled with diamonds.

Stunned, Vicky could do nothing but stare for long seconds before she dared to touch any of the stones. Somehow, she knew they were real. No fake stones could glitter, shine and reflect prismed rainbows the way these did. There had to be over fifty precious gems here. Maybe more. The value? It frazzled her brain to think about the possible value especially when a lance stabbed into her grey matter. She knew where this necklace came from. Knew who it had been given to. Sophia. Greece. The two men had ransacked Mum's house looking for this. Probably. Maybe. But how did they know about it? How could anyone possibly know Mum had this secreted away?

The funeral. The two strangers. There could only be one conclusion. Regina had to be Sophia which meant Vicky was the illegitimate daughter of K and he knew about her. Why else would two men from Greece be at Mum's funeral and search her home? But why now – after so many years? Could Regina's death be the key but who from overseas even knew about her illness and death?

Vicky slammed the lid down on the leather case, re-hooked the catches and dropped it back into the shoe box. Panic took hold. What if they came here looking for it? No, the sergeant said they had left the country. But they hadn't or at least one was still here and the original owner of these gems had to be someone important to be able to afford something so magnificent. Vicky wasn't stupid but now she was scared. Not having a clue about what else she could do, Vicky shoved the box at the very back of her wardrobe, covered it with a couple of large soft overnight bags. The necklace needed to be in a bank. Tomorrow. Tomorrow she would get the darn thing valued and shove it in a bank safety deposit box. No, it will be Saturday with banks shut. But she would still get it valued and maybe find somewhere to hide it: somewhere safe but not in this house.

All through her shower, a vivid picture of the jewels centred in her brain. The image was still there after a mug of hot cocoa which she thought would settle her mind and bring on drowsiness. Wild questions, ideas and thoughts chased each other through her brain while she tossed in her bed from side-to-side in the vain hope she would fall asleep. She got up, went to the bathroom, crawled back into bed. An hour later, after she was almost mesmerised watching the digital minutes flick over on the bedside clock, she went in search of a tot of Cognac, but doubled the dose after she stared at the small amount nestled in the bottom of a brandy balloon.

At some stage, the high-proof alcohol must have worked its magic for her eyes opened to sunlight peeking through the bottom edges of the window blinds. A woozy head sent a definite message about how much Cognac she had indulged in but it had worked, which was a relief – until she stood and the woozy turned into a dull ache and the contents of her stomach swilled from one side to the other. Fried food and too much alcohol did not mix. It was something she knew but sometimes you didn't think or care about the consequences. Feeling more than unsettled was the result in the morning.

With a wry grin, Vicky selected underwear, jeans and skivvy and headed for the bathroom where she lingered under hot jets of water until they had washed away a good proportion of her lethargy. Breakfast consisted of hot black tea with a piece of dry toast while Gina indulged in Muesli slathered in yoghurt followed by toast, butter and a thick layer of strawberry jam. Vicky tried not to look.

'I need to go to the shops this morning and want you to come with me.' Vicky eyed Gina.

'Why?'

'I don't want you staying home alone.'

'Mum, I'm seventeen, not seven.'

'I know, Sweetie but we were followed last night and the man who followed us knows where we live.'

'Mum.' The drawn-out single word rose an octave then down again. 'Why would anyone follow you? Get real.'

'I now know why and I don't appreciate your tone.'

'Sorry.'

'Come with me.' Vicky reached over the table to grasp Gina's hand. She had to stretch while she edged around the table when she tugged Gina from her seat, not letting go until they were in her own bedroom. 'Sit on the bed.'

'Why?'

'Only a suggestion.' Vicky slid the wardrobe door aside, reached into the back and retrieved the box she had hidden in the depths. She opened the jewellery case, paused, turned it around.

Gina's eyes popped as her jaw gaped. 'Oh, my, God. Are they real?' She plopped onto the side of the bed.

'I am almost certain they are and equally sure this is what the intruders were looking for in Granny's house. When they couldn't find it they must have assumed I knew about this necklace and had brought it here.'

'Do you think it is worth a bit?'

'I think it is worth more than a bit. Look at this huge ruby.' She pointed with a finger which shook like a pot of upturned jelly. 'It is enormous. That alone could be worth thousands and see how many diamonds there are. None of them are tiny chips. I had a diamond ring which I found in another box, valued. A cluster of five diamonds was valued at ten thousand. These diamonds are bigger and there are so many. It scares me to think of what this necklace is worth.'

'But can you keep it?' Gina reached out, stroked the jewels with reverence, her finger also shaking as though she was too scared to touch them but had to.

'Well, it was in Granny's belongings and she left everything to me. I have a written will to prove ownership and there is an old letter giving me a hint as to where it came from. It was a gift to Sophia.'

'But we don't even know who Sophia was or whether she is related to us.'

Vicky sank down next to Gina. 'From what I have discovered so far, I have a distinct impression Sophia is related to us. I mean, why would Mum have all these things from the one family? There has to be a reason she has them and an even stronger reason why she kept them hidden away. In fact, I think Mum was Sophia.'

'Really? Surely not. Why would she lie to us... to you all these years?'

'I don't have a clue. Maybe something really bad happened. Maybe there was a family rift. Maybe... goodness, anything could have happened. Lots of families split up, have feuds, don't speak to each other, or simply drift apart. There could have been a really bitter divorce. But there could be some answers. I found a box of letters and diaries last night but they were all written in Greek.'

'So we could have Greek roots.'

'Could do. It would explain my dark hair, dark brown eyes and olive complexion. But I don't know and maybe I don't really want to know. What if it is something really bad?'

'Ah, the secret life of Mrs Vicky Saunders.' Gina grinned but a frown quickly followed. 'But it would mean I'm not who I am.'

Vicky put her arm around Gina and tugged her close. 'Which would be a pity because I am rather fond of you exactly the way you are. Anyway, I want to visit the jeweller I went to earlier in the week to get this necklace valued and until I'm certain we are not in any danger I insist we stay together.'

'Okay, I will come with you but only because I want to know how much this is worth.' Gina sprang upright. 'Let's go. Now I can't wait.'

'Give me a couple of minutes. I have an idea. Wait for me in the car.'

A mixture of fear and excitement accompanied Vicky the entire journey to the jeweller. She had to force herself to keep her foot from pressing down too hard on the accelerator in order to maintain a sensible speed, to keep her thoughts on driving safely and away from the object she had stuffed into the pocket of her jacket. Terrified of being mugged with her handbag grabbed, she figured a mundane pocket with balled up tissues which looked like they had been used, packed on top, was a far safer option, even though the likelihood of being mugged was negligible. She had never been mugged before so why would it happen now? Karma, her sub-conscious answered.

At the thought, she flicked a glance in the rear-vision and both side mirrors but spied no obvious car following them. As if they would be obvious, especially after having been caught out last night. Despite her boozy getting to sleep method, she still managed to have a restless night, probably from fear of uninvited guests breaking in during the night, she guessed but it didn't dampen her over-sensitive agitation. Heavens but she felt like a fugitive desperate to keep one step ahead of the law.

'What's wrong, Mum?'

Vicky jerked her head around. 'What do you mean? Nothing is wrong.'

'Then why are you scrunched over the steering wheel looking like a hunchback and you keep looking in the mirrors?'

'Huh, I'm not.' But she was. She huffed out her breath on a long sigh, straightened her back and forced her body to relax back into the seat. On a long inhale, she relaxed the muscles in her arms, followed by the legs. 'See, I'm fine,' she said with a forced grin.

'Yeah, and I'm the big bad wolf ready to eat you up. Pity you're not wearing a red cape.'

There was no choice but to laugh at Gina's analogy. Maybe Vicky was acting like an over-anxious idiot. 'Sorry. Perhaps I am a bit uptight.'

Gina snorted. 'Only a bit?'

'Actually, I'm terrified.'

'Of what?'

'There is a necklace worth more than I want to think about, sitting in my pocket. A necklace someone else wants bad enough, they tore Granny's house apart to search for it.'

'But only you and I know where it is. Nobody else even knows of its existence.'

'The burglars do and we were being followed last night.'

'So, if they knew we were out, why didn't they break into our house and search while we weren't there? I think you are imagining things and over-reacting.' Gina leant forwards and twisted her body towards Vicky. 'Are we being followed now?'

After another quick glance in all three mirrors, Vicky huffed out her breath. 'Well, no, I don't think so.'

'Was there any car sitting in our road spying on us this morning when we left?'

'How am I supposed to know?'

'Come on, Mum, I saw you searching the street, peering down every driveway and double-checking every road as we turned each corner. It wasn't half obvious.'

Guilt flamed but not one she was game to admit to. 'I did not.'

Gina laughed. 'Did so, too. Liar, liar, pants on fire.'

'Yes, well, I had to be sure.'

'And there was no-one. Last night you saw one poor guy who happened to be going in the same direction as us, the same as all these cars.' Gina swept one hand in the direction they were going, pointing out the dozens of vehicles driving along the jam-packed roadway. 'Just because he was going to Alfred's Kitchen, the most popular eating place in the district, along with dozens of other locals, you tag him as following little old you.'

'Enough of the old, thank you and he didn't buy any food, which made it more obvious he was spying on us.'

'You don't know what he bought.'

'I didn't see any food in his hands.'

'You probably scared him to death by staring at him. Gave him the heebie-jeebies.'

'Now you are plain teasing me.'

'Well it worked. Got your mind off things.' Gina pointed to her left. 'Isn't this where we are supposed to be going?'

Stunned at the sight of them passing by the jewellery store, Vicky jammed her foot on the brake and winced at the blare of a horn from behind. Far out, she thought as she raised one hand to wave an apology and tried to stifle the flare of heat which rushed to her neck and cheeks.

'Good one, Mum,' came from her side. 'Becoming a bit of a habit.'

Vicky's cheeks incinerated while she edged forwards slowly, turned on the indicator and rounded the next corner. The drive around the block was sedate and silent apart from the giggles escaping Gina's mouth.

'Are you enjoying yourself?' Vicky finally asked while she turned into the small shopping centre parking lot.

'Sure am. It's not often I catch you being so flustered and the driving... well, I'm pretty sure you would have failed your test.'

Vicky straightened the car in a parking bay, ensuring the car was both perfect in alignment and centred. She didn't dare give Gina any more cause for her smarmy derision for Vicky's less than exemplary driving skills.

'Glad I could amuse you,' she said as she opened the door. 'Let's go find out exactly how much I am carrying around in my pocket. Have a guess. I reckon $75,000.

'Nah, the rubies are the biggest stones and they're not worth anything as much as diamonds. I'll go $50,000.

'Loser cooks dinner tonight.'

'Okay.' They high fived to seal the bet before they headed across the bitumen, along the footpath but paused at the door where Vicky sucked in a breath.

'Let's go.' With one open palm, she pushed the door open and strode to the woman who stood behind the counter at the rear wall, too keyed up to waste time gawking at the various items along the way.

'I spoke to the jeweller the other day. Is he in? Would I be able to speak with him again?' The words ran out of her mouth without pause. 'Sorry.' Vicky felt her cheeks heat up for the third time in as many minutes. 'I should start again. Good morning.' She smiled at the woman who wore a stunned look on her face. It was a different assistant, someone younger and now Vicky felt like an idiot.

'Good morning,' the assistant said with a smile. 'Let me see if he's not too busy.' She turned and vanished behind the door but was only gone for a couple of seconds. The elderly jeweller followed her out, his face lighting up in recognition.

'Ah, you've found another ring, or maybe a brooch.'

'No, a necklace. I hope you could give me a rough estimate of its value.' Vicky shoved her hand in her jacket pocket, felt around and drew out the necklace but had to scrabble mid-air to catch falling tissues before they hit the floor. With care she spread the necklace on the glass counter, then scrunched the tissues into a ball and stuffed them back into her pocket.

'Dear, God, where did you get this?'

Vicky jerked her eyes towards the man at the sound of his voice which had taken on a squeaky sound. He stared at the necklace with his jaw as low as it could possibly go.

'It was in a shoe box.'

'A shoe box?' The man stared at her.

'Yes, but it was in a leather case, which was in...'

'In a shoe box,' he finished for her.

'Yes but you seem... shocked.' Vicky eyed the man.

'Stunned would be a better word.' He reached out and stroked the stones with what appeared to be the same reverence Gina had used.

'You think it might be valuable?' Vicky managed to stutter out.

'Oh, no.'

'No? Aren't the stones real?'

'Oh, they are real but this piece isn't valuable, I would say it is more on the priceless level.'

'Priceless?' Gina looked puzzled. 'Does it mean it doesn't have a price?'

The man looked at Gina and grinned. 'No, it means there are few people in the world who could afford to buy it.'

'Excuse me?' It was Vicky's turn to drop her jaw and stare in stunned amazement.

'Let me look at these stones.' He withdrew a jewellers loupe from a drawer and held it to his eye but hesitated at the sound of the shop door opening. 'I think we should go somewhere a little more private.' In an instant the necklace disappeared into his gnarled fingers. 'Follow me.'

Vicky followed into the back room, Gina on her heels. The man shut the door and turned the key. 'I'd rather not let anyone know what you have here.'

'What I have, but it is only a necklace.' The words belied Vicky's nerves which had tightened to the level of a taut piano wire, stretched to its limit.

'More than a mere necklace. Please sit.' The jeweller drew out an old armchair and beckoned Vicky to sit before he dragged a stool from against the wall for Gina. He settled onto a wind-up stool at what was obviously his workbench with several watches in various states of repair or disrepair, backs opened. A long rectangular metal tin held a variety of fine-tipped tools. There was a polishing wheel at the far end with a pile of soft rags covered in greys and red polish traces. Soft fabric mats each held some form of jewellery from rings to chains. It looked like an orderly mess.

'Give me a minute,' he said with eyeglass to his eye.

Vicky was intrigued as she watched him study each stone.

'Flawless,' was mumbled barely loud enough to make it out. 'Magnificent,' came out louder. He turned the necklace over, studied the back, paused on one section, glanced at Vicky and peered again through the loupe. 'Unbelievable,' rushed through aged pale lips topped with wispy whiskers which hadn't been shaved off for a couple of days.

Vicky's knee began jerking rapidly, up and down. Gina's hand gripped hers. They glanced at each other, back at the man. If somebody made a sudden noise, Vicky felt sure she would explode like a nuclear bomb.

'Karl Faberge,' she thought she heard but with everything so tense, she couldn't be certain. She dared to look up.

'As in those super-expensive jewelled eggs?'

'Yes.'

At the single word, everything in her body stilled, even her breathing. Her mouth opened, but nothing came out.

'Mum, what do you mean?' Gina shook Vicky's shoulder.

Ever so slow, Vicky turned her gaze to Gina. 'It means you are cooking dinner tonight with champagne on the menu.'

'Huh?' Gina looked mystified. 'So the necklace is worth more than $75,000.'

A choked laugh came from the man. Both women stared at him. 'Even the ruby alone is worth more than $75,000.'

'Excuse me?' Vicky squeaked.

An ancient hand reached out and grabbed her tense fist. 'If this were up for auction right now, some super rich billionaires would fight to outbid each other. You are looking at seven, possibly eight figures here.'

For the life of her, Vicky could not breathe, could not move. Her brain was in lockdown.

'What does he mean?... Mum!'

Vicky roused at the yelled word accompanied by a strong tug on her arm.

'More than a million,' Vicky managed to stutter out.

'You're kidding.'

'Sorry, young lady, but your mother is right.' He caught Vicky's eye. 'You might not know this but there is a registry for famous lost pieces like this. Do you know where it came from?'

'Y... yes, sort of.' Vicky eyed the man, now afraid he thought she had stolen goods. Would he ring the police? It was all she needed – another bout with the same officers. First she was arrested for murder and now high-end larceny would delight them.

'There is a letter indicating who it was from and who it was gifted to. I am not certain but I think it was given to my mother – to keep her safe. But... but I have to do some more research... you see... a lot of the details are written in Greek.

I need to get more translations done.' She looked at the man before dropping her eyes back towards the necklace. 'Far out, I can't believe this.'

Crazy thoughts shot through her brain; muddled thoughts chased after each other before they became clear. No wonder someone wanted these jewels. Her house – it wasn't going to be safe any longer. Gina – what if they broke in during the night and attacked them, took Gina hostage? She eyed the jeweller. 'This,' she ran her fingers over the necklace, 'must go into a bank vault. I can't keep it safe. I don't have security… no safe… nowhere to hide it.'

Unnerved, Vicky stood, one hand clutched to the back of her head as she spun around, shot a glance at the man, the necklace and Gina in rapid succession. Her brain cells were too shocked to be able to think. She plopped back into the chair. 'I don't know what to do. I'm in shock.' Her hand had taken on a definite tremble when she reached out to stroke the starburst of rich red and shimmering white.

'My dear,' the jeweller reached out and patted her hand. 'It will be as safe at it has ever been. Only we three know you have it and the value. Take the necklace home until Monday when you will be able to put it in a safety deposit box at your bank.'

'Normally I would.' Vicky slid her hand free. 'But…'

'Mum thinks someone is following her,' butted in Gina.

'Following you?' The man reeled back but remained seated on his stool which whirred and rumbled as it slid backwards across the tiled floor.

'Mum's house was ransacked. I didn't know why… didn't

know about this.' Vicky stabbed a finger at the necklace. 'Until last night.'

The man listened intently while she related her suspicions.

'I have a solution,' he said. 'I have a secure safe. Have to in this line of work. Keep it here for the weekend. I will give you a detailed receipt, the same as I always do. We will both photograph the necklace – for insurance purposes. I can even arrange a security firm to deliver it to the bank at a time convenient for you to meet them.'

'You do such a thing?' Vicky asked with relief streaming through her body.

'Not normally but I have never had something of such value in my shop.'

As they drove, Gina sat silent, staring out of the side window. It was hard for Vicky to maintain concentration on driving so they would arrive in one piece at 28 Siesta Lane. A picture of the starburst of jewels kept over-riding oncoming traffic, pedestrians on crosswalks, traffic signs and lights. When she finally turned into her mother's driveway, a long hiss of tension escaped through gritted teeth. When Gina got out, Vicky sat for a moment, sifting through her thoughts until the reason for being here became central.

'Come on, Mum.' Gina leant back into the still open doorway.

'Coming.' Determined to keep her thoughts on the task for the day, Vicky opened the door, eased from her seat and stood. Before going inside the house, she opened the rear door, set the back seats down, eyed the space to figure if the chair would fit. She was hopeful but had serious doubts.

It took almost an hour to wrestle free-standing wardrobes and other furniture items into the sitting room with another fifteen minutes needed to wriggle the leather recliner into her car. Rear door shut, Vicky leant against it, swiped the sweat from her brow while she heaved in a couple of long breaths of air to get her lungs working properly. Muscles replicated her lungs, tired and a tad sore. She had thought she was fit but maybe a few months of gym work were needed.

With a wry grin at herself, Vicky followed Gina inside to gather their belongings and lock up. A bit more cleaning was required but the house was presentable enough to bring in a few agents to value the property. At the same time she would get advice on whether it was worth spending a few dollars to tizzy up the place. Her heart wrenched at the thought of a sold sticker stuck across a billboard but she didn't much care. With the death of Mum, a huge chapter of her life had closed. What hurt a whole heap more were the secrets Mum had never shared. What was so terrible it had been too devastating to reveal? Why couldn't Mum at least have written a letter to be opened when the will was read? Surely if there were some unsavoury skeletons hidden away, they were in the past and couldn't hurt anyone now. Besides, she had a right to know. So did Gina. It was also Gina's heritage, their missing DNA.

The entire drive home, Vicky went over the facts she had gleaned so far until they sorted themselves into a rough order beginning with Helena's birthdate. And the date of her death. She knew both. Even though it was imperative to find more about Helena's four children it was going to take some serious computer time – if any of them were still alive. It was possible since the oldest would only be in their seventies. Going back to work the day after tomorrow was going to impede any spare time for research but she still had this afternoon and all of tomorrow. Maybe luck would be on her side. She could only hope.

Lunch was past due after they re-arranged lounge furniture umpteen times to fit in the chair, which took up a lot more room than anticipated after allowing space for the reclined position, but happy at last, Vicky nodded before a wide grin broke out at the long, exaggerated sigh from Gina. They made do with salad sandwiches and hot chocolate to fill empty stomachs, neither of them having the energy to do any serious meal preparation. While Gina settled in her room to do homework, Vicky showered and changed into comfy fresh clothes, ready for an afternoon of internet research. After a much needed shower, she walked from the en-suite with a quick glance at the bedside clock but something about the table didn't seem right. She paused at the edge of her bed to study everything on the small three-drawer side table. Clock – tick. China tray of knick-knacks – tick. Book – hmm, what was wrong? One hand rubbed the side of her mouth while Vicky tried to figure out what was different. She sat on the side of the bed, reached out, touched the book, imagining lying in bed, closing the book and setting it aside.

'Damn!' hissed from between clenched teeth. The book was not only upside down but angled the wrong way, the exact opposite to what it should be. With her gut gripping tight, she whipped out the top drawer and swore at its emptiness. 'I knew it,' rasped out of her tense throat.

'Gina,' she called as she rose from the bed and raced across the room, down the passage to Gina's door. 'Gina, I want you to stand and take a careful look around. See if anything is out of place.'

'Uh, why? What's going on?' Gina spun around in her chair, which creaked and groaned at the speed.

'We've been burgled.'

'Excuse me? What... how do you know?' Gina shot up onto her feet as though stung by a scorpion.

Vicky crossed the room, slid an arm around Gina's shoulders and drew her close. 'Sorry, I didn't mean to scare you but my room... the red necklace case has gone.'

'You're kidding.'

'Sorry, no. Maybe it's the only thing gone but study everything in here, see if you think anything has changed since you left this morning but try not to touch anything you haven't already touched.'

'Why?'

'Fingerprints.'

'Far out. Are you serious?'

'Absolutely. I was so certain someone was hanging out watching me, I deliberately left the jewellery case in an easy to get to place. I need to confess something as well.'

'Mum, what did you do?'

'Well, you know the necklace we bought for your year twelve ball... I, um, put it in the box as a decoy. It was roughly the same shape and looked as though it belonged in the case.'

'Mum!' The shriek hurt Vicky's eardrum. 'I was going to keep my necklace as a memento.'

'I know, sorry but now we can afford to buy you the real thing with real jewels. To be honest I didn't really expect it to be stolen, it was only an idea I had in case they came here but really, I didn't believe they would. Seems I was right.' She sank her head into one hand, frustrated. 'I need to call the detective again. Maybe this time, whoever did this has left some trace.'

Gina wriggled free and turned to face her mother. 'Well at

least we know what they were after so maybe they won't come back again.' The shiver across her shoulders belied her wish.

'Yes, true, but what if they inspect the necklace and figure it's the wrong one? Even I can tell real jewels from the costume variety. I need to call the police.' At Gina's shudder, Vicky regretted spouting her thoughts but they were out now. Eyes closed on a long sigh of regret, she turned away to find her phone.

'Good job we left the real one at the jewellers,' Gina called after her.

'About the best thing that has happened,' Vicky called over her shoulder. 'Maybe you should still check the things in your room but try not to touch anything else,' she added while she searched for the card the police had given her. Fiddlesticks, but she hated this entire ordeal. When a person died, it was supposed to bring closure to the life they lived but her mother... oh, no, she had to go and create chaos along with a bucketload of mystery.

* * *

Frustration gnawed after Vicky had sat on the front veranda for two hours while police officers searched for traces of invaders: traces, Vicky was certain, which would not be found. There was no brilliant-minded autistic neighbour to take minute details of everything that dared to move outside the security of his bedroom window. The street where she lived was inhabited by young families where both parents worked. Today they all seemed to be out. Probably doing the weekly shop or attending children's weekend sporting activities, a task Vicky was free from this year for the first time since Gina began school. A doorknock of close neighbours had found hardly anyone home. Those few who were, had not heard nor seen any strange car in the street or someone lurking around Vicky's home.

At the squeak of the front flyscreen, Vicky twisted the top of her torso around. Her old nemesis, Sgt Phil Rogers, stood there with deep frown lines. Vicky sighed, 'No fingerprints, I presume.'

'No, apart from yours. The drawer had been wiped clean. Only your fresh prints on the handle from when you opened it.' The man stepped onto the veranda, letting the screen slam behind him. He stood in front of her, blocking the sun.

'How did they get in?'

'Spare bedroom window was jemmied but wiped clean. They were careful.'

'Or professional.' It hurt her neck to peer up so Vicky stood.

'More professional than our usual breed of burglars. Can you describe the man you think was following you?'

'Not think. Now I am certain. You already know who. The same man from the funeral. Same man who wrecked Mum's place.'

The look on the sergeant's face showed more than disbelief. It was mocking. Why can't they believe her? 'Those two flew back to Greece.'

'Did they?' To show her own disdain, Vicky folded her arms across her chest as she eye-balled the man. 'Did you check they both actually boarded the plane? They might have returned their hire car to the airport depot and had flight tickets but were they on the flight? They didn't find what they were looking for at Mum's place so decided to follow me around.'

Vicky jerked back at the glare she received. It was obvious the man didn't like being shown up for ineptitude and equally obvious she had managed to hit a raw nerve confirming they hadn't followed up.

'How do you know what they were looking for?' The question sounded more like a demand as though he was accusing her of something untoward.

Guilt washed through her but she was too scared to reveal what she now knew. No doubt these guys would demand to see the necklace, probably seize it as evidence. With its value, there is a chance it could go missing. Evidence did disappear. Vicky wasn't prepared to risk it but she needed to come up with something, quick smart.

'I didn't have a clue to start with but think I do now. The man I saw was definitely one of the men from the funeral. Logic tells me it is the same man responsible for both break-ins. Nothing went missing from Mum's house but now a single item has been taken from my place, but without my house being torn apart,' she added with emphasis. 'I have seen this man three times in the past couple of days. Since he has trailed me it makes it obvious he hadn't found what he was looking for.' Ah, fiddlesticks, she needed some quick smart fanciful thinking. To waste time, she walked to the end of the veranda, racking her grey matter for inspiration. When an idea came, she spun around.

'Mum had some stuff stored here so I decided to go through it. I found a leather jewellery case with a necklace inside. It looked pretty but I was sure it was costume jewellery. On the outside of the case was the insignia of a famous jeweller.'

'How famous?' Sgt Rogers stalked towards her and didn't stop until he was crowded into her personal space. Oh, he was good at intimidation techniques.

'Karl Faberge.'

The man's eyes flared as he reeled back. 'And this is what was taken?'

'Yes, but the necklace wasn't real.'

'How do you know?'

'Oh, for goodness sake, I am a woman. I can tell real from fake. To start with, there were no maker's marks anywhere on the metal.' Vicky sidled around the man to resume her seat. At least if she sat, she wouldn't feel so overpowered. So far she hadn't really told any lies but also hadn't revealed the truth. Discretion and gut feeling insisted she didn't reveal everything she knew.

The sergeant followed. 'Why didn't you tell us this?'

'I just did.'

'What else was in the boxes?'

'It really is none of your business.'

'Humour me.'

Vicky sighed, loud enough to make a point. 'Stuff of mine which Mum kept. Old school reports, certificates, silly things like shells we collected on a holiday. I've been through it all.

The necklace was in the bottom of the shoe box.' All true in a roundabout way. No guilt stabbed at her innards.

Sgt Rogers ran a hand through his hair leaving the thick strands standing on end. He spun around, walked to the edge of the veranda, bounced up and down on the balls of his feet, turned and came back. 'None of this makes sense,' he finally said.

Vicky sort of agreed but wasn't game to give any more away. Knowing what she now knew, most of it did make sense to her but she understood why the sergeant was confused. 'What do you mean?'

'How did they know what they were looking for? The P.I.'s came from Greece.' His hand went to the back of his neck, gripped hard. 'Why now? What relationship do you have with Greece?' The hand whipped down with one finger pointed at her: an accusing finger.

'None. I don't know a soul in Greece.'

'But your mother.'

'None I am aware of.' Now she was telling Porky pies and prayed her body language didn't give her away, although her knowledge wasn't factual, only supposition – so far.

'Your father?'

'Timothy Wakefield certainly doesn't sound like a Greek name to me but to be honest, I wouldn't have a clue. I never met the man.'

'Your mother's maiden name? Regina sounds more like a European name.'

Vicky couldn't help the snigger which slipped out. 'Jones. Can't get any more British than Jones. Welsh, I believe. She always insisted all of her family are gone so there is no-one I can contact to ask. Personally, I wish I could. This whole... thing... mess, is not only a mystery to me but being personal, it is more than upsetting. The last thing I need is some jerk breaking into my house, riffling through my things, creating havoc, tailing me for something I know nothing about. I have a daughter to protect.' Vicky caught the man's eye. 'How long are you going to be?'

'The guys are packing up now. I will check on those flights, see if you are right.'

It was another fifteen long minutes before Vicky was able to return inside where she rang Gina to tell her it was safe to come home from Sara's place to where she had escaped to do her homework. Phone call made; Vicky headed straight for the computer.

Twenty

Vicky sat hunched on the chair; her fingers poised over the keyboard. What to search for first? She typed in the family name, LEBTOS, waited. A Wikipedia notice about Lesbos, a Greek island nestled not far from the coast of Turkey, flashed onto the screen. Third largest Greek island in the Aegean Sea, she read while she scanned the description. It looked quaint but spectacular in the attached picture until she spied a second picture of a squalid refugee camp which held 20,000 people from the Middle East. Not so pleasant and terribly sad. Australia was still a lucky country. At least the article was about Greece so she was in the right country. There were many entries about Lebos, which seemed to be a clothing chain in the USA but she found nothing with the spelling she had. Disappointment settled into the pit of her stomach. She huffed out her breath, tapped one finger against her temple, scrambled for ideas.

Facebook. Why not search internet social sites? A shimmer of excitement caused her finger to tremble when she logged onto Facebook. She typed the surname in the *Search* area, deleted it and added Lukas before the surname. The few seconds wait felt like an hour before it came up with a hit. Stunned, Vicky stared at the name. Surely not... it couldn't be. She slid her eyes shut on an indrawn breath. No way could she be lucky enough to find the person she wanted on a first attempt. The odds would be phenomenal. She dared to open her eyes again to study the name, which had no profile picture. It wasn't unusual. Some people, including her, didn't like their picture made public but how she wished there was a picture of an elderly man sitting next to the name. How old would he be now? She had to rack her brain for dates. Lukas – 1948, she remembered. Wow, he would now be 71. Old but not so old.

Well, girl, she thought, there is only one way to find out if this was the Lukas Lebtos she wanted. She pressed on the invitation to be a friend, sat back and waited until she realised the person was on the other side of the world where it was probably in the middle of the night. A closer look at the details sent a shiver down her spine. Lukas Lebtos lived in Tinos, wherever that was. Could it really be Georgia's brother? Sophia's brother? Maybe a real live uncle. Did Vicky Saunders, only child of Regina Wakefield, actually have family out there? She plopped back into the chair, staring at the name, her eyes stilling on the word, Tinos. Everything led to Greece. To have a little peek-a-boo, she logged onto Tinos to learn a little about the place. Ah, another island in the inner Cyclades. Cute with a gorgeous harbour and not too touristy. The type of place she would enjoy.

Costas Lebtos was next on her list. She found two possible, living in the U.K. but two with the same name was okay since she was now certain the family had moved to England at some stage. Her hand had taken on a definite shake as she requested friendship on both. Even though she was sure she wouldn't find Georgia or Sophia, she typed in their names as well. If either were still alive, it was more than likely they had different names, Sophia could be married and Georgia, well, she would be Sister something. Definitely not Georgia. Somehow, she felt sure they never used their given name but were given a biblical name on the day they took their vows to be married to the church.

Shock was not a strong enough word to describe how she felt when a Sophia Lebtos showed up. Vicky could do nothing but stare at the name. It wasn't until she slid her eyes to the picture and spied a dark-haired beauty about the same age as Gina, she figured this was not the Sophia she was looking for. How could it be when she was almost certain her mother was Sophia. She was about to dismiss the name when a thought brought her hand to a standstill. Could this be a daughter or granddaughter? It was possible, even though the possibility was about as remote as Vicky ever flying to Mars. Despite her doubts, she clicked on the friend request as she heard the pad of footsteps on the hallway tiles. As she spun the office chair around on its spindle, she couldn't hold back the grin which had spread across her face.

With a bookbag grasped against her chest, Gina hesitated in the doorway, hoicked up one eyebrow and took her time to cross the carpet. 'What's so amusing?'

'Hi, to you as well.'

Gina blushed, bent over and planted a peck on Vicky's cheek. 'I've only been gone a couple of hours.' She knelt on the floor. 'Did the cops find anything?'

'No, but I didn't think they would. Entry was through the spare room window.' Gina's entire body trembled but she said nothing. 'It was jemmied open. I rang the insurance company. Because it is a safety issue, they will have someone here today or tomorrow to make any repairs needed. Now, look what I found.' Gina stretched up towards the computer screen when Vicky pointed towards it. 'Four people with the same surname. There aren't many. Might be an unusual name and given their age they might not even have social pages. I sent friend requests to them all. We can only hope at least one is from our family.'

The thought of these people belonging to *our family* sent a warm fuzzy sensation through her innards. If only it could be true. But the mere fact Mum had these papers must mean a closeness somehow, somewhere. And with so few people showing up with the surname... hope surged at the thought but instantly eased when she remembered there might be serious reasons there had been no family contact for years... except for those letters. She had forgotten about those dated letters – one each year. Therefore there must have been contact, so maybe the relationships were not so bad after all.

'Have you done a search for your dad?' Gina asked as she sank back onto her knees with a sheepish look.

'A long time ago.' Vicky wondered if Gina's request was because deep down, she wanted to know her heritage even though she always said it didn't bother her. Maybe she cared more than she ever let on. 'There were a lot of people from various parts of the world with the same name but without his birth date so I put it in the too hard basket. Maybe I was too scared to find out. In the end I figured if he wasn't interested in me... well, he wasn't worth the effort.'

'What about Granny's marriage certificate? Surely his date of birth would be on it.'

'I have never seen it.'

'Why not?'

'I don't know. I figured Mum was too hurt to care about it but now I'm not so sure.'

'What about those certificates in the shoe box? Could it be amongst those?' Gina rose, sounding a lot more eager about finding out than Vicky felt. Hmm, so Gina did want to know.

'I had a quick glance through the pile but thought they were all in Greek. I didn't notice any in English and to be honest, Mum's marriage certificate didn't even cross my mind at the time.'

'Can I look?'

'Sure, why not? Go ahead.' A quivery, sick sensation settled in Vicky's innards, which intensified at the squeak when she shifted her weight in the chair so she could go back to her search on the internet for any more people with Lebtos as a surname. Her heart was having a tug-of-war with her brain about whether or not she wanted Gina to be fruitful in her search. For a while, she sat back, eyes closed, while thoughts tumbled through her mind. This was the first time Gina had shown such an interest in her grandfather. Sure, there had been questions over the years, but never this much enthusiasm. Vicky wasn't sure how she felt about it. Not knowing about her father had bothered her when she was young but over the years she had become less and less concerned. But now? She thought. With so many hidden secrets coming forth, maybe her mum had lied about Timothy Wakefield as well. The idea hurt, more than she expected, with a stab of something sharp jolting her heart.

'Why, Mum, why?' she whispered while she escaped from the Facebook page to search other social media sites.

At a shout from Gina less than five minutes later, Vicky shot from the seat and scurried down the passage. 'What have you found?' she asked before she had even stepped into her bedroom.

A hand wavered in the air. 'Nothing. Someone is knocking on the door.'

Vicky scarpered, doing a half-walk, half-run the rest of the way to the front door. 'Coming,' she called at the loud tattoo. The man dressed in jeans, work boots and a khaki work shirt bearing a company logo, was a shock until she remembered the message from the insurance company. Middle-aged, his clean-shaven face was weathered but his brown hair was neatly cut and brushed.

'You have a window to be repaired,' he said as he shifted a metal toolbox from one hand to the other. It chinked and clanged before quietening when movement stopped.

'Yes, come in.' Vicky retraced her steps to lead the man to the rear of her house. An all-male aroma, tinged with oil and something woodsy, followed her. Heavy footsteps echoed from the ceramic tiles. It was a surprise when the man toed off his boots to reveal thick navy socks before he stepped onto the carpet. His consideration was appreciated. 'Thank you,' Vicky murmured with a smile.

'Carpet and boots don't go together,' he replied with a grin. 'Now, show me your problem.'

'Here.' Vicky drew back the curtains to reveal the splintered woodwork of the frame with a keyed lock hanging by only one screw.

'Hmm.' The man ran his fingers over the damage, tugged off the lock, pulling a hunk of wood with it. 'This piece of the outside frame needs to be replaced with a new lock. This one is bent. To straighten the metal will only weaken it which would make it much easier to break-in next time. A couple of hours but I'll have you secure by tonight. Not sure I can match the paint though.'

Paint. It was the last thing Vicky thought of or was concerned about. 'Near enough will be fine. This room hardly ever gets used so it doesn't matter. Besides, I will never notice it and if any guest is upset about a strip of not quite matching paint, I'm not sure I would want them here. All I care about is my daughter's safety.'

'Not your own safety?' The man moved the bed aside, set his toolbox on the floor and lifted off the curtain rod, taking care to lay the curtains across the bed so they didn't crease. Such a considerate man, Vicky thought. She liked him.

'Not so much. I probably wouldn't sleep much with a window unlocked but this is usually a pretty safe area. First time I have been broken into. I would be more concerned about my daughter and would probably hover outside her door most of the night.'

The man laughed. 'Typical parent. I have to admit, I would feel the same.' He held out one hand. 'Rick. Rick Johnson.'

'Oh, Vicky. Vicky Saunders.' After a brief shake, she

dropped her hand. 'Is there anything you need? Anything I can do?'

'Nah, I'm right.' He nodded towards the window. 'Good job they didn't break the glass or the frame. Makes it easier.'

'I suppose. I never thought of that.' Feeling awkward, Vicky left the man to do whatever it was he needed to do. She had more important things to discover. She bypassed the office to see what Gina was up to. 'Find anything?' she asked as she perched on the side of her bed next to Gina.

'Yes and no.' Gina held up a pile of certificates. 'No English wedding certificate for Granny but as you said, this pile is in Greek. But...' she made the word sound exciting by elongating the sound. 'These two are French.' She lifted the ones in her other hand.

'So you can understand them, since you studied French,' Vicky said with excitement mounting. Sophia had been in Paris.

'Yes, one is a birth certificate and the other is a death certificate. *Le Certificate de la mort.* The certificate of the death.'

'Who was born and who died?' Vicky asked but somehow she knew. Sophia had her baby. Please, please, please don't let the baby be the one who died, tumbled through her mind, but she didn't want it to be Sophia either, especially since she was now sure Regina was Sophia.

Gina ran her finger down one page. 'Baby girl born February 6th, 1982. Name is Kristina. Born to Sophia Lebtos. Father is... umm... Kristian Nesbloutas.' Gina turned to stare at her mother. The same year you were born.'

A shimmer ran down Vicky's spine. 'Yes, but I was born

on May 23rd. I have my birth certificate as proof and it certainly isn't written in French. What about the death certificate? Maybe the baby didn't survive. It would explain a lot.'

It felt like forever as Gina scanned the words, mumbling to herself between French and English as though she was translating in her mind. 'Oh, no, Sophia died only a week after giving birth. Oh, God, no, a car accident. 14th February 1982. St Valentine's day. Oh, how sad.' Gina lifted her head and stared at Vicky. 'Well there goes your theory of Granny being Sophia and besides Sophia couldn't have had two children born only three months apart.'

A churning stomach was uncomfortable when Vicky settled into the office chair and pressed the *on* button of her computer. Today's revelation answered more than one of her questions but at the same time created even more. At least if Mum had been Sophia, things would have made more sense than they did now. Now all she had was utter confusion with all of her theories now sent to the disposal unit to be shredded into a thousand pieces.

'Mum.' Gina ran into the room, excitement in both her voice and face.

'What?'

'Your birth certificate. Doesn't it have the names and ages of your parents?'

'Sadly, no. There is only something like, a female born on 23rd May 1982, my name and where the birth was registered.'

'Well, can you go to the place it was registered and see if there are more details. Surely they had to have the names of your parents and the dates they were born. Especially in England. I've seen certificates with occupations as well. They have all these family history search engines now where all those types of details are recorded.'

'I never thought of doing such a search. Maybe you are right but how come you have this interest in Timothy Wakefield all of a sudden?'

'I don't know but since we found all these mysterious names which must be super important since Granny has kept them hidden away, I guess it couldn't hurt to find out about your dad as well. It's only one more name typed into the computer.'

Vicky reached out and grasped Gina's hand. 'You really want to know about him, don't you? Why didn't you tell me this before?'

'I didn't want to hurt you.'

'Oh, Sweetie,' she tugged Gina close. 'If it is so important to you, I don't mind doing another search. I guess, deep down, I want to know as well but I gave up when I had no success before. Your idea of asking the registry district is a good one so maybe I can start there. See what comes up. We also have another name to look up – Kristian Nesbloutas. And there is the baby. Someone must have cared for her. Maybe she was put in an orphanage. God, I hope not. I have never heard anything good about what kids have to go through when they had to live in orphanages. Although in 1982 conditions might have been better. Leave me to it and don't forget, you are cooking dinner tonight. I have already put a bottle of champagne in the fridge to chill.'

'I'm not 18, Mum. You keep telling me I can't drink alcohol until my birthday.'

'Oh, I think you deserve... we both deserve to celebrate the necklace. One glass for you.'

'And the rest for you?'

Vicky laughed. 'Not all in one hit. I might save some for

tomorrow. Who knows, we could find some answers and have even more to celebrate.'

Gina stood. 'What would you like for dinner?'

'Surprise me. Anything is fine, even if it is only a decent toastie.'

'Toastie and champagne kinda doesn't sound right,' said Gina as she walked to the door.

'Well they have champagne breakfast where toast is a feature on the plate, but they have the fillings on the outside, piled on top of the toast instead of in between the slices. Search the fridge and freezer, see what you can find.'

When Gina left, Vicky began typing in names. Since she was born in Orpington, in Kent, it would be the perfect place to begin even though answers won't come through until at least Monday night since it was a Saturday and Kent was on the other side of the world. Nobody is going to work in a registry office on the weekend nor in the middle of the night.

It didn't surprise her when there was no hit for Kristina Nesbloutas. The baby would now be a grown woman of 38, more than likely married if she survived and if she were adopted there was every possibility her name would have been changed to that of her adoptive parents.

In between entries, Vicky couldn't help logging onto her Facebook page, hopeful someone with the surname of Lebtos was up in the wee small hours and would be scrolling through their messages. It was ridiculous to keep looking but the need to get answers outweighed common sense.

In the background, bangs, scrapes and rattles from the spare room worked in syncopation with kitchen noises until

Vicky could concentrate no longer. She shut down her computer on a long sigh, took a peek in the spare room to see a large drop sheet on the floor and Rick Johnson carefully applying a coat of paint to the new piece of wood. His hand was steady as it drew a slow line down the edge. When the brush reached the bottom and was carefully lifted, Rick glanced her way and grinned. 'Not long now. This paint needs to dry off a bit before I can fit the new lock.'

'Coffee?' she asked on a croak, the strong smell of paint tempting her nose to sneeze.

'Nah, thanks. I always bring my own. I'm right.'

'I will leave you to it.' Vicky sniffed away the oily smell as she backtracked, stuck her head in the kitchen where she was surprised to see an expertly arranged salad gracing two of the best china dinner plates. An eyebrow lifted at the sight of best china. A real celebration. Chopped lettuce had grated coils of carrot and beetroot centred on top. Tomato wedges fanned out around the lettuce with blueberries precisely placed in a pattern and crunchy chopped almonds scattered over the top. What smelt like garlic encrusted steak sizzled in the frypan, the delicious aroma managed to chase away the last vestiges of paint. 'That looks and smells amazing,' she said, grinning when Gina spun around on a squeal of fright. 'Do you want me to set the table?'

'Done.'

Vicky stepped further into the room so she could see the table. Her eyes popped. 'Wow, this looks gorgeous.' A white linen tablecloth lay under the best cutlery, paper napkins folded in a fan, crystal champagne flutes and a small vase of rosebuds Gina must have found in the garden.

'Well, it is a celebration.' Gina stood beside her mother. 'Are you ready to eat? The steak is almost done.'

'Sure am. I'll open the bubbly.'

Halfway through the meal, her mobile phone pinged. They both ignored it. The meal was too pleasant to interrupt and Vicky was the master over her phone and not the other way around like a lot of people she knew who could never ignore a message, despite what they were in the middle of doing. Even though their lively chat centred on mundane things, Gina's homework, her friend Sarah, school in general, Vicky's mind bubbled with every minute detail since she had received the phone call from the police telling her of Regina's death. Was it only three weeks ago? Enough had happened in those three weeks to fill three months. Like an onion, she peeled back the layers of her life from the items she had found in the chest. Hidden layers, hidden from her. For some unexplained reason she still needed to discover what lay behind many of those layers. A secret life. A mystery still unfolding with layers still begging to be peeled away to reveal the hidden core. The reason? She prayed the core was sweet and crisp and not slimy brown with rot.

A jolt to her arm jerked her mind back. 'Earth calling Mum!'

'What? Oh, sorry.' Vicky sent Gina a wry grin. 'I try not to think about what everything means but questions keep prodding, demanding my brain to think about them.' She glanced at her plate, surprised to see it empty apart from a few strands of wilted salad drowned in meat juices. She scooped up two small pieces of almond on the end of her finger, sucked them into her mouth. Roasted almonds are too good to let them go into the waste bucket. 'You outdid yourself, Sweetie. Dinner was delicious.'

Her wine too, was gone. She didn't remember drinking the last half but must have done so in a trance. While Gina collected dishes and cutlery, Vicky searched for a champagne stopper in her drawer of everything, plugged it into the bottle neck, snapped down the catches and returned the bottle to the fridge. Any other time she would have poured a second glass. Not tonight. Tonight she needed a clear mind to sort all the details she now knew, do more searches and list what she wanted to find out.

Rick Johnson appeared while she rinsed off the plates. At the same time her phone pinged again. She wiped her hands on a towel, grabbed her phone but instead of looking at the message she followed Rick to inspect the work, after which she signed the form he produced to confirm she was satisfied with his work. Insurance company protocol, she was told. With the finished product looking as though there had never been any damage, she was more than satisfied. Pity it wasn't so easy to resolve her family mystery.

After seeing the man off, she opened up her phone to see someone had sent her a personal message on her Facebook page. Her pulse quickened. While she ambled back to the kitchen, her finger pressed and slid on relevant icons. A prickly sensation ran down her spine. She stabbed at the icon with SL indicating the sender. 'Sophia,' slid out of her mouth.

Mid-stride, she stopped, breath held while she read the message.

SL. WHO ARE YOU? WHY DO YOU WANT TO FRIEND ME?

Vicky's breath gushed out at the curt but curious message. At least the woman was being cautious. A good thing given her age in this era of electronic social media with all the scams and cat-fishing. Even better – Sophia Lebtos had answered. Vicky couldn't figure out if her taught nerves were because she was scared or excited. What were the chances of this being from the family she was searching for? Remote to impossible, came back from her sub-conscious. While she stared at the message, she yanked out a chair from under the kitchen table and sank into it. Her finger resembled a pot of wobbly jelly when she typed in her response.

VS. I AM SEARCHING FOR RELATIVES OF COSTAS LEBTOS. BORN 1946. SON OF HELENA AND GEORGE.

The wait was interminable. Maybe Sophia had gone to bed. It had to be the early hours of the morning in the U.K. The minutes on the electronic timer of her oven flicked over. 1... 2... 3... 4... Ping.

SL. WHY?

VS. FOUND A BOX OF PAPERS RELATING TO THIS FAMILY IN

MY MOTHER'S BELONGINGS. HAS TO BE A REASON SHE KEPT THEM.

SL. WHO IS YOUR MOTHER?

VS. REGINA WAKEFIELD BUT FOR SOME REASON I DON'T THINK IT IS HER REAL NAME. DIED A FEW WEEKS AGO.

SL. NEED TO MAKE SOME PHONE CALLS. NOT TILL MORN-ING. GET BACK TO YOU.

Vicky could only manage to stare at the screen of her phone. Hope stabbed but so did fear. Excitement welled with her nerve endings tying themselves into tight knots of tension. Why were phone calls needed unless the name was important? But what was the big secret? If this Sophia knew the name, why was she being so careful? 'This is too much,' Vicky whispered to the empty room, hating all these unanswered questions.

'What is too much?'

Vicky bolted from the chair, her heart thundering. 'Gee whiz, Gina, you scared me half to death.'

'Sorry.' Gina crossed the tiles and stood beside Vicky. 'What is too much?'

'This.' Vicky restored the now darkened screen. 'I received a response but it really tells me nothing. Only adds to the mystery.'

Gina took the phone, scanned the messages and grinned. 'I bet she knows. Bet there is a Costas in her life. Maybe she needs to confirm if it is okay to pass on your message.'

'You think?' Vicky asked as she took back her phone and

switched it off. 'I want to believe it but am terrified it isn't who we are looking for. The odds are too remote for me to find them first time around.'

'Not if you consider how few people showed up with that particular surname.'

'Yes, maybe. I hope so but what if they don't want to talk to me? What if something is so bad they don't want anything to do with us? I don't think I want to know if it is really awful.

'Mum, we are good people. Granny was a good person, a bit wacko at times but still a good person.'

'Wacko?' Vicky interrupted.

Gina grinned. 'Yeah, a bit weird with the hair and clothes at times... well, most of the time but everyone loved her. She never did anything bad even though she was stubborn and always had to be right but she was always helpful and kind. She worked really hard all of her life. So if anything in her past was really awful it wouldn't have been Granny's doing.'

Vicky hugged her daughter. 'When did you become so wise? You are right, Mum was a really good person even if she wasn't the warm fuzzy, huggy type. I think I might get back to the computer, put in more names for the search engine. Kristian Nesbloutas next.

After searching several social media sites a whole heap of people had the surname Nesbloutas but only one had the first name of Kristian. For some reason, Vicky's finger hovered over the *Friend* button but wouldn't press it down. Overwhelmed, she dropped her hands in her lap as she stilled and stared at the name then re-read every word on the site, which were too few but he did live in Athens. Again there was no picture. After several minutes of hesitation, she closed down the page, deciding to wait for responses to the requests she had already put out there in the nether world of electronic media. Still, she wasn't sure if she really wanted to know. Fear, she finally figured. She was too darn scared to find out. At least not until she knew more about the Lebtos family.

Instead, she added details to all she had discovered onto a separate sheet of paper so everything was on the single page. Since tomorrow was her last day free from work, she decided an early night was needed so she and Gina could spend the day at Siesta Lane.

Twenty-Two

Armed with cleaning gear, each of which took on a mind of its own, with the broom handle going one way and the mop in the opposite direction, Vicky tried to follow Gina into her mother's house but had to stop, drop everything on the ground to re-sort them. She gave up on a groan when the broom head caught on the wall. To relieve her frustration she made two trips, carrying half at a time. Earlier, she had made a large sign to dangle on any items still good enough to warrant a new life in someone else's home. With the sun having chased away the winter blues and a forecast of rain not returning for several days, she guessed today would be a good day to do a kerbside take-away. Sunday drivers might pass, stop and hopefully grab. Tomorrow she would call the Good Samaritans to come and collect anything they considered worth their while. All the unwanted items left would go into the skip bin.

First task was to shift bed frames, tables and chairs onto the verge. They added a small wooden wardrobe, taped the large cardboard note to the door. After they spent an hour re-sorting boxes with like-minded objects in each box, they lugged out a carton of pots and pans, one of kitchen china and another of glassware which they placed on the table. While Gina arranged a row of books along one edge, the first people walked past, paused a while, came closer before scrummaging through the boxes. A frypan with lid went with the couple when they left. One item down with a hundred more to go, Vicky thought with a triumphant grin as she watched the couple walk away.

Over the next two hours while Gina and Vicky scrubbed, vacuumed and polished, they kept glancing out of the windows, amazed at the number of people who seemed to be avid in their search for some treasure which begged to go home with them. Every now and again they found something to add to the table, including a large box of kitchen gadgets, many only used once but as fast as they added, items were taken. It became more difficult when the kitchen table and six chairs were packed into a trailer and vanished around the corner. To take the table's place, Vicky and Gina struggled to heft a metal bench from shed to verge. Not five minutes after they had re-stacked boxes on the bench, the bench was emptied and taken away.

When they were both desperate for a rest, they wandered down the road to visit old George, hanging out for a caffeine fix. By the time they got back fifteen minutes later, the wardrobe had disappeared along with her mother's bed. Vicky stared at the empty spaces, stunned.

'Maybe we should have had a garage sale and made a bit of money,' Gina said.

'Hmm, maybe but this way everything is actually going and the little money we would have made would hardly be worth the effort. One of us would have to stand here all day, have a pocket full of change and it is possible things wouldn't go with such ease if people had to pay. All this stuff is old with little value even though a lot is still in good condition. Consider it our good deed for the day, giving to the needy.'

'Except most who have taken something don't appear to be all that needy,' Gina added with a laugh.

'True. Let's get back to work. The sooner we finish, the sooner we can go home.'

Three hours later, with only a short break to eat the sandwiches she had brought with her, Vicky locked the front door, happy the inside of the house was sparkling clean and forever thankful the house was only a basic small, three-bedroom place. There were still some larger furniture items stacked in the sitting room but it would be men from the charity shop who would lug them outside, not Vicky. As they walked to her car, Vicky detoured to add two boxes of canned and boxed foodstuffs to the roadside goodies. It would be interesting to see what was left in the morning when she did a drive-by on the way to work.

The first thing she did after they reached home was dump her handbag on the kitchen table, head for the shower where she stripped off and wallowed while scrubbing away the layer of grime and sweat. Clean, she headed for the computer, her nerves tingling with anticipation while she waited with her fingers doing a drum roll on the desk, for her Facebook page to boot up. She ignored everything but the little mark which denoted private messages. Her breath stalled when she spied the number 2. She pressed, waited, anxious.

SL. MY GRANDPOP IS THE MAN YOU ARE LOOKING FOR. HE WANTS TO MEET WITH YOU. HAS MUCH TO TELL YOU. BUT HE

CAN'T FLY. HAS EMPHYSEMA. ON OXYGEN. CAN YOU COME TO ENGLAND? DAD HAS SAME NAME.

'Oh, God, I don't believe this,' slid from Vicky's throat which felt as though a wodge of cardboard was stuck halfway down. 'Gina!' she yelled but immediately twisted her head back to stare at the message. Her eyes scanned the same short sentence over and over. *Has much to tell you.* What did he know? How was he related? It had to be the right person. Why didn't he message me himself? Message. Her eyes shot to the top of the page. Two messages. Frantic fingers clicked onto the icon. The air whooshed from her mouth when it was only a message from Marty's wife, inviting them to a barbecue next weekend. Never had she been so disappointed to hear from a friend she adored but she answered, accepted the invite, asked for time details and offered to make something.

Gina shot into the room, 'Why were you yelling?' she panted out.

Vicky went back to original message and pointed. 'This.'

Gina squatted beside her, read aloud, plopped onto the floor. 'Far out,' she said as she twisted her head to look at Vicky. 'It has to be them. Are you going? When?'

With her fingers clutched over her mouth and eyes shut, Vicky tried to unscramble shocked brain cells. Her eyes opened, fingers moved down, gripped the edge of the desk. 'I don't think I have any choice. I want... no... I *need* to find out the truth. Whatever this man has to say must be important if he wants to see me in person.'

'What about a phone call?'

'Maybe. I can ask.' She typed in the message, waited but nothing came back. 'Sophia is probably in bed,' Vicky murmured as she closed down the page and typed Qantas in the search engine.

'Qantas?' Gina asked.

'No harm in finding out when the soonest flight is.'

'But work.'

'I know. I go back tomorrow but I have a few weeks of holidays banked up. I can use them if I need to.'

'But I won't be able to go with you unless you wait until July. We have only been back at school for two weeks since the Easter break.'

'The man has emphysema, is on oxygen. When the disease gets to such a serious stage it means his time is short.' Vicky reached out, grasped Gina's arm. 'I can't lose this chance to find out. What if he dies before I get the information to solve this mystery? Deep down in my gut I know this is important. Has to be. There can't be any other explanation as to why Mum kept all these papers.'

'Aren't you scared? What if it's not good news?'

'Terrified, but I will never forgive myself if I don't find the truth while I have the chance. Not knowing good or bad news will eat away at me the same way knowing nothing about my father ate away when I was younger. It has taken me 37 years to let him go, to not let it worry me but now his non-existence has come roaring back with a vengeance.'

'This is why I never pushed you about him.'

Vicky took Gina's hands in hers. 'But I get the feeling Timothy Wakefield preys on your mind as well. Deep down. You asked me to add his name to the list we are searching for. You want to know your background as much as I do, don't you?'

'Yes,' quivered from her mouth.

'I *need* to talk to this Costas Lebtos. I want to see him in person, gauge his body language as he hopefully, tells me the answers to Mum's mysterious life. I have so many questions. Maybe he can also give me details about my father. And I don't think I can wait until July. What if this man dies before I get there? Do you understand?'

'Yes, of course. I want to know as well. It really sucks I have to go to school.'

'Any other year it wouldn't matter if you missed a week or two but not this year. It is too important if you want to get into university to do law. Now let me get back to figuring out how soon I can fly out. I need to make a list of everything we need to get done first. Granny's car should be ready to pick up. I need to pick up the necklace, arrange for time off, phone estate agents, organise the pick-up of the furniture, pack. Heavens, so many things to think about.'

'What about me? I don't think I want to stay here alone, not after, you know, the break-in.'

'What about if you stay with Uncle Marty? You will have your own car so will be able to drive to and from school.'

'Okay, sounds good.' Gina leant forwards, flung her arms around Vicky. 'I really don't mind you going. I understand how important it is for you. I would hate it if I never knew who my father was so go for it.'

Tears washed across Vicky's eyes, making everything blurry while a lump of emotion tightened all her innards. 'I am so glad I have the best daughter in the world, thank you. Now get out of here before I begin blubbering.' She forced a laugh and turned back to the computer to see another message had come through. 'Look,' she pointed to the icon.

SL. GRANDPOP WANTS TO SEE YOU IN PERSON. PLEASE COME. HE IS NOT WELL.

'Well, I guess this gives me an answer. I have to go,' Vicky said, going back to type in an answer.

VS. WILL ARRANGE A FLIGHT ASAP.

Next, she went back to the airline web site but ended up making a call when it became a little too complicated. Person to person was much easier since she could give reasons and more details on why a flight as soon as possible was needed. When told Tuesday, she had to pause to think. Could she possibly get everything organised in one day? It wasn't a hard decision when she figured if it were a matter of life or death she would make it work. And with this man's health so bad, maybe it is a matter of life and death. With a thundering pulse she made the booking, paid by credit card and dropped a long sigh when she hung up. It was done. She was flying to England... In 36 hours... Oh, far out.

Another message to Sophia was needed.

VS. NEED DETAILS ON WHERE I CAN MEET COSTAS.

Frozen pizza came to mind when she thought about dinner so she burrowed into the depths of the freezer, tugged, ignored the rattles and bumps as everything else settled into chaos. After her fingers turned numb while she wrestled with the adult-proof plastic cover and frozen cardboard box, she shoved the frozen circle on a tray and slid it into the oven between jotting down notes on a list. While she waited for the pizza to cook she dusted down a suitcase retrieved from the garage, packed necessities for a week, shoved dirty clothes in the washing machine and managed an essentials only quick clean of her own house. She almost forgot but managed to make a call to her boss; begged for another two weeks off work. By the time she fell into bed, exhausted, it was almost midnight. Despite the weariness of her body, Vicky's brain refused to let go of the myriad of thoughts which kept tumbling through. She tossed, glanced at the clock, lay still, turned and looked at the clock again only to find the digital numbers had only added another ten minutes. Yoga relaxation exercises didn't work, nor did the counting backwards trick. Finally, frustrated to the nth degree, she went in search of the cognac, doubled the nip to a good slug, sipped it slowly as she made her way back to bed and snuggled under the covers.

The events of the hectic day flashed through her mind while she drove to the jewellers. It hadn't been the most brilliant of starts when she overslept due to an over-indulgence of cognac. Now her head remonstrated to the tune of a dull ache and eyelids which were desperate to slide shut. She winced at the memory of arriving in the kitchen still tying the belt of her dressing gown in time to see Gina go through the doorway to catch the bus for school. Gina's laugh at her apology didn't help. Two more loads of washing had gone through the washing machine and now hung on the clothesline, hopefully drying in the wind since a few clouds had decided to gather. The weatherman, last night, said fine weather. What does he know? Karma knows better.

Phone calls had been made, which resulted in meetings every half-hour with estate agents after she collected the necklace and shoved it in a bank safety deposit box. At the same time, the Good Sammy's were due to arrive to pick up what they deemed suitable. Already she had visited with Marty's wife, organised for Gina to stay the week or maybe longer, made her apologies about the weekend barbecue and lingered too long over coffee while she related the saga of opening a simple chest. Packing was half done after she had to remove everything she had packed in a panic last night. This morning she had read a report on the weather conditions in London.

Half of the clothes she needed were now hanging on the clothesline, still damp but hopefully dry by the time she got home. Please, let it not rain, she thought as she pulled to a stop at the red lights.

Now Gina needed to pack as well, after Vicky picked her up from school to take her to the mechanics so Gina could drive her granny's car home.

The lights changed to green, Vicky picked up speed, drove through the intersection, passed the row of houses, turned left.

She had to be at school in time.

She slammed on the brakes when the rear end of the car in front came within a hair breadth of her front lights. She swore at her own stupidity and ignored the beep from the car behind who also had to brake suddenly. When her mind became determined to wander, Vicky forced it to concentrate so she could safely negotiate the heavy traffic. Where did all these people come from? It's Monday, for goodness sake. Everyone should be at work, including you, Vicky Saunders, she added as an afterthought. Oh, for heaven's sake, why would someone want to turn right in this traffic. Taking more care this time, Vicky pressed her foot on the brake pedal, drummed her fingers on top of the steering wheel, waited, waited, waited.

When the car turned, she released a long sigh and drove on to the next corner, flicked on the indicator to turn right. Different thing entirely when you are the one desperate to get over two lanes of continuous traffic. Fortunately, the wait was much shorter for her to find a gap. She spun the wheels, turned with a squeal, winced and drove on, turned left into the carpark of the jeweller. To make up time, she jogged to the door, shoved it open and strode to the counter at the far end. This time it was the very man she wanted to see, who stood there serving another customer. He glanced at her, smiled and turned back to his other customer who was pressing numbers in the machine which had a credit card poking out from the end. Transaction complete, small, beautifully wrapped package handed over, the jeweller stepped in front of Vicky. When he glanced around the store, Vicky twisted around to see what he was looking at. There was no-one else in the store. Her nervous tension skyrocketed.

'There is a problem with your necklace,' he finally said.

'Excuse me?' All she could think of was that maybe the jewels were not real. It would solve a lot of problems if it were true.

'I made a search on the internet. Most pieces by Faberge are recorded somewhere. Your piece, I'm afraid, is listed as stolen.'

Vicky reeled backwards, struggled to find her balance while her eyes stared at the man who looked as though he was sorry for being the bearer of bad news. His mouth was turned down at the edges and a frown deepened the wrinkles already resident between his eyes.

'Stolen?' Her mouth closed, opened and closed again, replicating a guppy. 'I have paperwork saying it was a gift to a woman who I now know is dead. Maybe the person who gave it to her wants it back. But I also know who gave it to her.' She paused, scrambled for logic to return. Maybe this man was going to keep the necklace to turn over to authorities. Would she get into trouble? Surely not. She only found the darn thing. How much could she disclose? Huh, how much did she really know to be true? But she had to say something.

'Over the past two days, my daughter and I have delved through all the paperwork I found. We have done a lot of internet research and have found names relating to us and the paperwork. I have made contact with a couple of the names we found and tomorrow I am flying to London to meet up with one of these people who can, I hope, answer all of my questions. When I have answers I can return the necklace to whoever is the true owner. Since everyone lives in Europe, I need to take it with me. But technically, right now, the necklace belongs to me for it was in my mother's possession and everything of hers has been bequeathed to me, according to my lawyer.' Better mention the lawyer to make it sound official. She was prattling, she knew, but what else could she do? 'In fact, I am certain my mother is the person the necklace was given to.' Liar, liar but she had to convince this man of her ownership. 'Do you know who reported the necklace as stolen?'

'Let me see, I wrote it down somewhere.' He flicked through a small pile of torn paper, each with writing scrawled on it. 'Yes, here it is. Vasilis Nesbloutas. An Athens address. International phone number. He is to be contacted should it be discovered.'

Vicky sucked in her breath at the familiar surname. But it wasn't Kristian, who she knew for sure gave the necklace to Sophia. So who was this other man? A brother? Or maybe a son. Couldn't be a father for he would be way too old to even be alive. 'I recognise the surname from my research. A man with the same surname gave it to my mother. I have written proof – a letter written and signed by him. I think maybe I should take it with me so I can track him down and give it back.'

'Very well but I must warn you, if you try to sell this piece, there is every chance you will be arrested.'

Arrested? For finding a simple necklace in an ancient shoe box? Whoopie doo. 'Gee, thanks a million. Look, I realise you may have doubts and I don't blame you. Everything I have discovered is a real surprise to me but you have all of my details, photographs even. If the mystery isn't resolved you will be able to notify the authorities. But I need at least a week, maybe two to find out the truth about my life and this necklace. Let me get over to Europe. I will call in here when I return to let you know what happens.'

'Wait here. I will get it for you.'

Everything inside her went limp with relief as the man disappeared into the back room. Vicky slid her eyes shut, breathed in deep and slow, released the breath through pursed lips. The myth about the opening of Pandora's box had nothing on her real-life story about opening a cedar wood chest. Good grief, what a complicated mess. An unbidden laugh snuck out. This was so ridiculous with mystery names and objects; each find addling her mind. She would think one thing then her thoughts were completely contradicted at the next discovery. She had to fight to bring her grin under control when the rear door moved, whooshed and opened. The tension in her strung-out nerves eased when the jeweller dropped her necklace into a pouch and drew the string tight. It felt a whole lot better when she slid the pouch into her pocket although it felt like a tonne of lead weighing her down while she walked to her car, eased in then ensured she locked the doors from the inside before she turned the key to start the engine.

As she drove off, she glanced at the time on the car clock and groaned. She was going to be late even though she had bypassed the bit about the visit the bank. Probably the last place she needed to go with a hot piece of stolen jewellery worth a small fortune burning a hole in her pocket and indecision about what to do with it, frying her brain cells.

Even though the next hour and a half was chaos with two men moving furniture around various estate agents, who scribbled down details while they did a minute study of every detail in her mother's home, Vicky's hand kept finding its way into her jacket pocket to ensure the hidden bulk was still there. Rough estimates on the home's value were almost the same, with each agent doing their best to wangle the magic number their counterpart had given so they could promise to get more in order to get the listing. Vicky knew how they operated. Too many calls to Legal Aid came in about the unscrupulous practises of a few agents.

'Email your estimates,' she said to each one as she ushered them out the door in readiness for the next arrival. If only she had more time.

Before the men from the Good Samaritans left, she begged them to help her dump the last of the items into the skip bin. There was little to retrieve from the verge. Roadside pickers had done a brilliant job in the past twenty-four hours. What was left wasn't worth saving in any case and she was more than glad to tip the last boxful of bits and pieces into the skip bin – box and all.

She was only five minutes late to pick up Gina from school but the lateness meant there was actually a vacant parking spot in front of the school. Gina's scowl for having to wait an entire five minutes received a grin in return. Vicky didn't have the energy or time to have a verbal wrangle of excuses and reasons.

It was an exact opposite in expression when Gina sat in the driver's seat of the car which now belonged to her, apart from the minor detail of having the legal ownership changed on the licence papers. Another couple of weeks wasn't going to make an iota of difference. So the legalities could wait until she returned. Vicky figured the wide grin was going to be set in place for the entire drive home. She waved back as Gina drove off, unable to wipe her own smile from her face. Not many seventeen-year-olds were able to own such a nice car without a substantial loan hanging over their heads or eating a huge hole in their parents' savings.

She couldn't help but grin when she arrived home to see Gina standing by the side of her car, tapping her pointed foot in feigned impatience for Vicky to open the garage door. Another job on the to-do list which had to be completed tonight. She would have to hunt down the second remote control which hadn't been used since... better not to go there. But the thought of Mike returned with a vengeance when she saw Vicky's car parked in Mike's spot. Fiddlesticks, it shouldn't still hurt so much.

Determined to keep sad thoughts at bay, she raced inside, placed the necklace next to her suitcase and set to work. First, she grabbed dry clothes from the line, folded them, dumped piles in the linen cupboard, on Gina's bed and then her own. She managed to pack most of the clothes she needed into her suitcase before emptying the contents of her refrigerator on the bench to figure out how to cobble together a meal using up most of what was on hand. Left over vegetables were diced, chopped and grated before being fried off. Whipped eggs with a dash of milk were poured over to make something which was a cross between omelettes and a frittata. Grated cheese on top melted to a creamy lusciousness. Bread toasted while eggs cooked before being spooned carefully onto the buttered toast. A pinch of salt and sprinkle of ground pepper over the top. Dinner was a tad early but filled empty holes and tasted a whole lot better than Vicky thought it would. A fridge door meal, she called it – open the fridge door and cook whatever is in there. Her go-to formula when the weekly shop hadn't yet been done.

She left Gina to do the dishes while Vicky retreated to her office, approached the computer with her nerves notching up in intensity. Would there be any more responses to the half dozen enquiries she had sent out to the magical electronic stratosphere.

Vicky sat, turned the computer on, waited with her breath held. The screen came to life. She typed in her password, clicked onto her social media with an immediate glance at the message icon. The message from Sophia gave the address of Costas Lebtos. Vicky found a scrap of paper, wrote down: 5

Winter Avenue, Orpington, Kent. Hmm, the county where she was born. Made sense if it was an old family home but it was something else she had never been told. Her heart twisted in pain at the thought of another fact having been kept from her.

With no other messages, she logged onto her email account. It seemed to take forever before each message came to light. An over-eager finger pressed on the message from the Kent Office of Registrations. Another lifetime was taken before the message came up. Eyes boggled as open as her wide mouth when her own full birth certificate filled the screen. This was no copy of her basic birth notification. This was the full enchilada. She scanned then read more slowly.

Mother: Regina Victoria Jones. Spinster. Victoria? Huh? How come Vicky never knew her mother's middle name was Victoria?

Date of Birth: June 9th, 1951. Year was the same as was the date so no surprises there.

Father: Timothy James Wakefield. Bachelor. Carpenter. Vicky sucked in a long breath, unable to believe this was true and yet here it was – right slap bang in front of her. The official details of her birth. So everything she had been told must be true and all those conclusions she had come to were nothing more than speculation or maybe vain hope. Vicky Saunders was not the daughter of Sophia and Kristian. She was nothing more than the daughter of Regina and Timothy – as she had been told. But then why were there so many papers hidden away about an entirely different family?

Date of Birth: 26th November 1930. 'What?' gushed out.

'No way. 1930?' He would have been over twenty years older than Mum. Over fifty when Vicky was born. Why would Mum marry a man so much older? Vicky slumped back into the back of the chair, staring at the screen with her brain cells trying to make sense of what was in front of her. Leaning forward again, she read on.

Place of Birth: 5 Winter Avenue, Orpington, Kent. United Kingdom. Good grief, the same address and it must have been a home birth, otherwise they would have listed the hospital name. Oh, wow. Her spine hit the back of the seat again on a sucked in breath. The shocks kept coming. Well at least her birth date was right, she thought as she read the next entry.

She scanned down further, surprised when the email went to a second page. Her lungs ceased to work when she realised there was a second certificate attached. When she saw it was her mother's marriage certificate, her heart hammered to make up for lost beats. She read, her eyes scanning left to right, left to right. The details re-iterated all she had only just learned but they stalled on the date. Her eyes closed in disbelief, opened again, focussed but the date read exactly the same: 22nd May 1982. The day before Vicky was born.

Now, things made no sense at all. Her dad was supposed to have high-tailed it out of Regina's life on the announcement of Regina's pregnancy, yet they married the day before the pregnancy bore fruit – the day before Vicky was born. So, here was a lie – a humungous lie. But why? Again, something didn't make sense which only added a whole lot more mystery to an already complicated mystery.

Twenty-Four

Vicky tugged the edges of her coat together to block out the frigid air. It was supposed to be spring here in England but this northern spring was far colder than autumn back home. The biting wind was relentless and managed to find every single miniscule gap between clothes and body to sneak in and chill to freezing status. Already numb with cold, she quickened her step to hurry into the relative warmth of Charing Cross station. Inside she searched for a sign which she hoped would lead her to the south-east mainline, whatever it meant. Already she had got onto one wrong train in the Underground system by not following the signs she hadn't seen because she didn't know where to look for them. Now she knew, but her mistake meant she was an hour late and she hated being late.

A flood of people scurried every-which-way. A few stood at pay machines, waiting to drop in coins, taking tickets and joining the melee. Everyone seemed to know what to do and where they were going, barely pausing in their continual race to get wherever they needed to be in as short a time as possible. Vicky didn't have a clue. She paused, spun around, searched for someone she could ask. A smile broke out when she spied a ticket booth manned by a human. The queue was short with only two ahead of her but the wait was long with an obvious language barrier making requests and instructions difficult to understand. Finally at the window, she gave details of where she wanted to go, paid the fare and made sure she understood the instructions on which platform she needed and how to get there. No more getting on trains which took her the wrong way.

It appeared every soul in the station was determined to cram themselves into the same carriage Vicky managed to step into. Free seats were non-existent so she wedged her back against a metal pole and held on. Twenty-five minutes later she released her death grip on the pole and nudged her way to the door, excusing herself as she went. It was a relief to step on the platform even though half the carriage spilled out with her.

Get a taxi, she was told, even though it was a walkable distance, so Vicky made her way through the entrance, spied a line of cabs, most of the famed black variety. With many passengers headed towards them, Vicky ran to one near the far end, gave the address and with a nod from the driver she climbed into the back seat. Still weary from jetlag, she let her head drop back against the top of the back seat and slid her eyes closed. Even though she was eager to see the town where she had been born, catching up on some shuteye was preferable. No sooner than she felt her muscles relax, the car came to a halt with a jerk, bouncing her back to alertness.

'Here we are, lady. That'll be three pound fifty.'

While scrabbling in her money purse to sort through unfamiliar coins, Vicky figured it must be roughly a pound per second since the ride was so short but it was better than walking, especially since thick clouds hovered less than two metres from the ground as though afraid to go any lower. As she stood on the footpath, she studied the two-storey brown brick house in front of her. It was a surprise to see it stand alone since she had visions of rows and rows of terrace houses as was so common in London. A short step up through an open gateway and onto a short well-weathered concrete pathway, led her to three more brick steps up to a painted wooden door. She paused, sucked in a long breath for courage, rapped the brass knocker three times and stood back, prepared to wait a while since Costas was on oxygen.

She had only just managed to plant both feet back on the ground when the door flew open and a sprightly elderly woman beamed at her.

'Vicky, oh my dear, at last we can meet in person.'

Her mouth gaped. 'You know who I am?'

'Of course. Come in, come in. Let me hug you.' Vicky's breath whooshed out when arms swept around her and squeezed so tight she couldn't draw in another breath.

'My turn,' came a raspy male voice.

Vicky managed to lift her head far enough to peer over her captor's shoulder to see a wide grin of a frail man with a plastic hose in each nostril. As suddenly as she was grabbed, the arms let go but grasped her shoulders instead. The woman stood back, studied Vicky from head to toe and back again before she released her hold. Immediately, the man approached but took a more gentle approach, with a gentle but long hug before he bestowed a kiss on her brow.

'Our beautiful Victoria,' he mumbled but there was a

hitch to his voice and when he glanced at her, his eyes were awash with tears.

Stunned by the reception, Vicky couldn't think of a thing to say. It took a few seconds for her mouth to connect with her brain. 'You know about me?'

'Of course,' the man said. 'Please, come inside out of this miserable weather.' He took her elbow and led her along a short passage.

Vicky had to shorten her steps to keep pace with his shuffles. One of his hands dragged a small trolley with an oxygen bottle attached. They entered a kitchen which was much warmer than the rest of the house. The heat seemed to emanate from a large cooking range with an enormous black kettle on top which had steam rising from the spout. The kitchen was spacious and recently updated if she took into account the modern countertops, cupboards and shining appliances.

'Sit here,' Costas said. His open hand indicated a wooden spindle-backed chair at the end of the table nearest the range. He settled into a cushioned cane armchair set on an angle to one side of the stove but within reaching distance of Vicky. By the shape of the cushions, she figured this was the favoured spot for a man so ill.

'You must be Costas,' Vicky said as she unhitched her stuffed backpack and dropped it on the ground at her feet.

'Yes, my dear and this is my lovely wife, Theodora, but she only answers to Dora. Welcome to our home which is also your home.'

Dora sat on the other side of the table but leant forward with her eyes showing anticipation.

'My home?'

'Yes, of course. You are family.'

'Family? Now I am confused and how come you know all about me when I knew nothing about you until a few days ago?'

Costas shook his head and looked so sad Vicky's heart managed a tumble-turn. 'Sadly, the old man is still alive.'

'Old man. What old man? I have no idea what you are talking about.'

'Vasilis Nesbloutas.'

Adrenalin spurted, flooding through her veins at such a speed her nerves twitched to high alert. 'I heard that name only two days ago. Who is he?'

'A murderer. He murdered my sister, Sophia.' Costas lifted his eyes, took her hands and stared at her. 'Your mother.'

It felt like she had been struck by lightning the way everything inside her jerked and tightened. 'Sophia was my mother?' she managed to rasp out of a throat which had something hard jammed in it.

'Yes.'

'But Regina... I now have the birth certificate. It was emailed to me the other day from your local registry office.'

'You really don't know, do you?'

'Don't know what?'

'Regina is your aunt. Your mother's sister, Georgia. She changed her name by deed poll to keep you safe from that murderer. She just swapped the letters of her name around and changed a couple.'

Everything in her body went limp. Now it was explained,

it was so darn obvious. If she weren't sitting she would have fallen to the ground. Vicky dropped her head into her hands, forced her lungs to work properly, while trying to make sense of things. Regina – Georgia. Mother - aunt. 'But how, why? Georgia is a nun. And there is an age difference. Georgia was born in 1947 while Mum was 1951. I found a photo of her when she took her vows.'

'My sister left the church after Sophia died, to raise you.'

'But if she was so religious, how come we never went to church? What religion was she? She left a letter asking for a religious funeral, which surprised me. It was an Anglican service because I had no idea.'

'We were Greek Orthodox. I am not sure she was such a believer but she became a sister of the church after an unpleasant experience. I believe it was her way of coping.'

'What sort of experience?' Vicky eyed the two when the silence was filled with glances between husband a wife. Obviously, it was something they didn't want to discuss. What could be so bad?

'Georgia was raped.' Dora finally said after a discreet nod from Costas.

'Oh, my goodness but why did she never tell me?' Vicky swung her eyes between the two.

'Back then it was a terrible shame. The attack was vicious. Georgia was badly beaten and after she came home from the hospital she found it difficult to cope. Blamed herself. The guilt ate away at her but she found solitude with the sisters,' said Costas with a wheeze after every three words.

'Rape is never the fault of the victim,' said Vicky. 'The perpetrator is the one who deserves the blame.'

'Easy to say, but when you are the victim, the very act gnaws at you. Georgia was in a terrible state. We were glad she found solace with the sisters but were even happier when she found a purpose for living when she took over your care. You saved her sanity.'

Vicky had to sniff back her tears but a sniff didn't work for they spilled over in a torrent down her cheeks. She searched her backpack for one of the travel packs of tissues she had shoved in at the last minute, withdrew one, wiped her eyes and blew her nose. 'This is so awful. Thank you for telling me, it makes a huge difference, believe me. This might explain why Mum... er, Georgia was never a hugging type of person. I think I understand her better now. But... I'm not sure I should tell you this but Mum did have relationships with men, later on in her life. You know, um, physical relationships. I know of at least one who asked her to marry him but she refused. So maybe she did get over her trauma. I hope so.'

When she glanced at Dora, there was a redness to the other woman's cheeks but there was a sappy kind of smile spread across her face. 'Such a delicate subject but I am glad.' Dora turned to Costas. 'Georgia never told us any of this in her letters did she, Dear?'

'Um, no.'

It delighted Vicky to see her uncle also blush but he did his utmost to hide it, making him appear all the more cuter.

'Why don't we have a cup of tea,' he added after a pause

during which Vicky saw him trying to bring his heated flesh under control. Dear, sweet man, she thought. So cute.

'And I am certain my Dora has made some cakes because this house has had delicious smells through it for the past two days. Then we can talk. But first, tell me about dear Georgia. It must be hard for you, first your husband and now Georgia.'

'My husband? You know about Mike?' Her hands were taken again, this time by Dora who stood and gripped tight before she let go and bustled over to the range.

'Of course,' she said over her shoulder. 'Georgia sent us letters and photos every few months ever since she took you to Australia. We know everything about you and your lovely daughter, Gina. Why didn't you bring her with you?'

It took a few seconds before Vicky could unscramble her brain cells from the shock of all these revelations. 'This year Gina can't afford to miss school. This is her final year with important exams to pass so she can get into Law at the university.'

'I understand,' Costas said but he looked sad. 'I would have loved to meet her. My great-niece.'

Vicky's heart twisted. With his condition, it was unlikely he would live long enough to meet Gina, even if she came over after her exams at the end of the year. But Vicky didn't know the details about how bad his condition was so maybe there was hope. Maybe she should make it a priority to bring Vicky to London for Christmas. It was doable, more so with the extra money from the sale of Regina's house. Heavens but she didn't know what to call the woman who raised her. Now not Regina, her true mother but Georgia, her aunt.

A plate piled high with a mixture of home-baked biscuits and cake slices was placed on the table in front of her. While Vicky related the details of her mother's passing, cups and saucers, a sugar pot, a milk jug and a large steaming teapot were precisely placed within reach of them all. Teapot was spun three times. Milk was poured into cups but Vicky held her hand over her cup to indicate no milk. Dora paused with the jug on a lean in the air but nodded and replaced the jug. Beautiful matching china plates were handed around and the goodies offered. Vicky took a piece of fruit cake to be polite but she doubted she would be able to swallow a single crumb, her stomach was so churned up. Finally, the cups were filled with well-brewed tea poured through a proper tea-strainer to catch real tea leaves.

Eager questions about her life were asked while they nibbled and sipped. Between answers, Vicky noticed how Costas ate little but drank three cups of tea. She guessed his appetite was not the best, hence his pallid features. It hurt to realise this man, her real-life uncle, didn't have a lot of time left and she had only just found him. To her it was criminal to be denied her family for so long. Surely one man's threats shouldn't have caused such a rift. If he was an old man, why weren't the police notified of his threats? He lived in Greece, for heaven's sake. How could he harm her from there? But then the picture of the two private investigators shot to her mind. How did the man know about her? She had to ask.

'Why was Vasilis Nesbloutas such a threat? How could he possibly harm me? I mean, I live in Australia, he lives in

Athens and why weren't the police notified? It has been 37 years, almost 38. Surely there is no longer any danger.'

Dora and Costas glanced at each other again, the worried eyes giving Vicky the heebie-jeebies.

'After Georgia took you away, it took several years for the man to find you. When he did, he had photos taken of you without Georgia's knowledge. The first was of you on a swing in a park. He sent her a copy of the photo with a note. *I know where she is.* A picture of a speeding car was attached.'

Vicky sucked in her breath on a hiss.

'At random times, two or three pictures would arrive each year, always with a threat. After Gina was born, the picture often included your daughter.'

'Gina?' Vicky croaked as she shot from her chair with anger pulsating through her. 'The man took unsolicited photos of Gina? Why didn't Georgia call the police? Mike was a lawyer for goodness sake. He would have put a stop to it.'

'Georgia was terrified.'

'I don't care how terrified she was, she was wrong not to tell me or Mike,' Vicky shouted. 'I have been denied my family, knowledge of my real parents. My whole life has been one enormous lie. Everything about this is so wrong,' she added. She plopped back into the chair which caused the legs to screech on the flagstones. She winced at the noise, huffed out a long breath and tried to calm. 'Who is Timothy Wakefield?'

'An old friend. The marriage was real but in name only to give you legitimacy. Tim was... how do you say? Did not prefer women.'

'He was gay?'

Dora whimpered at the word while Costas glanced away for a second, making it obvious homosexuality was not as easily accepted from these elderly people who were brought up in a much stricter time. 'Yes, but he was a good friend. It was his suggestion for Georgia to change her name, for them to marry to make everything legal and to help hide you. He even paid for the journey to Australia. The family sent Georgia money for the first couple of years so she didn't have to work while you were still a baby. Timothy gave her enough to pay the deposit on her house.'

Her head fell into her hands at these new revelations. She'd had no idea about any of this. Regina had never let on she didn't work in the early years and Vicky couldn't remember so far back. To her, Regina always worked. 'But he was so much older than her,' Vicky said.

'Yes, but it meant nothing. He was never going to marry in any case. It was only to give you a name. He was not a well man at the time. What we now know as Aids. He died only a few years later.'

Overwhelmed, Vicky buried her head in her hands again. There were so many facts to absorb, to understand. Now she wasn't so sure it had been a good thing to open the darn chest. Maybe she would have been better off never knowing any of this. 'Give me a minute,' she muttered. 'I need time to make sense of all this.' Around her, china clattered as it was collected and put on the sink. Water flowed but Dora and Costas were silent except for the continual rush of oxygen every time Costas inhaled. Still she only really knew half of the story.

'Kristian Nesbloutas is my father,' she finally said aloud.

'Yes, but how did you know his name?' asked Costas sounding surprised.

'Long story. You said Vasilis is still alive. Is he my grandfather?'

'Unfortunately, yes, which is why Georgia couldn't tell you the truth.'

'Why?'

'If you ever found out, he was going to kill you.'

'Kill me, why?'

'He is extremely wealthy.'

'So what? I don't understand and how would he ever find out if I knew the truth?'

'You would seek out your father. It is only natural.'

Vicky eyed the man. 'Not necessarily. Kristian knew about me. I know this for sure. But obviously he didn't give a damn so why would I want to seek him out? He didn't want me.'

'How do you know these things?'

'Letters Mum... er, Georgia, kept hidden away. I found them locked away in a chest. There are some diaries written in Greek along with certificates, photos, newspaper cuttings, even some jewellery. Rings, a brooch.' Something kept her from mentioning the necklace.

'The rings belonged to my mother. They were left to Georgia so now they are yours. I have no use for such things.'

'Two wedding rings are much larger.'

'My father and grandfather. Keep them but I would like to see the letters and diaries. Did you bring them?'

'Yes, I have them here. Would you translate them for me?' Vicky picked up her backpack, undid the catch and fossicked around, ensuring she only showed what she wanted. She withdrew a file containing the letters and certificates then placed the six diaries on the table.

Costas reached over, took the first diary, opened it out and began scanning the words. He glanced up. 'It will take me some time to write the words down. Can you leave them with me overnight? Dora can help me.'

'Dora is Greek?' Vicky asked.

Costas grinned. 'Certainly, we Greeks tend to stick together. You also are Greek.'

Vicky laughed. 'I might have Greek blood but I now know I was born in France and raised in Australia. More of a combination omelette.'

'Definitely Greek.' Dora added with a gentle grip of Vicky's shoulder but her hand dropped all of a sudden when a strange whoosh of oxygen came from Costas.

'Costas are you okay?' Dora asked as she dropped to her knees beside him.

He wavered a hand in the air, smiled but it seemed to be forced. 'Yes, just a bit tired.'

Sensing he was more than tired and needed a break, Vicky figured it was time to go. 'I have a suggestion,' she said while placing a hand on his arm. 'Why don't I leave now, return to London so I can explore and see some of the sites? It will give you both a chance to read all these papers and write me some translations. What if I come back some time tomorrow? Maybe the afternoon to give you more time.'

'Come for dinner. Around six,' said Dora.

'Okay, sounds good. I think I might walk back to the station if you give me directions. I need time to digest all I have learnt today and want to set the picture in my mind of this town where my mother's family have lived for so long.'

Instructions given and goodbyes said, Vicky set off with a brisk walk to the corner, turned left and strode all the way down Tubbendon Lane which took her to the station without having to turn any more corners. Impossible to get lost and much easier to negotiate than the Underground. Despite her brain churning, she took the time to study the town her mother's family had lived in for years. Her town, she thought, although she didn't have even a twinge of feeling to tell her she belonged here.

Twenty-Five

Several cars stood parked along the edge of the road when Vicky turned in Winter Ave not long before six. While she studied them she slowed but dismissed them as belonging to the various houses along the street. Everyone would be home from work by now. When she stepped through the open gateway at number five a thrum of voices greeted her and grew louder after she mounted the last step. She lifted the brass door knocker on the panelled door. Oh, please, let there not be a party of neighbours and friends. Still suffering the effects of jetlag, highlighted by a night with little sleep, she didn't feel like being sociable to strangers. Maybe she shouldn't have spent the day trawling the streets of London from Westminster Bridge to Harrod's in Knightsbridge, but with so little time and so much to see, it had been a way to keep her mind occupied by amazing sights rather than tumultuous facts of her life.

The knocks seemed to echo, followed by hurried footsteps. The door opened. A grinning Dora stood there.

'Come, come inside, everyone is waiting.'

As she stepped through the doorway into the carpeted passage, Vicky swallowed the groan which wanted to rumble out from deep down. Her hand was tugged, giving her no choice but to hurry, keeping pace with the excited woman who was dressed in her Sunday best. Dove grey hair had been curled and carefully combed with not a single wispy strand out of place, unlike Vicky's which was now windblown into what felt like woven straw after the chilly walk from the station. She ran the fingers of one hand through the strands, hoping to create some sort of order. Dora's soft pink cardigan toned with the pink slashes in her tweed skirt. Darn, she had even worn stockings and smart low-heeled leather shoes while Vicky's feet were clad in thick socks and sneakers, although they were of the expensive but super-comfortable walking variety. The jeans she had worn for two days now felt grubby, wrinkled and inadequate. Should have asked if they dress for the evening meal, she thought, but too late now.

The kitchen bustled with bodies, half of them seated while the other half fiddled with platters of food spread out along the kitchen bench as well as the table bearing what Vicky figured was the very best in china, glassware and cutlery. Feeling like a frump, she paused in the doorway as silence descended and at least two dozen pairs of eyes bored into her.

'Vicky, my dear,' came from the edge of the range which still pumped out heat. Since there was no fire, Vicky figured it was oil or gas heated but it sure was effective, instantly wiping away the chill from her face and hands. She glanced at the man who sat in the same cane chair which hadn't moved an inch. An instant path was made with bodies parting ways so Vicky could see Costas. He also wore his best smartly pressed trousers, a white shirt and red-striped tie. There were even gold cuff links holding the edges of starched sleeves together. She went towards him, the silence so dense it rattled her. 'Meet your family,' he said when she reached him.

Her family? All of these people? She turned and glanced around, eyeing each person in turn, overwhelmed. Her eyes stalled on a familiar face, one she recognised from the computer. 'You must be Sophia,' she said to break the silence. Hubbub ensued as people were named and hellos were said. As far as she could figure out, there were three cousins, Costas junior, called Con to differentiate him from his father, Eleni and Anna, children of Dora and Costas. Sophia had a brother and sister, names already forgotten. In the melee there were the five offspring belonging to Eleni and Anna plus various partners, boyfriends and girlfriends. There had to be at least thirty people jammed into this room, Vicky figured when she was finally offered a chair, right next to her uncle Costas.

Food was piled onto plates with a filled plate handed to Costas and another placed in front of Vicky giving her no choice but to taste every single dish since a scoop of each had been piled onto her plate. People forked food into mouths between eager questions Vicky barely had time to answer before another question was fielded. She didn't get a chance to use her own fork until Dora shushed everyone and demanded they *let poor Vicky eat.* The noise dropped several decibels to intermittent murmurs while the guests – her family, for goodness sake, shovelled an enormous amount of food into their mouths. She knew Greeks partied well with generous dishes but this was ridiculous. Red and white wine was poured into glasses then topped up. After two glasses, Vicky filled her glass with iced water from a large jug. Not a good idea to get tipsy, especially when she had yet to make a return train trip to her hotel.

After plates were cleaned of food, they were stacked and removed along with the various dishes of leftovers, only to be replaced by half a dozen different kinds of desserts. Dessert plates and spoons appeared and the plates were soon filled. Vicky chose her favourite, baklava and two different types of honey drenched delicacies. One she knew was kataifi and the other was custard filled filo pastry with honey dripped over the top, name unknown but who cared when it tasted so heavenly. Yum, they were so good she had no hesitation in going back for another roll of kataifi. These treats she could get used to but too many and she would need to join a gym. But after the miles she had walked yesterday afternoon and today, she figured there were a few calories to make up for. She certainly needed a boost to her energy levels even though sugar was not the best sort of energy to have.

While women washed dishes and returned to kitchen to pristine cleanliness in what seemed like mere minutes, the men took it in turns to sit in a chair opposite Vicky while the others stood crowded around, all eager to talk and make themselves known. What shocked Vicky the most was how they all knew about her and had done so all their lives. A spear of hurt managed to worm its way into her heart and continued jab as the evening wore on.

When coffee of the Greek variety was served, the men trailed away, taking Costas with them. 'He needs to rest in bed,' his son said as he led his father, trailing his oxygen cart, from the room.

No sooner had the men gone to another room they were replaced by the women who crowded around, all eager to have a piece of Vicky. They butted in to each other's conversation so much it was obvious they all wanted to get to know Vicky and for her to know where each of them fitted into her family. It was after ten before people began drifting away to go home.

'I will drive you back to London,' her cousin, Con, said after Sophia and her boyfriend gave Vicky a hug goodbye. 'Dad asked if it was possible for you to come back tomorrow so you can talk. He was worried about some diaries he hadn't given you. I told him I would ask.'

The request threw her plans awry but she figured what Costas had for her was far more important than seeing more landmarks. Besides, she thought, coming back with Gina was no longer a possibility – it was definite. These people were Gina's family as well. No way was Vicky going to deny her daughter a relationship with her heritage the same way she had been denied for thirty-seven years. 'Sure, I can come. I have a whole heap more questions to be answered.'

'Let me tell Mama, so she can put Dad's mind to rest. Are you ready to go?'

'Actually I am exhausted. So many people with so much information, my mind feels like a tumble drier on high speed. But I can catch a train. I don't want you to go out of your way.'

'I live on the other side of London in any case. It might seem like a long way but it's not much more than twenty kilometres from here to central London. Just give me a minute.'

Despite her desperate need for sleep, Vicky enjoyed the pleasant car drive back to London, chatting quietly to Con, finding out more about this one cousin in the twenty-minute drive than she had about any other person in the previous four hours of mayhem.

'You are a doctor, like George was, who must be your grandfather,' Vicky said when he hinted at patients.

'You know about him?' He glanced her way before turning his attention back to the road.

'Yes, I found a newspaper cutting with his death notice. What happened to him? How come he was in Greece when the rest of you were in London?'

'During the Greek civil war, Granddad worked as a medic, caring for anyone who came to his surgery, despite which side they came from. Apparently it wasn't a very happy time, with Greeks dobbing in their fellow man if their politics didn't agree. Some were unhappy with him giving medical attention to the other side. In the end, he was arrested for consorting with the communists and put in jail where he continued to treat inmates, again despite their politics. Somehow, he managed to send Dad, Georgia and Lukas to relatives in England. At the time Grandma was pregnant with Sophia and unable to travel. She stayed in Greece until after Sophia was born. She never saw her husband again. He was murdered in jail by a gang of thugs who disagreed with his treatment of a couple of Germans, men the prison authorities refused to give medical attention because of their nationality. Life in Greece was not very good at the time.'

'What about your uncle, Lukas? Where is he?'

'In Greece.' His left hand reached out and gripped her knee. 'He's your uncle too, you know. He is also a doctor but now retired. He lives on one of the islands of the Inner Cyclades - Tinos. He wasn't able to come at such short notice but sends his regards. He would love to meet you. How long are you staying?'

'Not long. I have to get back to work and to Gina. My ticket is open at the moment but I need to finalise a date tomorrow or the day after.'

'Pity, but I understand. Here we are. Your hotel.'

Before she alighted, Vicky needed to ask a few more questions in case she never got to catch up with Con again. 'Your wife isn't with you.'

'No, she had the afternoon and evening shift. Paediatric surgeon in the E.R.'

'Another doctor. Have your children followed suit? I never got the opportunity to ask what career each had. Too much going on.'

'It was a bit overwhelming wasn't it? To answer your question, no.' Con laughed. 'They all wanted something with more realistic hours. My son works in I.T. A bit of a computer nerd. Sophia is training as a teacher and her sister is studying business management at university.'

'Not sure teachers have such realistic hours. My friend spends more time at home marking and preparing lessons than she does in the classroom.'

'Yes, well, Sophia will discover this for herself.'

'Before I go, could you please give me your dad's phone number so I can ring him in the morning to make a time to visit?'

'Certainly, but don't ring before nine. It takes him a while to get through his morning ablutions and get dressed.' Con withdrew a pen from his pocket before lifting the console where he took out a prescription pad and scribbled a number on the back of a blank prescription.

'I am afraid to ask but how bad is his condition?'

'He will never get any better. Mesothelioma. He was a building contractor. Back when he began, masks were never even thought of when working with things like asbestos. There is no cure, we can only treat the symptoms to make life more comfortable. I doubt he will see Christmas.'

Vicky reached over to grasp her cousin's hand and gave it a squeeze. 'I am so sorry. I was thinking of bringing Gina over after her exams at the end of November. She deserves to know her roots, to meet her family.' She shook her head. 'I am angry about the way I was kept in the dark. It was wrong.'

'But old man Nesbloutas is still alive. His threats to Georgia were consistent and terrifying. He knew where you were. He threatened your daughter's life as well and there was your husband.'

'Excuse me?' Her heart jolted and body stilled. Vicky stared at Con, who looked away but not before Vicky noticed the regret in his eyes. She didn't miss his muttered swear words.

'What do you mean?' she demanded.

'God, I'm sorry. I didn't realise you didn't know.' He turned back, this time with pain etched on his face.

'Georgia was certain his death was not an accident but was deliberate because of the message and photo she received the day after.'

Everything inside Vicky froze. 'Vasilis Nesbloutas?' she

managed to squeeze out of a throat jammed with a wad of cardboard.

'Yes.'

T he last thing Vicky felt like doing was to visit with Costas and Dora, which required being all happy and cheery. She felt like crap after she had spent too many hours of the night weeping bucketloads of tears, ranting in anger and cursing the world. Sometime well after midnight she had fallen asleep, probably through sheer mental exhaustion. It had helped to write a long email to Marty, outlining all she had learned, getting it off her chest instead of bottling it up to let it fester inside. It made sense to blame Mike's death on someone else entirely since there was not, and never had been a skerrick of evidence his death had been caused by the bikie gang. Poor Marty had given up his lunch hour to reply with a whole heap of questions and suppositions, his quick lawyer's mind coming up with logical angles. His biggest and scariest hypothesis was a wakeup call for Vicky, something she still couldn't get her head around and found it almost impossible to accept but it did make a whole lot of sense. Mike had been driving her car the day he died, because his was at the mechanics for a service. Which meant she had been the intended victim.

When her heart stabbed so hard she became breathless, Vicky paused mid-stride in her walk along Tubbendon Lane. She glanced around in a desperate search for a car heading towards her. Her nerves were twitchy and had been since she left the hotel room but for an entirely different reason than previously. How safe was she? Did Nesbloutas know she was here, in London, finding out the truth of her birth? She so wanted to face the man, beat him to a pulp and worse, but only after she found out the reason for his hatred. Money, her uncle had said, but was it the only reason and she sure didn't want a cent of money from such an evil person. Shame? Could her illegitimacy be a stain on the family name? They were Greek where maybe such things held more importance but surely not in this day and age. But no-one knew. Well, maybe that wasn't quite true for she now realised her entire family knew about her and how she came to exist. But being born out of wedlock didn't constitute a reason to be murdered. How was it her fault her biological parents had an affair?

Deep in her gut, she knew her mind would never give her rest unless she found out the truth. All of it. Which meant a detour to Athens on her way home. Since she had dragged her eyelids apart at the sound of the alarm on her mobile phone, the detour to Athens had been on her mind. She had tossed numerous arguments for and against, desperate to figure out the best way to confront the man. Somehow she would need security. Hmm, she could hire a personal bodyguard. She snorted at the thought. Little old Vicky Saunders, who was nothing more than a mother and legal advisor on the end of a telephone line, needed a bodyguard. It was beyond ridiculous. Bodyguards were for royalty or highfalutin movie stars and high society people who were always in the news, not common everyday mums who kept to themselves.

She turned left into Winter Ave, hurried to number five

and strode up the steps. This time the door opened before she had a chance to lift the brass knocker. Put on your big girl pants, Vicky Saunders. Make out you are delighted to be here, be nice, smile. She attempted to swallow her negativity by forcing a smile, spreading the corners of her mouth wide. 'Hi, I am so glad to see you again. How is Costas today?'

'The same but anxious to see you. Come in.' Dora stepped aside to let Vicky in then closed the door behind them.

'In the kitchen?' Vicky asked, heading towards the rear regardless.

'Nearly always,' said Dora from behind. 'He is most comfortable by the range where I can keep an eye on him.'

'My dear,' Costas said, his eyes lighting up in pleasure when she stepped into the kitchen which today seemed to be overwarm. 'Come here, sit by me,' he added as eager hands reached out to take hers in a warm grip.

With her heart hitching at his obvious pleasure, Vicky forced everything about last night from her mind to give this frail man her heart and soul while she was here. He deserved as much enjoyment of life as she could give, especially now she knew his time was so short. 'It is so lovely to see you again. You have no idea how happy you have made me. Thank you for last night. I am certain I won't be able to recall everyone's name but now I know I have such an extensive family they will live in my heart forever.' She leant over to give the man a hug, careful not to dislodge his lifesaving tubes. 'And just so you know,' she sat back in her chair keeping hold of his gnarled fingers, 'as soon as Gina has finished her final exams I will bring her to London to meet you all. We will be able to spend three months here before she begins university.'

'Oh, how wonderful,' said Dora, as she paused in tea-making activity.

When she saw the moisture wash across her uncle's eyes, Vicky's own eyes itched with tears. With her emotions still raw from her breakdown in her hotel room it was difficult to hold them back. Change the subject, she chided herself. 'Now I have a question for you. How come I have two different birth certificates? Surely my French one, which is the real one, was enough.'

'Your father's name is written on the original. For Georgia to hide you, we decided you needed an entirely new identity.'

'But how did you get away with it? I would have been a few months old when the second one was formalised. Certainly not a newborn.'

'Georgia and Tim went to the registry office with their wedding certificate a week after they married. Told them it was a sudden home birth the day after they married with no time to get to the hospital. The registry office didn't want to see you. It was a lot easier than they thought it would be. Georgia took you to Australia the day after both of your passports arrived.' We sent her by sea, a wooden chest filled with only the important things she needed.'

Trying to absorb his words, Vicky sat back with her eyes shut and both hands gripping the sides of her face. So much information to make sense of. When she opened her eyes again, Dora slid a full teacup in front of her. 'Thank you,'

Vicky said although she didn't feel like any refreshment. Be nice, a voice in her head said, so she took a tiny sip.

'We have translated the diaries. It took a while. Young Sophia helped us by typing everything on the computer. They are not daily entries but it appears Georgia only wrote important details when they happened over the years. The first started not long after she was raped. There are things in them which we did not know, including the name of the man who molested her. I think writing everything down was her way of healing but some of the entries were a shock to us. You need to study them.'

A fist clamped around her heart. After last night's bombshell, Vicky knew what one of those entries was going to be about. 'Thank you, I will read them with utmost care but not right now. Now is our time to be family. Tell me whatever comes to mind or ask any questions you like.'

'The letters you gave us,' Costas jumped in. 'They were our annual Christmas letters about what had happened in the family during the year.'

'There were two different handwriting styles.'

'Yes, Lukas wrote the first few before he moved back to Greece to live and work. I wrote the rest. But this year, maybe I don't need to write one since you are here and dear Georgia is with God.'

Poor man looked so sad. Vicky grasped his hand, squeezed gently. 'I would love to receive one but only if you write it in English. It doesn't have to wait until Christmas. I will be delighted to receive one any time. And I promise to write back straight away. We need to make up for lost time.'

He squeezed her hand back in a death grip. 'There is so little time left for me.'

It was a struggle to hold back a fresh bout of threatening tears. To hide her angst, Vicky knelt in front of him. 'Every day is precious. You have to hang in there so you can meet Gina. Now, no more sadness. Today is a happy day.'

'We have photos. Would you like to see them?'

Vicky twisted her head up and around to Dora. 'Of course.' She wriggled her way back up into the chair. Within seconds two albums landed on the table in front of Vicky. It was obvious this little exercise had been planned. Trawling through photograph albums wasn't her favourite social activity but her breath stalled when she realised the albums contained a history of her own life. All those photos missing from the shoe box back home were stuffed into this record of her life from babyhood, through childhood, her teenage years, marriage, followed by Gina's life. Each photo had a little neatly printed description underneath. A stab of pain shafted through her heart at a picture of Mike, more so when she turned the page to find a photo taken at his funeral. Vicky had to pause as she ran her finger along the coffin. Seeing this picture hurt a whole heap more after last night's revelation. It should have been her in the coffin.

'Oh, God,' slipped out as she flipped over the page to get rid of the scene.

'I am so sorry,' came from Dora. 'Maybe this wasn't such a good idea.'

'It's okay,' Vicky stuttered before sniffing back her tears. 'Nothing will ever bring him back but it still hurts.' Soft, warm arms went around her and held tight. 'I keep telling my daughter we have to be thankful for having him in our lives for as long as we did. We need to remember and appreciate the good times,' she mumbled against Dora's shoulder, desperate to stay there, relishing in the most motherly embrace she could recall ever receiving.'

'Then let us talk about the good things.' Dora gently pushed Vicky's head back. 'Georgia wrote how wonderful Mike was as a husband and father. I think she was a little in love with him herself.' Dora's grin was contagious.

Vicky grinned back, swiping at the few tears which managed to escape. 'I think so too.'

'You loved him a great deal, didn't you?' Dora's face turned serious.

'Yes, very much.'

'I know this to be true. Your Gina was created from much love the same way you were created from the deep love between your parents. Stupid traditional customs and a bitter man forced your parents apart but I know you were born from love. Your father came here looking for her but already Sophia was dead and you were in Australia. He didn't know about you and we didn't tell him because of the evil threats from his father. You were our family's priority, keeping you safe.'

'Thank you.' Vicky went in for another hug before saying her goodbyes. There was a mad scramble to hand over the diaries and letters along with a wad of neatly typed translations which she managed to stuff into her small travel backpack. It wrenched her innards to see their disappointment when she informed them she was flying out the next day. 'I don't want to go but must. I have a daughter at home and a job I need to get back to. I promise I will be back late November. Cross my heart.' She grinned as she made a childish cross sign over her chest. Somehow, she didn't think it was wise to tell them she was making a detour to Athens on her way home. After her emailing session with Marty, she had plans to confront both Kristian and Vasilis Nesbloutas. This sadistic relentless pursuit had to stop.

Twenty-Seven

The cab was as tired as the driver looked. The seat was shiny and flat from thousands of backsides which had slid across the vinyl, compressed the stuffing and constantly buffed the surface to a slippery sheen. But inside was clean as though this car was vacuumed and polished at the end of each shift. A slight aroma of cleanser and polish was pleasant to the nose but there was a putrid sweet smell emanating from the Christmas tree shaped air freshener which hung from the inside rear-vision mirror. Two and fro it swung, in time with the meter ticking over as though they were mechanically joined.

Outside, the dry heat was already stifling and dusty, despite it not yet 10 a.m. It had been a relief to settle into the air-conditioned taxi after only a short wait standing on the kerb outside the hotel. The temperature was no different to a summer day back in Perth but was a bit much to handle after the wet autumn day when she had flown out from Australia and an even cooler, damper few spring days in England.

Every second shop they passed was an eatery of some sort, abutting clothes and shoe boutiques, pharmacies and souvenir galleries. Some had wares which spilled onto the sidewalk while others barely had a window large enough to display their goods. The buildings looked old and classical in style with stone, marble or rendered frontages. Here bright colours seemed only to be attracted to doors and window frames, giving life to earth-hued buildings.

Despite the heat, the city bustled. Much more than yesterday when she had walked the streets for a few hours after a rest day to catch up on sleep, study the translations and send frantic emails to Marty. Besides, it had been Sunday when businesses were closed and the only address she had for Kristian Nesbloutas, was a business address.

Traffic this morning was chaotic. If drivers were following road rules, those rules were incomprehensible to Vicky but the locals seemed to know what they were doing. Despite regular beeps from horns and more near misses than Vicky wanted to think about, there were no bingles. More than once her seat belt was tested, jerking tight to keep her plastered to the back of the seat when brakes were stomped on. Thank goodness her driver took things in his stride and wasn't aggressive with fist pumps and curses.

Two-legged traffic seemed to be orderly congestion, hurrying along footpaths in two opposing lanes until they milled at crosswalks in a heavy pause before they streamed in various directions over intersections. There were often news reports back home about the number of refugees who had fled war-torn countries to seek a safe haven in peaceful countries like Greece. The thousands of people with African or Middle Eastern appearance who begged or tried to sell cheap wares from ragged stalls or simply stood around looking haunted, was a shock, giving grim realism to the reports. It had been the same in London but here in Athens it appeared to be much worse. So many people torn from their homeland, who wanted nothing more than to feel safe with a better life. With such an influx of desperate people, what were their chances in a country so overwhelmed with homelessness and poverty?

When the taxi came to a jolting halt, Vicky sent a questioning glance to the driver's image staring at her in the rear-vision mirror.

'There.' The single heavily accented word was accompanied by a finger pointed to her right.

Vicky swung her head around. The building was much like all those they had passed but was obviously an office block with dark marble pillars supporting four storeys. In the centre, modern, tall glass doors reflected the bustle of the street and opposite pathway.

'How much?' she asked although the meter gave the amount. Handing over a Euro note of almost double the value she added, 'Keep the change.' After she managed to unfold stiff, tired legs from the cramped rear door, she stood, stretched and let her eyes roam up and down the building. It wasn't new, with classical Greek Corinthian pillars but looked to be well-maintained. Two well-worn marble steps upwards gave a truer indication of the age but they were clean with a small puddle residing in a foot-worn dip from an early morning wash-down. Now she knew a little about one of the business owners, she figured he would only have offices in an upper-class building. Amazing what one could learn from the internet.

Before she was game to take the first step up, Vicky drew in a long, deep breath, letting her chest expand and shoulders rise before slowly releasing it through a pursed mouth. Despite willing her body to relax, her stomach clenched as she ascended the steps and shoved the door with one outstretched hand.

Inside was modern elegance with polished black marble floor tiles, stainless steel fittings and a gorgeous, polished wood reception desk. Since there was nobody in attendance Vicky searched for clues as to where she was supposed to go. A list of businesses to the left of elevator doors told her she needed level two. *Nesbloutas Industries.* Vicky pressed the button, stood back and waited with her breath held. Inside the carpeted car, she leant against the back wall, willing her stomach to quit broiling. She couldn't recall ever being this scared in her life. A ping, the car stopped, doors whooshed apart. Vicky opened her eyes, stepped out and stared at yet another reception desk, this one attended by a middle-aged woman who wore typical business attire of a white blouse under a smart black jacket. What she wore below was hidden behind the desk.

Every nerve in her body tied itself into knots as she approached the desk, now knowing what it felt like to approach a guillotine. A welcome in foreign words was spouted.

'I don't speak Greek.' When her words came out husky, she cleared her throat.

'Can I help you?' The woman's English was excellent with barely an accent.

'I would like to speak to Kristian Nesbloutas, please.'

'Do you have an appointment?'

'No.'

'I am sorry but Mr Nesbloutas is very busy. He cannot be disturbed. You must have an appointment.'

'It is important. I have come a long way.'

'Sorry, but it is impossible.'

'I have something which belongs to him. It will only take a minute. Can you please ask him if he can spare a single minute... half a minute?'

'I can pass anything you have on to him.'

A vision of the necklace centred in her brain. More than a million dollars. No way could she entrust such an expensive piece of jewellery to anyone but the owner and it had to go back to him since it was listed on an international stolen register – something else she had searched for and found. With a will of its own, her hand reached into her pocket, burrowed under the tissues to finger the warm gemstones. 'I can't. It is only to be handed over in person. Please. Could you please ring him? It won't hurt to ask. It is of vital importance.'

Her plea must have worked for the woman lifted a telephone receiver, spoke in Greek, turned to Vicky. 'Your name?'

Her name. Vicky Saunders would mean nothing to this man. Inspiration hit. 'Tell him... Sophia Lebtos.' Stunned at her own audacity, Vicky spun around, ready to flee. It was amazing how heightened her senses were for she heard a door swing open, followed immediately by quick footsteps which came closer and closer, each step a tad louder and each step pinged her nerves tighter and tighter. This man was her father, for heaven's sake. A man who never wanted anything to do with her... wanted her aborted. He sent spies to ransack her mother's house in search of valuable jewels. Which he must be desperate to get back since it had been listed as stolen.

Her shoulder was grasped, tugging her around. A hiss came from compressed lips. 'You are not Sophia. How dare you pretend.'

Anger bubbled up from deep down at the fierceness of the man's stare. 'No, Sophia is dead, murdered by your father.'

'Excuse me?' The shock on her father's face could not have been staged. He reeled back a few steps, found his balance and straightened.

Vicky felt sure her own face showed the same amount of stunned amazement for she was staring at an older version of herself. Same colour hair, same eyes, same skin tone, same shaped face only hers was far more feminine and he was way taller with a dark shadow already covering his beard line. It took a moment to gather her wits together. Before she lost all of her courage she plunged her hand into her pocket, fisted the necklace and held it out. 'Since you recognised Sophia's name maybe you will also recognise this.' She dropped it onto the reception desk turned and rushed towards the elevator door, desperate to get the hell out of there. 'Now you can call off your henchmen and leave me and my daughter alone,' she called over her shoulder as she stabbed at the button.

Her arm was grabbed from behind. 'Where did you get this? What henchmen? What are you talking about?'

His hand bit into her upper arm as he twisted her around. 'Please, we need to talk. I need to know how you got this. Who are you?'

'You know who I am since you sent your men to steal this

from me.' She pointed to the necklace dangling from her father's fingers.

His head shook rapidly from side to side. 'I have no idea what you mean. I don't have a clue who you are but obviously you have something to do with Sophia or else you wouldn't be here or have this necklace in your possession. And I don't have any of your so-called henchmen. Why would I need them? It's not the way I work. And since you are obviously from another country with that accent of yours, how can I possibly know anything about you? Come, we need to talk. There is a little trattoria over the road. Join me for coffee so we can make sense of things.' He turned and spoke rapid Greek to the receptionist, but still he had hold of Vicky's arm although his grip had lessened to firm rather than biting, as though he didn't dare let her go. The necklace went into his trousers' pocket before he punched the elevator button.

When the elevator doors opened, her arm was released but a splayed hand guided her inside. Vicky couldn't figure out how she felt. This was her father, for goodness sake. The father she had searched for all of her life. The father who never wanted her. Joy vied with regret and anger and surprise and relief and every other emotion she could think of. Things got blurry and she realised tears had flooded her eyes. She fought them back. This man didn't deserve her tears.

The doors opened, the hand returned to her back, guiding her across the marble tiles, through the doorway and remained there while they waited on the kerb for a gap in the traffic. A slight nudge and she strode across two lanes of bitumen, onto the opposite pavement, into the wide opening of an eatery. Large posters of ancient Athens' landmarks adorned the walls. Well-worn wood of the tables gleamed with polish. Bare wood floors were brushed clean but held aged scrapes and chips from chairs and table legs. A loud screech from a chair being pulled – she fumbled as she sat. She lifted her head as her father settled into the chair opposite.

'Coffee?' he asked, his voice sending something squishy to her innards.

'Please, with milk.' Vicky couldn't help studying his face, a familiar face.

'Something to eat? Maybe baklava.'

'That would be nice, thank you.' Baklava was something she knew, something she liked so why not although she didn't think she would be able to swallow a single crumb when her throat seemed to have something wedged in it and her stomach clenched so tight she wanted to throw up.

Order given to a young waiter, her father settled back in his chair, staring at her. 'Now, who are you and don't tell me I know for I don't even though there is something familiar about you.'

She squirmed at his words. Surely he could recognise himself if she had seen the similarity so quickly. 'Vicky Saunders.'

'And you are from where?' He seemed to be studying her face. How long before he realised?

'Australia, Perth to be exact.'

'Somewhere I have never had to good fortune to visit. Now I need to know where you got this necklace from.'

'I found it in my mother's effects a week ago.'

He stilled as a deep frown formed. 'What is your mother's name?'

'Regina Wakefield.' Vicky wasn't sure whether or not to disclose more.

'Not a name I am familiar with which leaves me with a quandary. This necklace. How did your mother come by it?' He drew it out from his pocket, spread it across the table. 'And how did it lead you to me?'

'You recognise the necklace?'

'Yes, I gave it to the woman I loved.'

'Sophia Lebtos.'

'Yes, but how did you know?'

'There were some papers, letters, notes, diaries hidden in boxes, which I found after my mother passed away a few weeks back. This note gave me a clue.' Vicky delved into her backpack, withdrew the papers she had brought with her, flicked through the pile and withdrew his letter to Sophia. She opened it out, held it out to him and watched as he read it.

'Sophia,' hissed from his breath on an anguished moan. He glanced at Vicky but his face had changed from anger to sadness. 'My name is not on this.'

'But you wrote it and gave Sophia the necklace.'

'Yes. I went searching for her afterwards. I was told she had died.'

'Yes she died in France. It has taken me a lot of research to find out the truth. She was deliberately run down in the street in Paris.' Vicky paused, sucked in a breath while she peeked under her eyelashes to see his reaction. 'By your father. He murdered her.'

He shot from his chair, knocking it to the floor with an almighty clatter. 'You lie. You cannot possibly know such an horrendous thing. My father is not the nicest of men but he would never do such a thing.'

Vicky searched through the papers, took out the relevant diary. 'Maybe you need to read this. I had it translated for me. There is a witness statement in the entries.' It had taken her too long to read the translations yesterday, in between long email conversations with Marty.

It took a few seconds before her father made the decision to pick up his chair and sit. While he scoured the diary entries, their coffee was served, his of the Greek variety while hers was a large cup of what looked to be cappuccino. Vicky sipped, stirred in the froth and sipped again, barely tasting it, all the while eyeing her father's face, waiting for the moment when he figured out who she was. Her gut believed him when he said he had no idea who she was which was a bit of a relief. Maybe he really didn't know she had been born.

Two plates were placed in the centre of the table. The baklava looked and smelt far better than any she had eaten back home. Vicky drew one plate towards herself, picked up the tiny cake fork and sliced off a corner. It was so moist, it dripped. She slid the corner onto her tongue, tasted and felt like drooling. God, but this was a little bit of paradise. Still watching, she ate until she had to scrape the remnants from the plate because it was too delicious to waste even a skerrick. The fork paused in mid-air when she noticed the man in front of her stiffen.

'She had the baby, my baby, my daughter? *The ei mou*, I do not believe this.'

Vicky was certain the words were not meant to be heard. They were sighs of surprise and wonder. So, he really didn't know. Tears threatened again making it fuzzy when he lifted his eyes, stared at her.

'You?'

She could do nothing but nod.

'You are my daughter? Kristina?' He buried his face in his hands, choked out something she couldn't understand, then wiped one hand down his face. When he looked at her again, his eyes were definitely awash with tears. '*The ei mou*, I had no idea. I...' He reached across the table, grasped her hands in his. 'I am so sorry. I never knew. Why did no-one tell me? I can't believe this. But you said your name is Vicky.'

'My name was changed to protect me. I never knew either until two days ago.'

'Protection? Why did you need protection? From whom?'

'Your father.'

'Excuse me? No, this I don't believe.'

'He knew. He threatened the woman who raised me. If I ever showed up he would do the same to me as he did to Sophia. Sophia's sister, Georgia, raised me. She also changed her name by deed poll, took me to Australia. But after a few years he found her, threatened her so I was never told the truth. I only discovered the truth after finding a whole heap of papers in a chest after Mum... Georgia died a few weeks ago. And the necklace. It was in a shoe box.'

His mouth gaped, closed, opened and closed again. 'I

don't know what to say. I need a minute.' He gulped down his coffee in one swoop, drew his food close, pushed it away again. It took a few minutes with him flicking through pages of the diary, glancing at her, drumming a finger on the scarred wood of the table while seeming to think before he seemed to relax and settle back into the seat. 'I am so shocked I cannot think clearly but I am delighted you managed to find me. I am overwhelmed with joy to have you here but also I am sad because I never knew. Why did I never learn about you?'

'Your father's edict. Apparently I was never to be told.'

'Why? You are my child. I don't understand. Maybe if I explain what happened, both of us may be able to make sense of all this.' He glanced at his food. 'Here, I can't eat this, you have it.' He pushed the baklava towards her but with her nerves so on edge she didn't think it would be wise to eat more.

'I was several years younger than Sophia when I met her at the university here in Athens. She was studying for her PhD in Greek history. I loved her from the minute I met her. We dated but my parents didn't know. You see, it was arranged from a young age for me to marry someone else. Tradition. The old ways. My father found out about our relationship. Anger is not a good word to describe how he reacted. Fury would be a better word. He threatened to disown me and cause trouble for Sophia if I didn't stay away from her. But already she was pregnant... with you.' He smiled at the same time he lifted her hands from the table and gently rubbed his thumbs across her skin. 'My daughter,' he murmured as though in awe.

'I begged my mother to intervene because I knew in my heart that my love for Sophia was the best. She owned my heart and still, to this day, lives in it. But Mama was more of a pawn in my father's abusive demanding ways than I was. I must point out, he was, still is, a cruel man. For Sophia's safety, I had to let her go. I had no choice. We talked, discussed every detail. Sophia understood. I gave her money, a ticket for Paris. Mama helped to hide everything from my father. Mama understood but she was helpless. Our wealth came from my mother's family, not my father's. He was a pauper, married my mother only for money. He lied about his past and pretended he had vast wealth. He was a true gentleman until after I was born, their only child. It was then his abuse began to the extent Mama refused to have any more children, refused to share his bed. She has since divorced him because of his cruelty. My father negotiated my marriage with the daughter of one of his cronies, a man whose wealth would have benefitted my father in some shonky business deal. I didn't know until I was twenty. Hated the idea, disliked the family, knew they were not the most honest of people. I later learned they operated against the law.'

'Where does the necklace fit in?' asked Vicky.

'My grandmother, Mama's mother, left it to me when she died. She had extreme wealth, left to her by her husband. It was to be given to my wife. In my heart, Sophia was my wife, still is. I wanted her to have it, to use it to give her a good life. It was her idea to have an abortion, not mine.' He caught Vicky's eye. 'I never wanted you to be aborted but Sophia insisted, I think because her heart was broken, like mine.' His eyes closed as he lifted his face to the ceiling. '*The ei mou*, I am so glad she didn't go ahead with it. You are our daughter, born of such sweet true love.' Tears washed across his eyes again, causing her own tears to re-appear. 'I have missed so much,' he cried in anguish, causing her heart to tumble-turn.

'I agreed to the arranged marriage under a great deal of sufferance but the woman, my promised fiancée, was in love with another man. She refused to marry me. I was overjoyed, agreed to accept the blame for us not marrying, which caused a furore with my family, especially my father. I went in search for Sophia but I couldn't find her. I ended up hunting down her family, found her brother but was devastated when I was told Sophia had died. I was not given any details. He was an angry man, blamed me for her death but gave me no explanations. Now, if what you say is true, I understand his anger. My heart was shattered to the extent I was not interested in marriage until I met my wife many years later. She was in much the same place as me. Her fiancée had been killed in a work accident. She loved him as much as I loved Sophia. We dated, both knowing the other's heart belonged to someone else but grew to enjoy each other's company and decided marriage would work. We have learned to love each other but not with the same intensity we had with our true loves. A more gentle love borne from friendship and respect. We have three children, two girls and a boy.' He grinned. 'You have a brother and two sisters but they are quite a few years younger than you.' He drew his wallet from a pocket, opened it out.

Vicky's eyes boggled at the picture. 'Sweet mercy,' gushed

out. 'This one,' she pointed to a girl in the centre, 'is the spitting image of my daughter.'

'You have a daughter?' He looked puzzled for a second. 'Yes, you said daughter earlier.' He grinned. 'I have a granddaughter? The shocks keep coming. Do you have a photo?'

'Sure but get ready for another shock.' Vicky took out her mobile phone, punched, slid, searched and brought up a recent photo of Gina. She handed the phone over.

'*The ei mou,* she looks so much like my Sophia.'

'Sophia?'

He grinned. 'Yes, I named my daughter after your mama. My wife's idea. Our son, Nickos, is named after the man she loved. You did not bring your daughter with you?'

'No, she is in her final year at school. She can't afford time away from her studies. Wants to be a lawyer, like her father.'

'And your husband? He could not come either?'

Vicky slid her eyes closed at the sudden onset of pain. 'He died three years ago,' she said, choking on the words.

Her hand was taken again. 'I am so sorry. You loved him a great deal?'

'Yes, he was an amazing man, the best.'

'Then maybe you will understand my love for Sophia for it was of the kind a person can never recover from. The agony goes but there is always a twinge in the corner of your heart. And now, we have so much more to discuss.' He paused, eyed her, shook his head. 'My daughter. I still cannot believe this. I wish for us to spend the rest of the day together. I want you to meet my family which is also your family. There is so much for us to talk about. I want to know everything about you.'

'But you are busy.'

'I have already told my receptionist to cancel all of my meetings for the day. When I heard Sophia's name and saw the necklace I knew I would not be able to concentrate on work with so many memories taking over my mind. But now the reason has changed. Nothing can ever be as important as spending time with my daughter.' He laughed, a disbelieving type of scoff. 'I still cannot believe you are here, that you even exist. Come.' He rose, took her hand and stepped around the table. 'I need your permission to hold you close, feel you in my arms. Please?'

When he held his arms wide, Vicky stepped into them. She was tugged close, her head against his heart. She heard his heartbeats, thundering like her own. A bevy of emotions over-whelmed her. Unbidden tears welled. She fought them back but they tumbled out. A kiss landed on her head. 'My sweet daughter,' she heard before he stepped back, held her at arms-length and eyed her with eyes as wet as her own. Everything inside her felt like it was going to explode with emotion.

'I still find this hard to believe but now I know why you look familiar. It is like looking in the mirror when I was a few years younger. But I can see Sophia in you as well. *The ei mou*, this is unbelievable. I should have asked for I do not know of your plans. Are you able to spend time with me?'

'I hadn't planned on it...'

'No, why not?' He looked hurt.

'I always believed my father knew about me but wanted nothing to do with me. I hated you because you didn't care I was even alive. All I was going to do was give you the necklace and leave.'

'But why? The necklace belongs to you, not me. It was a gift to your mother.'

'There is a world-wide report about it being stolen. The jeweller I took it to, to get it valued, suggested I would never be able to sell it. If I tried I would be arrested. I figured if I gave it back to you, you could take it off the stolen list.'

'I don't understand. It was mine to do with as I pleased. I certainly never registered it as stolen. Nobody knew I gave it to Sophia and it was nobody's business.'

'But men, private investigators from Greece, came. They destroyed my mother's house searching for it. When they didn't find it they broke into my house.'

He reeled back. 'Believe me, they were not sent by me. I knew nothing about you so how could I send people to look for a necklace?'

'Maybe, your father. He knew.'

'My father? *The ei mou*, I will kill him if this is true.'

'You didn't read all the diary. My mother… Georgia… gosh, I get so confused about what to call everyone now. Further in the diary, she details how Sophia died. She saw it happen. Your father spoke to her, threatened her, threatened me… you need to read it all.' She was dragged against his chest again, preventing her from saying more.

'Maybe you will let me keep it for tonight? I need to know everything.' He held her out again. 'Now, will you come with me. Meet my wife and my mama. She is frail but still alive and will be delighted to meet you. Please?'

Family. It was such a difficult concept to understand. She had never been a part of an extensive family with brothers, sisters, grandparents or even a father. It felt weird. The largest family she had ever experienced was with Mike, her and Gina. Well add on her mother who now wasn't even her real mother but an aunt. So much had changed, had turned her life upside down and inside out. 'Okay, yes, I would like to meet them.' What else could she say?

'Come. We will go in my car. It is not far.'

All the while she fielded innumerable questions about her life, Vicky took in the passing scenery, especially once they moved from the congestive city crawl to a less crowded area her father called Alimos. It was a pleasant surprise to see the brilliant blue of the ocean as they drove along the highway, especially since they hadn't been driving very long. But Vicky figured, after she managed to visualise a map of Greece, Athens was not very far from the coast in any direction since it sat in a peninsula. Her eyes boggled when they turned into a massive driveway and pulled up in front of a mansion which overlooked the water.

'You live here?' Vicky asked.

'Yes, why?' came from over her shoulders as she stared at the gorgeous scenery. A perfectly manicured garden filled with various shades of green and a rainbow of bright colours from flowers tumbling over each other in flower beds, sat along the front of the white brick fence. Behind was the ocean with barely a white crest of wave, the water was so still. Above it the sky was even brighter giving realism to the word azure.

Vicky turned back, scanned the front of the stark white, two-storey building in front of her. Five wide, semi-circular steps led up to a massive carved door. Groomed potted shrubs sat on each end of all five steps, which looked to be marble. Evenly spaced large windows glinted sunlight back at her.

'This place is ginormous.'

'Our family home. *Papou*, my grandfather, built it for my grandmother. It was passed to my mother and now me. Mama still lives here with us. This would have been your home had I known about you. My regrets will live in my heart for the rest of my life. Come.'

Vicky watched him alight, watched him walk around the front of the car. She should get out but something, fear, probably, held her super-glued to the seat. The passenger door opened. A hand wavered in front of her face. Her eyes closed as she tried in vain to calm nerves which raced full-pelt. None of this was what she had expected and she wasn't sure she was ready to meet family she had done without all of her life. Weird, she felt downright weird as though she had been transported to some alternate world. Maybe she had landed in the twilight zone between worlds.

She heard a rustle at her side a split second before her hand was grasped. 'You seem uncertain,' her father said.

'To be honest, I am terrified.'

'Why?'

'Everything about the past few weeks has turned my life upside down. I don't even know who I am any more. I now have two different birth certificates, with different names and different birth dates, from different countries. My mother wasn't my mother, nor was my so-called father. I have never had a man in my life to call Dad. I...'

'You can call me Dad,' he said as he gently tugged her from the car, took both of her hands, stood back, eyed her with a half-smile on his face then tugged her into his arms again, hugging tight. 'You have no idea how much I would like to hear you call me Papa as my other children do but I realise Dad is the word used in your country.' He stepped back again. 'But if you find it too difficult, how about using my name, Kristian. Whatever you are most comfortable with. This entire situation is as hard for me to believe as it is for you. I am still in a state of shock, finding it difficult to believe you are really here.'

'But don't you have any doubts? I could be making all this up. People do.'

He laughed. 'How can I doubt you when you look so much like me, have Sophia's necklace and so much proof. Even more, our daughter's look as though they are twins so we must have the same genes. We could do a DNA test if you like but, *kore mou*, my daughter, I already know the result.'

A splayed hand settled against Vicky's back which told her she had no choice but to head up the five steps to her doom. Nerves, muscles, sinews, blood vessels, all twisted and tautened into an uncomfortable tangle when the door opened and they stepped inside. Her held breath whooshed out at the magnificence of the vast entry hall with a wide staircase heading up to the next level and four open doorways leading to various rooms, one to each side and two either side of the stairwell. This was no ordinary up-market house. This was a magnificent mansion.

'You must be wealthy,' slipped from her lips. 'Oops, sorry,' she added as she glanced up to see his shock turn into a smile.

'Yes, very, but you must have known this.'

'No, I knew nothing about you until my uncle told me

two days ago. I had no idea you were my father. I was always told and believed it was a man called Timothy Wakefield. My uncle never mentioned anything about money. Well, he did but I thought it was your father he was talking about. I don't even know what you do. He did say you owned a business but my local grocer owns a business. It doesn't mean he is wealthy.'

'I am in the process of selling off the various branches of my company so I can retire and spend time to travel, relax and enjoy the company of my wife instead of always working. Marika,' he called, but he didn't stop, instead guiding Vicky to the doorway on the right of the steps. The room behind was vast, furnished to look like what she would call a family room with comfy looking couches and chairs set in a semi-circle around an enormous flat screen. None of the items looked as though they came from the sort of furniture warehouse she bought furniture from. Everything in here looked to be of a quality Vicky could only dream about. The house might be old and classical on the outside but the inside was elegantly modern.

'Kristian... oh.' A petite dark-haired woman paused mid-stride, staring at Vicky. Her eyes didn't move from examining Vicky while explanations were made, but they widened at the same time her jaw dropped at the word, daughter.

For long seconds, Vicky couldn't make out whether the woman was angry, happy or plain stunned, pretty much how Vicky had felt for the past week so she understood the shock on the woman's face.

'Sophia's daughter? Your daughter?' Marika finally said in

such a way it gave Vicky the impression anger was the predominant emotion.

The silence said so much. Vicky slid her eyes shut, waiting for an outburst of angry words. The earth opening up and swallowing her would be a fantastic thing right now. It had been a humungous mistake to come here, to even think she would be accepted. Oh. God, why hadn't she done what she had intended and fled after dropping the necklace on the counter?

'This is a mistake. I think I should leave,' she said a split second before she spun on her heel and raced through the doorway, across the entry hall to the main door. Before she could grasp the handle, a large hand spread out on the panelling above her head.

'No, you cannot leave when we have so much to talk about. Why do you run?'

Vicky had to suck in her breath to fight back another bout of tears. She wanted to answer but didn't have a clue what to say. 'I feel as though I am intruding. I don't belong here.' Every impulse to run and keep running was tempered with an even stronger desire to stay, to get to know this man, her father.

'No,' a female voice said at the same time a smaller hand grasped Vicky's wrist. 'Of course you are welcome. I am sorry you felt unwelcome by my reaction but this was such a shock; I think to us all. It took me a minute to process what Kristian said. Come. Please come inside.' The hand tugged gently, turning Vicky around. A warm smile greeted her, which eased her discomfort a little but still her stomach was making a great impression of being a tornado.

With her father one side and Marika the other, both with a hand on her, Vicky had no choice but to walk between them, back through the door into the family room. She was led to a large leather lounge chair. Both waited, one either side until she sat. Her father dragged a matching chair across the room until it was on an angle within touching distance. A slight *whoof,* echoed as he plopped into the seat, sending up a pleasant leathery aroma. It was kind of comical the way he settled in so close, as if to prevent her from fleeing again. Marika hovered by his side.

'Would you like something to eat or drink,' Marika asked, now with a smile which meant her hesitancy must have disappeared.

'Thank you but no, we have not long had coffee,' her father said before Vicky had a chance to open her mouth. 'Join us,' he added, as he indicated the two-seater sofa on the other side of Vicky.

'Are you sure?'

It warmed Vicky's heart to think Marika was considerate enough to think father and daughter wanted to be alone. Maybe she wasn't so angry at the sudden imposition. Vicky glanced at her, smiled and indicated the sofa. 'Please join us. And you are right, finding out I have a real live father after so many years of believing an entirely different story has been more than a shock. I still can't believe it even though I know it is true. It feels like I am in the middle of some fantasy tale because everything about what I have learned in the past few days is so unbelievable.' She caught Marika's eye. 'I have a stepmother, two sisters and a brother when two days ago, I had no-one except my daughter. On Sophia's side I have two uncles, their wives and a bevy of cousins I never knew existed.' Her head fell into her hands. 'I feel so overwhelmed.'

'Why don't you start at the beginning? Tell us everything,' her father said. 'I can fill in my side as we go.'

For the first time since she had arrived, Vicky forced her body to relax. She fell back into the soft cushions of the leather. Unsure where to begin, she briefly outlined her life up until Regina died. Her story became more detailed when she related the past three weeks. Despite her father saying he would fill in, he said little apart from asking a few questions when she glossed over things and he wanted more detail. The more she talked, the more comfortable she felt. Somehow, talking seemed to release built up tension. 'So, here I am,' she said at the end.

'And I am beyond glad you found me,' her father said as he leant forwards and gripped her hand. 'We have lost so much, will never make up for what is lost but you can be sure, you will be a big part of my life in the future. You and your daughter.' He sat back with a curious look on his face. 'I cannot believe I have a granddaughter who is not much younger than my own children.'

'Do you have a photograph?' Marika asked.

Vicky glanced at her father when he snorted. It was obvious he was trying not to laugh. She grinned back at him as she took her mobile phone from her pocket, logged onto her photo gallery and brought a recent shot of Gina to the screen.

When she leant over to hand the phone to Marika, the woman had a questioning look on her face. She probably wondered why her husband was so amused, Vicky thought.

'Oh, my,' came out on a shocked gasp from Marika. 'So like Sophia.'

'Do you think there is any doubt about Vicky's story?' her father asked as he settled back in his chair with a smug smile.

'Only the eyes are different,' Marika added, still studying the image.

'Gina has her father's eyes and his smile,' said Vicky.

'How old?' asked Marika.

'She turned seventeen in January.'

'Sophia is nineteen. Angeliki, twenty and Nickos is twenty-two.'

'So close together,' said Vicki with a stab of pain lancing her heart. How she would have loved the opportunity to have been able to have more children.

'I was forty when I married,' said her father. 'We wanted children before I was too old to enjoy them as youngsters.'

'And I was thirty-five with not so many years to be safely able to have a family,' added Marika. 'It was hard work when they were very young but once they went to school it was a blessing to have them so close in age. More so now.'

'But now,' her father stood, 'we have three more important things to address. First, I wish you to meet my mama but I need to have a word with her to prepare her. The shock may be too much for her fragile heart.' He smiled. 'My heart is still recovering and my brain is attempting to catch up. Next, we have to solve this problem.' He drew the necklace from his pocket, ignoring the gasp from Marika. 'I honestly don't know how it could have been declared as stolen but I will find out. Vicky, this belongs to you. It was a gift to your mother and you are her heir. I promise it will be returned to you to do with as you wish.'

'It's not something I would ever wear, especially since the jeweller told me the value is astronomical. I would be too scared to even take it out of a bank vault and besides, I never go to any sort of formal function where such an item could be worn.'

'Then maybe you could sell it. I am certain the money would be of far more use to you.'

An unladylike snort escaped through Vicky's nose at the very idea of her having a clue how to sell such an item. 'I wouldn't know how. I don't live in your kind of world.'

Her father jerked back. 'Was that an insult?'

'Oh, no, of course not. I… oh, heck… how do I explain? Georgia struggled financially to raise me. She worked hard as a shop assistant, earning nothing more than a basic wage. At the same time she saved hard for the occasional treat. Wealth was never a word we could use to describe any aspect of our life. We didn't live… oh, far out, I'm making a hash of this.'

One arm swept her close in a hug. 'I understand. But the necklace belongs to you. Let me sort things about it being listed as stolen but finally, there is the issue of my father. If what you say is true, he must pay for his crimes. I need to tell you, I have not seen or spoken to the man for many years. He is an evil man; an abuser, a cheat, a liar but I never thought he would resort to murder.' He paused at an even louder gasp from Marika, turned and nodded to her. 'Vicky has been told he murdered Sophia. Says there is proof, which I still need to study to verify. But with everything I have learnt so far, I am afraid her story is true, which cuts at my heart to know his blood flows through my veins.'

'I would believe it.' The harsh statement from this serene woman was a shock. Vicky stared at her. 'He is the nastiest man I have ever met,' Marika added as she knelt on the floor in front of Vicky. 'I have never allowed my children to speak with him. He is never welcome in this house.'

Vicky could think of nothing to say but rampant thoughts tussled with each other while they galloped through her mind. The story must be true. If he is so mean, it must have been him who sent the private investigators. He must be the reason all these secrets were kept. But still she thought, if the police had been told, surely they could have brought the man to task, ended his tyranny.

'Let us not even think of the devil. Marika, how about taking our guest to the kitchen for some refreshment while I speak to Mama? It is past time for lunch.' He strode away, through a door at the end of the room.

Twenty-Nine

The tiny woman who sat amongst plumped-up pillows looked so frail with porcelain white skin so thin, blue veins were visible. Still thick hair was the silver-grey of steel but brown eyes sparkled as they bored into Vicky while she crossed the dense soft carpet. As she neared, the woman's eyes opened wider.

'Oh, my, so much like you, Kristian, when you were younger. Come here my dear, let me look at you.' Long, bony hands reached out and wavered as though begging Vicky to hurry. 'You are so beautiful,' she said in a voice much stronger than she looked, sounding as though she was as overawed as Vicky felt.

'Thank you.' Vicky knelt on the carpet, with a rush of something squishy flooding through her when her hands were gripped tight. She had a real live grandmother. Unbelievable. Words defied her. All Vicky could do was look and feel the warmth of this woman... her grandmother's fingers wrap around her hand. 'I've never had a grandmother before,' she managed to get out through a tight emotion-blocked throat.

'Yiayia, is the Greek for grandmother,' said her father as he drew up a chair next to them both.

'Yiayia,' Vicky repeated, smiling at this amazing woman while still trying to get her rampaging emotions under control. 'For thirty-seven years I have had a grandmother I never knew about.' Tears washed over her eyes but she managed to fight them back. 'I wish, with all my heart, things had been different. My daughter has a great yiayia.' She grinned, glanced at her father. 'I feel sure that wasn't right.'

'Progiagia,' he offered.

'You have a daughter?' Her grandmother's eyes lit up.

'Yes, her name is Gina.'

'Show her a picture,' said her father.

For the third time in as many hours, Vicky pulled up the same photo and turned her phone around.

'Oh, my goodness, so like Sophia.' She glanced up but peered over Vicky's shoulder. 'Ah, here comes our lunch. Please, my dear, you will eat with me so we can talk?'

Before Vicky could answer, her father said, 'We will all eat together. I don't want to miss a second of Vicky's presence.' He stood, moved across the room and carried a small table back, which he placed in front of his mother. Next, he arranged lounge chairs in a semi-circle.

Marika placed one dinner plate on the table and waited for Vicky to sit before she handed the other plate to Vicky. Immediately she turned and was back seconds later with two other plates. Chopped tomatoes, deseeded chunks of cucumber, red onion and sliced red pepper were topped with hunks of feta cheese and black olives, with olive oil and balsamic vinegar drizzled over in a typical Greek salad. A fork sat nestled to one side.

Eating seemed to take forever with so much chit-chat in between mouthfuls. So many questions were asked, much like Vicky's experience in London. It felt weird repeating so many facts of her life, facts these people should have known had circumstances been different. Long before Vicky had managed to eat half of her meal, she noticed how her grandmother began to flag with her eyelids drooping.

'Mama needs to rest. Her heart is not so strong nowadays. She tires often.' Her father stood, moved the table aside and gently assisted his mother from the chair. With her leant against him, she took tiny steps across the carpet. Before they passed through the doorway to what must have been her bedroom, her grandmother paused and turned around.

'Please forgive me for not being able to talk any longer. I know you are not here long but I beg you to come to see me before you leave.' She paused as though trying to find her breath. 'I have already made a place for you in my heart, my dear granddaughter.'

As she turned away, Vicky buried her head in her hands, overcome with a sensation of warmth and love for this ancient but still beautiful woman who was *her grandmother,* for goodness sake. It took a few minutes before Vicky was able to stand to help Marika clear the room of plates and forks and replace furniture to their homes, the indents in the carpet guiding her. While she assisted with dishes in the kitchen, her father re-appeared.

'I don't want to lose any time with you but I need to confront my father to find out the truth.'

Vicky almost dropped a plate when she jerked around. To save it from imminent destruction she slid it onto the sink. 'I want to come with you. I have his address.' Her father's eyebrows rose. 'I intended going there after we met this morning.

I have much to say to him. None of it pleasant. This torment he has put me through must stop – today. There is more I haven't told you about.'

'What do you mean?' He stalked closer, looking irate.

'My husband was a lawyer, in partnership with his best friend, Martin St James, who is now my lawyer and Gina's godfather. He and his lovely wife have been amazing friends and support since Mike died. Since I found out some shocking details in London and in those diaries written by Georgia, he and I have emailed information between us. I spent most of the last two nights and yesterday on the computer. Already he has made some enquiries, found scary information and I need to confront your father with what I know. Since you don't believe he would resort to murder, I think you, also, might receive a few more shocks.' She paused when a thought came to her. 'You don't happen to have a personal bodyguard do you?'

He reeled backwards at the same time Marika dropped a handful of cutlery onto the floor, the clatter on marble tiles, echoing. 'A bodyguard? Why?'

'Security.'

'My father is almost ninety-years-old. Harmless.'

A choking snort escaped Vicky's mouth. 'Not so harmless if he can commit murder and ransack houses although I believe he hires thugs to do some of his dirty work. If you say he is harmless maybe you can stand between him and me while we talk. Oh, and bring the necklace. I have a feeling he isn't going to appreciate you having it in your possession.' Vicky was as stunned as her father at the way she was acting but a new determination seemed to have overtaken her body. Crunch time. Time for payback which she knew would hit home with the old bastard after what Marty had found out over the past twenty-four hours. She owed Marty big-time for all the over-time hours he had put in on her behalf.

* * *

Her determination stayed with her until they stood in front of a small, terraced home which was squished between two others, none with the same elegance of her father's mansion, which was a bit of a shock. 'I expected something bigger, more up-market,' Vicky murmured as her father knocked on the door. 'My uncle said he was a rich man.'

'When my mother divorced him forty years ago, she paid him a substantial settlement to not contest the divorce. For a woman to divorce a man back then, in our culture, was not acceptable. I am unaware of what he did with the money. If he were wise, which I don't think he was, he would have invested it but I think he enjoyed the trappings of money too much to be wise. This is not the home he bought back then. I think he had to sell a much better home when money became short. This place does not surprise me.'

Her renewed bravado seemed to disappear in a flash when the door opened to a middle-aged woman. Vicky left all con-versation to her father, the rapid-fire Greek incomprehensible to her but there seemed to be a bit of confrontation because he ended up barging past the woman, tugging Vicky in after him. He stalked down a dingy dark passageway, paused at doorways only long enough to peer in. Vicky couldn't make out whether he was trying to figure out what each room was or whether he was simply looking for his father. The former, she thought, when she remembered he had told her there had been no contact between the two for many years. She almost ran into his back when he ground to a sudden halt at the doorway to a much brighter room.

'What... Kristian?' The voice was definitely an unwelcoming growl.

Her nerves returned with a vengeance by sending a wave of nausea rising up her gullet, Vicky wanted to turn around and flee but her hand was tugged and she was pulled inside the room, a kitchen at the back of the house, if she took into consideration the large windows above a long bench and sink. She had to swallow hard to keep the nausea centred in her stomach instead of half-way up her gullet. A grizzled old man sat at the table, a fierce frown taking up residence on his face. He didn't look anywhere near his age and a darn sight healthier than his ex-wife. It was weird the way the man winced when he saw her. His eyes flicked from her to the back door a mere two metres away from him. Good, he knew who she was and was scared but not half as scared as he was going to be.

Vicky dragged her eyes away from the man to take in the features of the room. It was neat and clean, probably courtesy of the woman who was now nowhere to be seen. Maybe hidden behind a corner, eavesdropping but if she was sensible she would have left.

A long wooden table in the centre looked good enough to be antique with a beautiful, polished patina covered only in the centre by a strip of embroidered linen. Eight matching chairs sat evenly spaced, three down each side and one on each end. Her eyes honed onto something on a shelf covered with odds and ends along with a pile of opened mail. She held back a gasp when she recognised something familiar it but it confirmed her suspicions. Not wanting to get caught she flicked her eyes back on the man.

'What are you doing here?' Vicky couldn't make out if Vasilis spoke to her or his son but she was going to take the lead.

'You know who I am.' It wasn't a question.

Vasilis looked away. 'No.'

'Liar.' A sucked in hiss of breath came from beside her. 'He knows. All my life he has sent Georgia pictures of me, taken without her knowledge, always accompanied by threatening letters. Not happy with taking unsolicited photos of me he also used my daughter to threaten Georgia.'

'Not me,' the man yelled.

Vicky dared to step closer, pointing her finger at his chest. 'Yes, you and I have proof.' He tried to stifle a wince but Vicky caught it. 'Georgia kept every single one of your letters, hidden where your henchmen couldn't find them. But...' she paused for effect, 'my lawyer found them yesterday.' She turned to her father. 'The location was in the diaries. I emailed the information to Marty. He went by the house, found them all hidden in a cardboard box in the ceiling space.' She turned back to Vasilis, delighted at the sucked in lips indicating his frustration. 'Exactly where Georgia said they were.'

She leant closer, grinned when he flinched. 'Guess what else is in Georgia's diary. Her witness statement which detailed exactly how Sophia, my mother, died. Georgia was there, watching through a café window while she held me in her arms. She was waiting for Sophia to arrive.' Vicky bent closer and whispered loud enough to make a point. 'Car registration number even. Greek number plate. Belonged to one Vasilis Nesbloutas according to the research my lawyer did last night.'

'This is true?' her father roared from behind her, making her jump. He rushed past her, grabbed Vasilis by the front of his shirt and yanked the old man from his seat. 'You murdered Sophia? How could you? She did nothing to you.'

'She ruined your promised marriage to Soula. You broke a vow. Discredited our family name. Destroyed the chance of a lucrative financial opportunity. I lost face because of her.' Vasilis spat but managed to break free with a strength belying his age. Kristian shoved him back into his seat and spun away.

'Soula was the one who refused marriage, not me.' He spun back to glare at his father. 'To be honourable and the man, I took the blame. The only person to discredit your name is you. You are a murderer,' Kristian yelled.

'Not once but twice,' Vicky added quietly. Her father spun around and turned his glare on her.

'Excuse me? What do you mean?'

'In his endeavour to get rid of me, he was responsible for the head-on collision which killed my husband. Only things went wrong because on that day, Mike was driving my car. It was supposed to be me who died.' Vicky turned back to Vasilis. 'Big mistake you made when you sent a photo of the car crash with another threatening letter. I believe it is in the hands of the police right now. Could be you might get a visit from Interpol in the not-too-distant future.'

'They will be lucky to find him alive,' Kristian growled as he closed in on his father. 'You are nothing but pure evil. Maybe I should testify at your trial about the beatings you dished out to Mama and me. Hmm?' He grabbed the shirt again, tugged, not letting go until Vasilis started changing colour from lack of oxygen. Kristian shoved him away again and began pacing around the room while Vicky pulled out a chair at the other end of the table, taking a minute to settle her anger to a level less than violence inducing. Never before had she felt this type of white-hot anger.

'How did you know about the necklace,' she asked as calm as she could.

'What necklace?' The belligerent response said far more than the words. He knew.

'Oh, come on, the one you had Georgia's house destroyed while looking for it.' Keep calm Vicky, keep calm. She sat on her hands to prevent herself from using the cocky old man as a punching bag. The sneer on his face needed to be wiped off.

'I have no idea what you are talking about.'

Deliberately, Vicky sprang from her seat, startling both Kristian and Vasilis, who jolted at her movement. She reached up to grab what had caught her eye before. 'Then how come, you have in your possession the case belonging to the Faberge necklace but which contained a cheap piece of costume jewellery when it was stolen from my bedside table? Pity your henchmen couldn't tell fake from the real thing isn't it?' When Vicky opened the case for dramatic effect, she was surprised to see Gina's necklace still inside. 'Well, look at this. Gina's necklace. Now I wonder how that could possibly be in your kitchen when last week it was on the other side of the world in my bedroom? Hmm? Amazing.' Vicky dangled the necklace in front of his face, as she sent him a gloating grin. 'I have a photo of my daughter wearing this at her school ball.' She made a deliberate show of dropping it into her pocket before handing the case to Kristian.

Desperate to appear calm but inside she felt anything but, Vicky sauntered back to the chair she had sat in before and took her time to sink down. Three slow breaths, in and out, in and out, in and out. 'I think it only right to inform you of a couple of things. First, my lawyer has spoken to the two men you sent to Georgia's funeral. They were stupid when they used their real names when they hired a vehicle. The police did not hesitate to pass on their names. These were the same men responsible for the destruction of Georgia's home and stealing this from my home.' She turned to her father who had taken the seat next to her. 'They were paid twenty thousand euros plus costs for their efforts. They have confessed all after they were told the truth which apparently was vastly different to the story this... this cockroach spun them.' She wavered her fingers towards Vasilis before turning back to Kristian. 'At the moment there is a forensic auditor looking into your father's bank accounts to trace down other payments to the men he hired to take the photos and kill Mike.'

A crash stopped her in an instant. Vasilis had shoved back his chair so hard it broke against the wall. The man was so angry he shook and looked as though he was unable to form words. His face was beet red with foam dribbling from his mouth. It was sick, she knew, but she prayed he would drop dead from a heart attack. She just hoped it was agonising. To make her vindication even better, she pointed to her father's pocket. It appeared he understood for he nodded, shoved his hand in his pocket and drew out the necklace, spreading it out in all its glory on the table. It was such a pleasure to see the old man's eyes widen and his jaw drop.

'Stolen, I believe, according to the internet,' Vicky drawled. 'Yet here it is, in the hands of the man to whom it was bequeathed. Seems to me, Kristian has had it all the time but your greed and truly nasty nature has turned you into a vicious murderer, liar, cheat, blackmailer and even a paedophile for isn't that what they call dirty old men who go around taking photographs of little girls? And I have the proof with the photos you took of my daughter when she was so very young.' Vicky stood, turned, walked to the door and spun around. 'Have a great day for I have had a brilliant day and I must warn you, by the time I get home, the police will have in their hands every single detail about you so if you even think about continuing your little game of evil deeds, beware. My lawyer has even sent the French police the details of Sophia's murder.'

Vicky spun around and high-tailed it from the den of iniquity, not waiting for her father. She wanted nothing more than to get on the plane first thing in the morning and get home. Her seat was booked. All she had to do was fill the seat.

t was such a pleasure to be free of unanswered questions, to know the truth. Vicky towelled her legs dry, folded the towel through the rack and ran a brush through her hair. In her bedroom, she glanced at the bedside clock, catching sight of the pictures beside it. In the three weeks she had been home, she had printed off pictures of family, a word she still found hard to comprehend. Her father stood behind her step-mother and three half siblings. A sense of belonging washed over her. For the first time ever, she looked like someone else and didn't feel like the odd one out. There was some innate connection with other people. Two other pictures had taken up permanent residence. One featured her Uncle Costas and darling Aunt Dora who had such a kind warm, heart. Vicky could still feel the motherly hug Dora had given her. The impact of that sensation was something she would always relish and never forget. The entire extended family from Kent, stood crowded together in the other photo. Vicky grinned at them, still unable to remember all of their names or who went with whom but she would rectify the situation come Christmas. The air flight was already booked.

She withdrew clean underwear, slipped them on, recalling the last few hours with her father and his family. Initial hesitancy between her and her siblings had turned into joyous discovery of similar likes and dislikes. The night ended late with Kristian begging her to delay her flight. Much as she had wanted to spend more time with them, a deeper need was to get home to Gina, to have time to sort through and come to terms with her overwhelming jumble of emotions. The normalcy of her work routine had settled the turmoil to a more serene calm.

It still stunned her how quickly Marty had set legal matters into motion with results from overseas still coming through. She grinned at the memory of the report on Vasilis' financial report. His assets had been frozen, pending further results. Nothing more than he deserved she thought, as she shoved legs into clean black jeans. She paused at the sound of the front doorbell. She stuck her head out the door to call Gina.

'Can you get the door, please, Sweetie? I'm not decent.'

'Sure thing.' Footsteps raced down the passage while Vicky took out a warm skivvy.

'Mum!' Gina screeched so loud Vicky shoved arms in sleeves at the same time she tried to tug down the fabric while she pelted from the room.

'Why are you yell... oh!' She stumbled the last few steps when she saw her father and his family crowded around the front door. After she managed to regain her balance she could do nothing but stare until her brain cells aligned. 'It's not polite to scream at visitors,' she said to Gina who stood there with her mouth gaping.

'But, Mum, she looks just like me.' A finger pointed to Sophia.

'I told you how much you looked alike.' Vicky couldn't suppress her grin.

'Alike and identical don't mean the same thing.'

'Your eyes are different; you have Dad's eyes. Are you going to invite your family in or leave them standing on the doorstep? I thought you had better manners or are you trying to show me up as being a bad mother?' Vicky turned to her father. 'How come you are all here in any case?' She stood aside, beckoned everyone in, lead them into the only room with enough seats, the kitchen.

'Every summer, we take a family vacation. This year we decided Perth was the place to explore, although summer seems to have disappeared with all this rain.' There was a clatter as chairs were tugged out, filled with bodies and scraped back in. 'The girls have a two-week semester break but Nickos only one. Marika and I can stay as long as we are welcome.'

An overwhelming sensation flooded through her. Vicky wanted to both laugh and cry. Instead, she made introductions which sounded so formal it felt ridiculous. When she finally plonked into a chair because she didn't have a clue what else to do, it was to see her father frown.

'I am disappointed, *kore mou*, my daughter.'

Her heart managed a hop, skip and jump. 'Why? What is wrong?'

Kristian stood. 'No hug from my daughter?'

Vicky flew from her chair into is arms and grabbed him around his waist. 'I'm sorry. It was such a shock to see you all here.' Tears leaked. 'Now look what you made me do. I am so overcome.' She stood back and swiped at her eyes, forcing a grin for being such a sook.

When she resumed her seat, Kristian turned to Gina. 'And

now, I get to meet my beautiful granddaughter. Come here.' He reached out with one hand to draw Gina from her seat. For a minute, he studied her face, a gradual smile breaking out. 'Beautiful like your mother. I still find it difficult to believe I have a granddaughter but be sure, I am so incredibly honoured you are both in my life. Am I allowed to hug you as well?'

Something warm and squishy replaced the shock inside Vicky as she watched the two embrace each other for the first time. The very fact he asked Gina's permission said a lot for his ethics and the type of man he was despite coming from such a despicable human being as his father. Her own tears made themselves known again when she spied the ones in Gina's eyes as the two parted but stood back eyeing each other while they still held hands.

The minute they sat, a hubbub of chatter broke out with questions and answers crossing the table. Feeling a really weird sense of contentment, Vicky filled orders for tea and coffee, made crackers with cheese and felt guilty at the packet of common supermarket biscuits but with work, she hadn't baked since coming home.

After she and Gina cleared away the remnants of the simple supper, she sat, only to find her hands taken by her father who had a serious look in his eyes. Oh, oh, what has happened?

'And now let me tell you one of the reasons we came. I can't call Vasilis my father for no man would want such evil in his genes but unfortunately he provided half of mine. But he is dead.'

Vicky sucked in her breath, an audible hiss which silenced the room.

'The only honourable thing he has done in his entire life was to take his own and rid the world of his wickedness. I am not sorry and feel no regret for his passing. In fact I am over-joyed he is no longer on this earth to carry out such inhuman-ity. I have detailed his criminality to your brother and sisters and now they understand better the reason Marika and I re-fused any connection with him. He was not only cruel to you but also to me and my mother, especially to Mama. The beat-ings she received were horrific until she was brave enough to walk away. To her, the financial cost of the settlement, which was considerable, was worth every cent. I believe the punish-ment she received is the reason for her fragile health now. He also beat me as a child but didn't dare once I grew big enough to fight back. But the emotional abuse continued until I also, found the courage to dismiss him from my life.

'The deep regret I will have to live with for the rest of my life, is the time you and I and young Gina have missed being together. This will change, I promise you. You will always be equal in every aspect of my family.' His hand went into his shirt pocket and withdrew a piece of paper. 'This is the other reason I need to see you in person. The necklace is rightfully yours. It was a gift to your biological mother, the woman I gave my heart to, and you are her heir as well as mine. You said you would never have use for it. I understand and agree with your reasons so I sold it to some mega-billionaire whose need to own precious things far outweighs common sense.

You never had the benefit of my financial assistance as a child, which saddens me a great deal.

'My initial wealth was inherited but it has never been something I took for granted or wasted on frivolous things. I invested and used the profits to build up a respectable industrial empire, which I have now sold so my beautiful Marika and I can enjoy the benefits. We have more money than we will ever be able to use. I hope I have brought up my children to respect money, to understand the pitfalls of wealth if they are not wise and to value every cent. Vasilis had no respect at all, allowing greed and envy to turn him into the pitiful human being he ended up. Money can't and never will buy love or happiness. I can never buy your love but you are my flesh and blood and sadly you missed out the benefits of the life I was born into, of the life you were entitled to. I calculated the support you missed out on up until the day you married and have added it to the price I received for the necklace.

'After the torment you have been through at the hands of Vasilis, you deserve your life to be a little easier than it has been. I am incredibly proud of you, the way you handle yourself, the way you have fought to give the very best you could for your own daughter. I saw the way you gave your heart to Mama, showing me you have a beautiful soul, much like that of your own mother, Sophia. I also saw the way you fought with tenacity, despite being terrified, for what is right when you confronted Vasilis. I wish I had the same guts when I was younger. I think you are the only person he feared, which delights me. You have more courage than I did. He knew he had been caught in a web he would never be able to get out of, thanks to you. Be proud. His death was an act of cowardice because he was unable to face up to the results of his evil acts.'

He reached over with both of his thumbs, swept the tears which had left a trail down Vicky's face. 'Like Marika, Sophia, Nickos and Angeliki, both you and Gina live in my heart.' He pointed to the piece of paper. 'You might need me to come to the bank with you to confirm the amount is legitimate and the cheque won't bounce.'

Vicky had no control of the shake in her hand when she unfolded the paper and stared at the number. 'Oh, my...' Words fled. She had to blink then concentrate to get her eyes to focus but the number after the dollar sign said the same. 'This is way too much. I...' Her hands flew to her face to cover eyes which threatened a forty-day flood.'

'Mum, are you okay?' Gina called before she rushed around the table. She took the cheque and swore. The embarrassed apology was followed by a different unladylike exclamation.

'Gina,' Vicky scolded, desperate to gain some semblance of control.

'Sorry, but ten million is a bit... unbelievable.' Gina dropped to the floor with her mouth in a permanent wide-open position and her eyes glazed with staring.

Finally after she managed to get her brain to function, Vicky grabbed her father's hand. 'This is too much. I can't accept it. The necklace wasn't worth even a quarter of this.'

He laughed as he grasped her hand. 'Vicky, there was a bidding war for the necklace. Jewellery items made by Karl Faberge himself, coming onto the market are not very common but are highly sought after. I put the necklace onto an on-line auction. I received bid after bid after bid within minutes of each other. It stalled at the nine million mark so I snapped up the offer. It took a couple of weeks for the funds to clear and necklace to be delivered.'

'Truly?' Vicky had to ask.

'Truly. I could show you the paperwork if you need proof.'

'I won't know what to do with so much money.'

'Invest most of it. I can show you how. But first, enjoy some of it. If you want a different house, or a holiday or a new wardrobe of clothes, go for it. Real estate is an investment if you buy the right place. You can give up full time work, live on the interest and dividends. Make your life a little easier. You certainly deserve it. But let's not think about it right now. What is far more important is to enjoy being a family.'

Kristian stood, drew both Vicky and Gina up into his arms and hugged tight. The other four joined them, linking arms around the outside.

'Family,' they chorused together, a single word which left Vicky so overwhelmed with emotion clogging her innards to such an uncomfortable level. After thirty-seven years of having so few people in her life, she had more family than she knew what to do with.